Y0-CJE-923

A Poisonous Silence

THE DEADLY TWENTIES MYSTERIES

A Deadly Endeavor

A Poisonous Silence

A Deadly Twenties Mystery

Jenny Adams

CROOKED LANE

NEW YORK

This is a work of fiction. All of the names, characters, organizations, places and events portrayed in this novel are either products of the author's imagination or are used fictitiously. Any resemblance to real or actual events, locales, or persons, living or dead, is entirely coincidental.

Copyright © 2025 by Jenny Adams

All rights reserved.

Published in the United States by Crooked Lane Books, an imprint of The Quick Brown Fox & Company LLC.

Crooked Lane Books and its logo are trademarks of The Quick Brown Fox & Company LLC.

Library of Congress Catalog-in-Publication data available upon request.

ISBN (hardcover): 979-8-89242-038-9
ISBN (paperback): 979-8-89242-240-6
ISBN (ebook): 979-8-89242-039-6

Cover design by Jessica Khoury

Printed in the United States.

www.crookedlanebooks.com

Crooked Lane Books
34 West 27th St., 10th Floor
New York, NY 10001

First Edition: May 2025

10 9 8 7 6 5 4 3 2 1

For Ellie—I hope you'll always remember that we can do hard things.

Chapter 1

September 30, 1921
Manayunk, Philadelphia

Gilbert Lawless checked his bag for what felt like the tenth time that morning. He had his notebook, neatly stowed in its pocket beside three perfectly sharpened pencils. A magnifying glass, tweezers, measuring tape, and calipers. A change of clothes and a first-aid kit in a Bakelite case, for the worst-case scenario.

Everything was exactly as it had been the last time he'd checked it, on the drive over, and the time before that, at his desk in the Philadelphia Morgue first thing that morning. The same as it had been on his last excursion into the field.

"Ready when you are," Marco Salvatore said. He came around the side of the truck, hat in one hand as he slipped his camera strap around his neck with the other. His dark hair, slicked back with pomade, glistened in the September sunshine. "Do you need me to carry the bag?"

"I'm fine," Gilbert insisted. Marco, his partner, had been hovering over him like a worried mother hen all morning. It had been just over five months since Gilbert had been shot while stopping the killer made famous in the papers as the Schuylkill Slasher. Gilbert had faced a long recovery—first in the hospital, then at his parent's snug row house in Manayunk, just a few blocks away from here. He'd returned to his job as an assistant in the office of Philadelphia's coroner earlier in the summer, relegated to desk duty as he healed.

Until today.

He ignored Marco's creased brow and took the steps to the porch quickly, his heavy bag knocking against his leg. He nodded at the small gathering of women clustered on the adjoining porch. A blond woman muffled a sob in a handkerchief and turned her back on them.

A uniformed officer opened the front door. Gilbert didn't recognize him.

"Dr. Salvatore. Dr. Lawless. Detective Pyle is waiting in the dining room." The man was young, fresh out of the Academy, with pale, pimpled skin and a thin wisp of mustache barely visible on his upper lip.

The interior layout of the house was familiar in the identical way of most of Philadelphia's lower- and middle-class row homes. They passed through a narrow vestibule, tiled in black and white, that opened into a large front room. Directly ahead, stairs rose to the second floor. The living room was neat as a pin and nicely decorated—a blue sofa with a curving back sat beneath the billowing lace curtains on the open front window, and an upright piano was beside the tiled fireplace. A pair of pocket doors led into the dining room, where Detective Finnegan Pyle stood talking intensely with another uniformed officer who was frantically scribbling notes on a small pad. Pyle glanced up as they approached. His serious, hangdog face broke into a grin.

"Bertie!" he said. He crossed the room in three steps and held out his hand. Gilbert shook it. Despite knowing each other as boys, Gilbert had mixed feelings about the man Finnegan Pyle had grown into. But Pyle had helped save Gilbert's daughter, Penelope, and had sat for long hours at Gilbert's hospital bedside as Gilbert recovered from the gunshot wound that had nearly killed him. "How are you feeling?"

"Fine," Gilbert said automatically, and it was true enough. He turned his attention to the rear of the room, where the body of a man stretched on the rug beside an overturned dining chair. "What do we need to know?"

Pyle watched as Marco fitted a flashbulb onto his camera for a moment, then spoke. "Homer Byrne, age thirty-seven. A teamster. The wife found him like this when she came down to start breakfast about two hours ago, and called it in. He was out late on a job last night—she said she was in bed before he came home."

Gilbert frowned. Pyle was a homicide detective; he wasn't called in without a reason. There were no obvious signs of trauma to the body—no blood, no wounds. "Why'd they call you?"

"Courtesy. I knew the guy." Pyle's words were carefully chosen. "He was a friend of Tommy's."

Ah. Gilbert knew that Pyle was still close with Tommy Fletcher, the gangster who ran the streets of Manayunk. They'd all been close, once, but Gilbert kept a careful distance these days. He'd seen enough of Tommy's crew come across his autopsy table to know how quickly a life of casual violence could end. Gilbert was sure, that, upon examination, the dead man would have a shamrock tattoo on his right arm, with the letters *C S C* on the heart-shaped leaves.

Pyle continued speaking. "There was a strong smell when I got here. Sweet. Like those Christmas cookies your mother makes. The ones with the cherries. What are they, sugar?"

"Almond," Gilbert corrected. "You think he was poisoned?" He set the bag down on the floor and squatted to take a closer look. Someone had opened the windows, probably to air the smell of death from the room, which meant that the telltale bitter almond scent of cyanide had also dissipated. But if Pyle was right, it pointed to something more sinister than a natural death.

"Shit, you're the doctor, Bertie. You tell me."

Marco lifted the camera. "Ready?"

Gilbert appreciated the warning. He steadied his hands on his knees, bracing himself, as the camera's bulb popped and the flash burned bright through the room. Neither Pyle nor Marco said anything else as the shudder worked through Gilbert's body, remembering the other blasts etched on his soul.

It's a beautiful day in Philadelphia, Gilbert reminded himself. He took deep, even breaths, in and out, and focused on the scene in front of him. *It's September. You're safe.*

The lace curtains billowed in the breeze. The dead man's fingers curled inward, his clouded eyes staring off into nothing. Rigor mortis—the stiffening muscles after death—hadn't yet set in, so he'd been dead for less than eight hours.

"Was he like this when you arrived?" Gilbert asked. "On his back?"

"Yeah," Pyle said. "The wife said she found him in the chair, and when she tried to wake him, he fell over onto the rug."

Gilbert lifted the hem of the man's trousers, revealing mottled reddish skin around his ankles, where the blood had pooled after death. He'd been dead for at least two hours before she'd knocked him out of the chair, based on the staining. Gilbert pulled his pocket watch from his vest pocket and checked the time—about five to nine—and calculated backward. "Time of death was somewhere between three and four this morning," he said. "Roughly."

He looked up to see Marco and Pyle watching him expectantly, their faces wearing twin expressions of cautious concern. Irritation prickled over his skin, and he stood, scowling. "What?" he demanded.

"Nothing," Marco said quickly, but Gilbert caught the flash of teeth as his partner suppressed a smile. "It's just nice to have you back, Lawless."

"Yeah," Pyle said. "We missed you, Bertie."

Gilbert's scowl deepened, and he turned back to his work. As much as it pained him to admit it, he had missed them too.

By midafternoon, Gilbert's abdomen ached, and the tremor in his hands had turned his notes illegible. Ink pooled beneath his pen nib, smearing the word, and he swore. He dropped the pen and dug his fingers through his hair in frustration. He shouldn't be this tired already. His job demanded long hours and steady concentration, and even at his lowest—strung out on morphine and haunted by the ghosts of his past—he'd never faltered. Not like this.

He wasn't about to start now. He just needed a breath, to gather his thoughts and . . .

"I don't know about you," Marco drawled from his side of the desk, "but I could use an ice cream right about now."

Gilbert lifted his head to stare at his partner. Marco leaned back in his chair, his fingers linked behind his head, his feet resting on a haphazard pile of papers. "You could always use an ice cream," Gilbert said. "And we have work to do."

"You've done plenty," Marco countered. "You've spent the last three months organizing every file in this place. You even cleaned my desk," he added, knocking his shoe against a clear spot on the tabletop, as if to illustrate his point. "You survived your first trip back to the field this morning. We should celebrate."

"We should not," Gilbert said. "We haven't even started the Byrne autopsy yet."

"The body is in full rigor mortis. We'd have to break him to autopsy. Best to wait until tomorrow."

"You're not going to let up, are you?"

"Like a dog with a bone," Marco said, grinning. His feet hit the floor, and he sprang up, unfolding to his full height. "Or a kid with an ice cream."

"Fine." Gilbert capped his pen and grabbed his hat. "And then I'm going home. My father's been teaching Penelope how to play cards, and I'm worried she's actually good at it. Next thing I know, she'll be hustling kids on the playground."

"Atta girl." They wove through the maze of desks in the office they shared with the other assistants. Most of the desks were empty; the job was demanding, sending assistants across the city at all hours, paired with long days in the refrigerated autopsy rooms downstairs. "Next time I'm over, I'll play a hand with her."

"Don't bet anything you're fond of," Gilbert warned, but Marco waved it off. They'd grown close in the months since Gilbert's hospital stay. Marco had visited daily at first, bringing toys and treats for Penelope, and conversation for Gilbert. The visits had stayed steady even as Gilbert moved back to his parent's house. Marco had even been the one to help Gilbert's sister clear his belongings from Gilbert's former boarding house in Spring Garden.

Marco had become more than a colleague, or a partner. He'd become a friend.

"Where do you two think you're sneaking off to?" Cecelia, one of the secretaries, teased as they reached her desk. She was a pretty girl, with big blue eyes behind wire-rimmed glasses and an obvious crush on Gilbert that he tried to gently discourage. She fixed her gaze on him, pouting slightly. "And you didn't even invite me?"

"Bassett's," Marco said. "Think you can join us?"

She glanced down at her desk, then called over her shoulder, "Maria! I'm taking a break!" To Marco and Gilbert she said, "Remind me to bring her back something."

The other secretary waved her off. Cecelia grabbed her own hat and coat, and within a few minutes they'd made their way the few blocks south and east to Reading Terminal Market. Trains rumbled overhead as they walked, drowning out Marco and Cecelia's pleasant chatter. They pushed their way through the heavy brass doors and inside the market.

Noise and smells assaulted Gilbert from every angle. Butchers haggled with housewives over the price of their dinner. An Amish family, in their old-fashioned clothes and long beards, sold donuts and breads. Small boys—the market brats—darted between the crowds, hands full of boxes tied with string, on their way to make the day's deliveries, feet crunching over the sawdust on the floor. Some of them weren't much older than Penelope.

They reached the ice cream counter. There were other shops closer to the morgue, but Bassett's, centered in the midst of the chaos of the market, was Marco's favorite. They each took a stool at the slim counter, and Gilbert looked up at the list of flavors scrawled on the chalkboard. A harried-looking young man in a vest and white cap turned, scoop in hand, ready to take their orders: mint for Marco, chocolate for Cecelia, and a hot fudge sundae for Gilbert, with whipped cream, peanuts, and a maraschino cherry on top.

He ate the ice cream slowly. Since he'd woken up in that hospital bed, he had been worried about his return to the field. War had changed him irrevocably, robbing him of some memories while making him relive others over and over again until memory and reality crashed together. As he recovered physically from the gunshot wound, he waited anxiously to see if that night in the crypt would haunt his waking hours in the same way. He'd nearly lost his daughter.

He'd nearly lost Edie.

Now *that* was a thought he pushed down quickly. Edie Shippen, his sister's employer and darling of the city's high society, had saved them all. She was the most ridiculous and brilliant woman that Gilbert had ever met. Which is why, after one short visit on her birthday to thank her for her efforts, Gilbert had avoided her entirely.

He'd been accused of being a coward for years—coming home from war with tremors and fits and a mind that stayed in the trenches had guaranteed that. And he was certain beyond a doubt that he was too much of a coward to see Edie Shippen again. It was easier to avoid her and the swirl of feeling she stirred in him. To avoid the way she drove him to distraction.

He had to focus on his daughter. On his work. He couldn't afford distractions.

He'd been worried about his return to the field, but riding with Marco today, assessing the scene—it all felt so blessedly normal. His hands and his mind cooperated, and that was definitely worth an ice-cream sundae.

Beside him, Cecelia laughed at something Marco said. Her shoulder brushed Gilbert's, and he looked over at her. She caught his eye and smiled, and he smiled back.

"It's really swell to see you back in the field," Cecelia told him. She licked her spoon and dipped it into her glass. Her cheeks pinked the way they always did when she spoke to him. "You seemed so miserable, cooped up in the office with me all summer."

Cecelia was the type of woman he should be interested in. Someone who moved in his world, who understood his job, his family, and his priorities. Someone he might even come to love, in time. A comfortable kind of love. Not exciting, but steady.

Safe.

He'd loved his late wife, Sarah, with a need that had set their entire worlds ablaze and then left him standing in the ashes.

He couldn't let himself be consumed like that again.

"I wouldn't say it was miserable," he said, his voice rumbling out of his chest. He met her gaze, and her flush spread down her neck. "I was thinking . . ."

She leaned toward him, spinning on her stool. Her knee pressed his, and Gilbert felt nothing. Which was fine. She was pretty and smart and funny. He didn't need the rest.

Behind her, Marco shook his head furiously, and mouthed, "Don't you dare."

He didn't need Marco's approval. His spoon clinked as he set it on the counter, and he looked up at Cecelia. But she was looking beyond Gilbert now, somewhere over her shoulder, her hand pressed to her throat, her eyes wide with terror.

"What . . . ?" Gilbert spun in his stool, the question dying in his throat. A man, twitching and jerking, stumbled down the aisle toward them, moaning. He stumbled against a display of cans, knocking it to the floor with a soul-splintering crash. A woman screamed.

The man fell.

Gilbert shuddered. *Stay here.*

"Come on." Marco was already moving, his hand gripping Gilbert's elbow, tethering him to the present. They hurried to the fallen man, who convulsed on the sawdust-covered floor, his eyes rolling wildly in his head. His limbs twitched as if jerked by a mad puppeteer, foam spewing from his lips.

Gilbert crouched over the man, searching desperately for a pulse. But as the man suddenly fell into an eerie, aching silence, he knew what he'd find even as he pressed his fingers to the man's neck.

He was already dead.

Chapter 2

Edie Shippen titled her chin, studying her reflection in the mirror. She wasn't sure about the hat that her assistant, Lizzie, had suggested, a cloche in a deep umber shade. The color was fabulous, especially atop her perfectly styled black bob. The bell shape was darling too. But it was missing something.

"Maybe a ribbon?" Edie wondered. She traced her fingers where the body of the hat met the brim, then sighed. She placed it back on the wooden stand to her left. "What else do you have?"

"Perhaps this one, Miss Shippen? I know it might be a bit much." The shopgirl was young and pretty in an eager sort of way. The hat she presented was a lovely dove gray in a cap style, with a turned-up yellow brim and a large plume of yellow curling over the top.

Edie loved it instantly. She placed it on her head carefully, turning this way and that as the feather danced above her left ear.

"It's perfect," Lizzie said, clapping her hands under her chin. Lizzie's own taste in hats was more demure, which made sense considering her cascade of copper curls. If Edie's own hair commanded that much attention on its own, she'd probably go without the feathers.

"I'll take it," Edie told the girl as she handed it back. The girl beamed and bustled off to wrap it up. The bell over the door danced merrily as Edie set her own hat back on her head, a feathered cloche with a wide brim, trimmed with a velvet ribbon in the same shade of hunter green as her coat. Lizzie followed the girl to the counter, where she'd make sure the account was settled.

"Hello, I—my word, Edie Shippen, is that you?" The woman in the doorway pressed a hand to her chest, and her perfect cupid's bow mouth dropped open in surprise.

Edie blinked, momentarily stunned into speechlessness. The last time she'd seen Ava Sylvester . . .

No. She wouldn't even let herself follow those memories, dappled in California sunshine. And yet Ava stood here, with freshly bobbed hair, wearing a chic black dress and matching embroidered shawl, looking as perfect as the day Edie had boarded the train back to Pennsylvania.

"Ava," she managed to say, "you cut your hair."

"So did you, darling." Ava's pretty face brightened into a smile as she closed the distance between them, brushing a kiss to each of Edie's cheeks in quick succession. She reached up and touched the wave closest to Edie's face with one gloved hand. "It suits you."

"What are you doing here?" Edie asked, recovering some of her senses. Ava had been her dearest friend in California. She'd lived next door to Edie's late great-aunt Mae. They'd bonded over their love of fashion and quickly become inseparable, though their letters had become sporadic since Edie had returned to Philadelphia. "You didn't write."

"I wanted to surprise you," Ava said, her eyes twinkling. "I landed a leading role in one of Harold Fox's pictures. We're shooting in Port Kennedy, just outside of town. I've been neck-deep in Shakespeare for months, believe it or not. You're looking at Juliet herself."

"How wonderful!" Ava's joy was contagious, and Edie found herself beaming back at her friend. Ava had spent the last few years working as a model, with bit stage roles here and there, but Edie knew how hard she'd worked to try to break into film. "How long will you be here?"

"A few more weeks. Are you free this weekend? We're throwing a little party at the Bellevue on Saturday, and I was going to surprise you with an invitation, but it looks like the cat's out of the bag. We'd love for you to join us."

"Here you go, Miss Shippen." Lizzie was already at Edie's side, producing a slim white card. "Your card."

"Thank you, Lizzie," Edie said. She passed the card to Ava, who read it and raised one perfectly arched eyebrow.

"'Edie Shippen, lady detective.'" Ava's eyes twinkled. "It seems I'm not the only one with news."

"We'll catch up," Edie said. "I promise."

"I'll hold you to that," Ava said. "Now, I heard Madame LaBelle is the person to see about a hat?"

Ava's invitation arrived at the Shippen's city house the next morning. Lizzie brought it to Edie as she took her breakfast in the library, which had, over the last few months, become Edie's office.

"I can't believe you've known a film actress this entire time and never said anything, Miss Edie," Lizzie said. She glanced out the window, down onto Chestnut Street, as if Ava had delivered the invitation herself, instead of the postman.

"I know plenty of actresses," Edie said. She sipped at her tea as her little pug, Aphrodite, snored in her lap. "I lived in Los Angeles for three years, Lizzie. I couldn't go to lunch without meeting at least a dozen actresses."

It was the truth. The film industry had exploded over the last decade, with studios opening all over the country. The highest concentration of them seemed to be in California, as more of the East Coast studios closed and headed west to shoot in the more predictable weather of the Southern California coast.

"Still." Lizzie flipped open the small black notebook she'd taken to carrying since she'd become Edie's assistant, and pursed her lips. She took her duties seriously.

"What's on the schedule for today?" Edie asked.

"Lunch with Miss Frances at the Crystal Tea Room," Lizzie said.

"Anything else?" Edie refused to look at the envelope from Ava, and instead focused her attention on her redheaded assistant. They did this every morning, since the day Edie asked Lizzie to take on the job. After her disappearing act in the spring, the housekeeper at the Chestnut Hill house, Mrs. Smith, had refused to rehire Lizzie. Edie thought it a terrible injustice and promptly hired her to be her right-hand gal. Never mind that she didn't actually have a detective agency or any clients—just a stack of business cards and piles of money in her trust fund. She liked Lizzie. They could figure the rest out together.

"Sorry, miss." Lizzie looked disappointed. "That's all I have."

"No apologies, Lizzie. We'll find something to amuse ourselves with today, won't we? We can go shopping."

"We went shopping yesterday."

"So?" Edie tilted her head. "People go shopping every day, Lizzie. We can get you a new coat, and I need a dress for Ava's party."

Aphrodite groaned and rolled over, presenting her belly for scratches. Edie obliged.

Lizzie made a small noise of frustration in the back of her throat and pressed her hands to her face. Edie looked up, a trickle of concern unraveling in her chest. "Lizzie? What is it?"

Lizzie kept her hands pressed to her face. "It's nothing."

"It's clearly not." Edie sat up, causing the dog to grumble, and placed her tea on the table beside her. "Tell me."

"It's just . . . aren't you *bored*, Miss Edie? I've been your assistant for three months now—"

"Four," Edie corrected.

Lizzie lowered her hands and placed them on her hips. "Fine. *Four* months now, and we haven't had a single client. We spend every day shopping or taking walks around the park or perhaps going on a picnic—"

"Don't forget our trip to Atlantic City," Edie said. "That was great fun. And the way Leo showed up to surprise you! It was very romantic, wasn't it?"

Lizzie flushed as scarlet as her hair. "It was, wasn't it?" Then she shook her head, as if reminding herself to get back on track. "No. Wait. We aren't talking about me, Miss Edie.

Well. I suppose we are, but really, I'm talking about *you*. Are you all right?"

"I'm fine," Edie insisted, her voice sharper than she meant it to be.

Lizzie stared at her.

Edie stared back. The trickle of concern widened, spreading into a torrent of emotion that Edie didn't want to deal with. She was fine. She had no other choice. If she started to think about what had happened in May, she'd never stop thinking about the way the blade sounded as it hit bone. The way the blood had felt hot as it splattered over her hands.

The way she'd been certain, completely certain, that if she hadn't acted, she'd be dead, along with Gilbert and his young daughter, Penelope. As dead as Edie's cousin Rebecca and her friends Ophelia and Athena, and poor Dottie too.

"I'm fine," Edie said again.

"Well, I'm not." The words left Lizzie in a rush. "I'm grateful to you. I am. But I won't take your charity, miss. You don't need an assistant. You don't need me."

"Lizzie, that isn't true—"

Lizzie wouldn't be stopped. "It *is*, Miss Edie. I wish you'd let me place an advertisement in the papers," Lizzie pressed on. "Drum up some business. We can't just wait here and expect for a case to stumble into our laps. We should be proactive."

"That feels a little common, don't you think? We should be more exclusive."

"So exclusive no one knows we exist," Lizzie grumbled.

"I—"

A soft knock on the library door interrupted them. Aphrodite awoke with a bark, leaping off Edie's lap to zoom to the butler at the door. He bent down and scratched the pug between her ears. "Caller at the door for you, Miss Shippen."

Lizzie flipped the datebook back open. "We weren't expecting anyone."

"Who is it, O'Mara?"

"A Mrs. Charles Patterson," O'Mara said. "She apologizes that she doesn't have an appointment, but she says it's an urgent matter, and insisted on seeing the detective at once."

Edie's mouth fell open. "The detective?" She could have kissed O'Mara, despite the fact that he was old enough to be her grandfather. He was still petting Aphrodite, though, and Edie figured she'd let the dog have her moment.

"Bring her up, O'Mara," Edie said. "I'll go get dressed."

"I'll get her settled," Lizzie said. She was already sweeping through the room, clearing Edie's breakfast tray and adjusting the chairs.

Edie slipped down the hall, her entire body fizzing with delight.

Her first client. What was she going to *wear*?

───────◆◈◆───────

Less than five minutes later, Edie had dressed in a navy frock, trimmed with black velvet, and found her way back to the library, where her first client was waiting. Her first client!

She smiled at the middle-aged woman sitting in the chair opposite, a darling half-barrel thing she'd ordered from Paris, upholstered in a cheerful spring-green damask. The woman was less cheerful: she sat with her spine ramrod straight, her manicured fingers clutching the carved wooden arm like they were the only thing keeping her tethered to the firmament.

"Are you comfortable, Mrs. Patterson? My assistant will be in with water and tea shortly," Edie said, raising her voice slightly at the end so that Lizzie would be sure to hear her. Edie knew that Lizzie would have her ear pressed to the door just outside, eavesdropping.

"No, no," Mrs. Patterson said. She gave a forced, brittle laugh. "I'm not even sure why I'm here, to be quite honest with you. But my niece said you could help, and gave me your card, so here I am. You know her, I think? Colleen Spencer."

Edie leaned forward slightly. "Colleen is a friend of mine," she said. "My cousin, Rebecca, was her roommate at Bryn Mawr."

The woman crossed herself. "Poor child," she said. "That whole thing . . . just terrible business. And to think they never found out who did it."

Edie pressed her lips into a thin line, and it was her turn to clutch the arms of her chair. She knew the truth, of course. She was the one who had asked the police to keep the whole story out of the paper to spare her sister, Frances, the scandal so that they could put it all behind them and move on with their lives. Even so, the omission felt like a lie.

"Thank you," she said, forcing herself to keep her tone light. "Now, how can I help you?"

Mrs. Patterson leaned forward. "I'm here, Miss Shippen, because I have reason to suspect my neighbor murdered her husband."

A thud came from the hallway, jolting through Edie. But she was just as surprised as Lizzie. A murder. Edie had assumed her first official case would be something mundane—a lost necklace or a missing dog. She'd even let herself hope for a cheating husband—she had really been looking forward to providing a sense of feminine justice.

A few seconds later, Lizzie came into the library, pushing a tea cart. She set the cups and kettle down on the table between Edie and Mrs. Patterson, then retreated to her chair off to the side, where she picked up her own notebook and pen.

"That sounds like a matter for the police," Edie said carefully. She poured two cups of tea and pushed one toward her client. "Have you taken your concerns to them?"

"Useless, the lot of them," the woman said as she picked up her cup. She gave a sniff, her expression sour. "They fell for the girl's act—hook, line, and sinker. Suckers for a few tears and a pretty face. But I'm no fool. Lily Byrne had something to do with that sweet boy's death."

Edie picked up a pad of paper from the end table beside her. She wrote down *Lily Byrne*, then took a deep, centering breath. "All right, Mrs. Patterson. Tell me everything."

"Peter was a good boy from the neighborhood," Mrs. Patterson said. "I went to school with his mother. He had a good job with the teamsters, and all the girls loved him. He took my Daisy to their senior prom, you know. I had thought . . ." She waved a hand. "It's no matter."

"It all helps," Edie said. She was glad Lizzie was also taking notes; they'd have to compare them later. "Why do you think Mrs. Byrne would want to kill him?"

"She's an odd duck, that one. Italian," she added. "I can barely understand a word she says, and she never smiles or says hello. Doesn't talk to any of us on the block, but there's a steady stream of strangers in and out of that house at all hours. Rough-looking strangers."

"Being Italian doesn't make her a murderer," Edie pointed out. Mrs. Peterson made a small noise of protest, but Edie kept going. "How did Mr. Byrne die?"

"I don't know," Mrs. Patterson said. "That woman woke the entire block up this morning with her screaming—she found him dead on the dining room floor. The police were there within the hour, and the coroners too."

Coroners. Edie's head snapped up. Their presence was expected, but Lizzie had mentioned something about Gilbert returning to the field this week. Edie hadn't spoken to him in months, not since her birthday. *Completely understandable,* she'd told herself. After all, she'd been busy starting her business, and he'd been busy trying not to die. Still, she couldn't help asking, "What did they look like?"

"Mr. Byrne was tall, handsome. Red-haired and—"

"No, not the victim. The coroners."

"Oh." Mrs. Patterson thought a moment. "Two young men, both strapping. Dark haired, tall. One was swarthy. Italian too, by the look of him. The other was thin, pale. Had a look about him—he seemed sad."

Gilbert and Marco. It had to be. "Thank you, Mrs. Patterson," Edie said, flipping her notebook shut and standing. "I'll look into it."

"Just like that?" Mrs. Patterson blinked. "You're sure?"

"Absolutely," Edie said. "Lizzie?"

Lizzie snapped her own notebook shut, a smile on her face. "This way, Mrs. Patterson. I'll see you out."

When Lizzie returned a few minutes later, alone, Edie stood near the window, deep in thought.

"Our first client," Lizzie said. "How exciting! What do we do now?"

"We have to talk to your brother," Edie said. "We'll kill two birds with one stone."

"You think he knows something about this dead man?"

Edie held up the envelope from Ava, a smile breaking across her face. "Yes. And it turns out that I'm in need of a date."

Chapter 3

"There was nothing any of you could have done to save the man from yesterday," said Dr. William Knight, coroner of the City of Philadelphia, as he closed the manila folder on his desk and looked up at Marco, Gilbert, and Cecelia. "Dr. Harrison returned the lab results this morning. It seems the poor fellow was poisoned. We've referred the case to the police."

Gilbert nodded at this. Dr. Harrison, the newest assistant in the office, and the first Black man to hold the job, had quickly established himself as a fixture in the morgue's laboratory. Never far from his microscope, the doctor was whip-smart; and thanks to his training in Paris after the war, he'd lent his invaluable experience in helping to identify a seemingly unidentifiable body during Gilbert's last investigation, by using dental records.

"You're—you're sure?" Cecelia's voice wobbled as she spoke.

"I'm sure," Dr. Knight assured her gently. He stood from his desk and came around the front to look at her directly. "There were traces of cyanide in his system. There was nothing anyone could have done to save him."

Cecelia gave a miserable nod. She wiped at her cheeks. Gilbert dug out his handkerchief from his pocket and handed it to her; she accepted it with a watery smile. "Thanks, Gil," she said. "I just . . . you'd think I'd be okay with what happened. I see dead bodies all the time! I work at the morgue! I don't know what's wrong with me."

"There's a difference between seeing someone dead and seeing someone die," Gilbert said. "I'd be more worried if you weren't upset by it."

"Dr. Lawless is absolutely correct," Knight said. "Why don't you take the rest of the day off, Cecelia? I'm sure Maria or Bette can cover the phones."

"Oh no. I'll be fine." Cecelia did not look fine—her normally pink cheeks were pale, and her eyes were dull behind her wire-rimmed glasses. She blew her nose noisily in the handkerchief. For a half moment, Gilbert was almost sure that she was going to hand it back to him, but she tucked it into her skirt pocket instead. "It's better than sitting around at home and dwelling on it, isn't it?"

"Can I have the rest of the day off?" Marco asked, his lips twitching. "I'm terribly traumatized as well, Boss. I won't ever be able to eat an ice cream again without thinking about it."

"I think you'll manage, Dr. Salvatore," Dr. Knight said dryly. "Cecelia, if you're sure you're all right, I need to talk with Dr. Salvatore and Dr. Lawless for a moment."

"Of course, Dr. Knight," Cecelia said. The three men watched in silence as she hurried out, shoulders slumped.

Dr. Knight cleared his throat. "I'll have Maria keep an eye on her." When neither Gilbert nor Marco responded, he continued. "Let's walk to the lab. Tell me about the autopsy from your teamster."

Gilbert and Marco exchanged a glance, but they followed their boss out of the door and into the corridor, heels clicking on the polished marble floor beneath bronzed chandeliers. Every inch of the morgue building at 13th and Wood streets in Philadelphia was intricately designed, even in the office wing, far from public view. The first time Gilbert had come to work at the morgue, he'd been instantly reminded of his late wife's family estate in Chestnut Hill—a looming stone mansion, ornate in its opulence. He'd only been inside twice: once, when he asked Sarah's father for permission to marry her, and again, several years later, after Sarah's death, their infant daughter in his arms. Both times, he'd been thrown from the house.

He rubbed his left thumb against the slim gold band on his ring finger and turned his attention back to the conversation.

"It was routine, sir," Gilbert said. "No signs of violence or trauma to the body."

"Detective Pyle mentioned a strong smell of maraschino cherries," Marco added.

"How was lividity?" Knight asked. He led them down a flight of stairs inlaid with black and white diamond tiles, a hand on the curved brass banister. He pushed through the door on the basement level, one floor below the autopsy rooms and cadaver storage. A low rumble, like faintly crashing waves, vibrated through the air, and the temperature dropped further this close to the massive refrigeration system in the subbasement level that kept the entire morgue cool. Few people came down this far, and yet the floors and walls were heavy sheets of marble dotted with electric sconces.

"Nothing out of the ordinary," Gilbert said, raising his voice above the humming machines. "But if Pyle thought the smell was worth mentioning, it's worth running the tests." The detective was corrupt, but he wasn't a liar.

"Harrison will be able to tell us for sure," Knight said. He pushed open the door to the laboratory that had quickly become Isaiah Harrison's domain.

Dr. Harrison looked up from his microscope. He was a slim man, dark-skinned and neatly dressed, from the sharp part down the center of his hair, to the deep blue of his bow tie, just visible beneath his pristine white lab coat. He smiled, standing, and held out his hand. "Glad to see you back with us, Dr. Lawless," he said, his Georgia drawl as deep as Gilbert's own Irish brogue. "Feeling all right?"

"Right as rain," Gilbert said, his own hand cool against Harrison's warm skin. "But please, Dr. Harrison—call me Gilbert."

"Only if you call me Isaiah," the doctor insisted. He turned to Marco and Knight, beckoning them all over toward his table, where a beaker hung suspended over a Bunsen burner. "You're just in time. I'm about to test a sample from your patient. I just need to check the temperature . . . Ah, perfect. Dr. Knight said your detective smelled cherries. Have either of you done this before?"

Isaiah posed his question to Gilbert and Marco, who both shook their heads. Knight watched carefully, his face impassive.

"All right," Isaiah said. "I'll walk you through it. I took a small sample—about ten milliliters—and added it to a solution of five percent sodium hydroxide. Once it was mixed, I added it to a solution of five percent ferrous sulfate, and one percent ferric chloride. Let it cook for ten minutes, and then I add this." He picked up a second beaker, filled with clear liquid. "Hydrochloric acid. If there's any trace of cyanide in the sample, we'll know immediately."

"How?" Gilbert asked. He'd been a passable chemistry student but had focused his medical studies on anatomy and surgery, which had served him well on the battlefield and in the autopsy room. Chemistry had never been his strong suit.

"Watch." Isaiah dipped a dropper into the acid in the beaker in his hand and held it over the vessel on the Bunsen burner. He squeezed.

The droplet of hydrochloric acid fell swiftly, breaking the surface of the clear liquid and instantly turning as dark as night. Solid strands of inky navy blue swirled through the clear liquid. Isaiah added another drop, then another. Each turned equally as blue, settling into sediment at the bottom of the beaker. Marco let out a low whistle.

"Prussian blue," Knight said. "I'll be damned."

"Your detective's nose was right," Isaiah said. "Your patient ingested cyanide, probably only a few moments before his death."

"So he drank the cyanide," Gilbert said. "Either intentionally or accidentally."

The four men stared at the deep blue sediment settled on the bottom of the beaker. Isaiah reached forward and flipped the switch, turning off the flame.

"A suicide?" Marco asked. "Or a murder?"

"That's not our job," Dr. Knight reminded his trio of assistants. "Good work, all three of you. Let Detective Pyle know your findings—he'll handle it on his own. Is that clear?"

He focused on Gilbert's face, his gaze serious. Gilbert looked down at his shoes, heat crawling up his collar. Gilbert's recklessness in the spring had nearly cost him everything—his job, his daughter. His life.

"Yes, sir," Gilbert said. Beside him, Marco nodded.

They'd do their jobs and leave the investigating to Finnegan Pyle.

Gilbert wouldn't get involved. Not again.

It wasn't worth the risk.

"Gil, you have visitors," Cecelia said, drumming her fingers on the doorjamb to the autopsy room. Some of her color had returned, flushing her cheeks, but she didn't look happy. Her mouth was turned down, and something hard flickered behind her gaze.

"Oh?" Gilbert set his pen down. He had just finished notes on his latest patient, an elderly woman who had collapsed on the trolley. She'd suffered an aneurysm, and her adult son was scheduled to arrive later in the afternoon to identify her. He couldn't possibly be the visitor. "Is everything all right?"

"Just dandy," Cecelia said, though her voice was tight, implying it was anything but dandy. "They're waiting at your desk. Marco said it was fine."

Now that was curious. *They?* Gilbert closed the folder and shrugged out of his white lab coat, hanging it on the hook by the door. He held out the folder containing the notes. "This is for you, Cee."

She took it without comment and turned on her heel, letting the door swing closed between them. He stood still for a moment, perplexed. Had he offended her in some way? Had she known that he'd planned to ask her to dinner? Was she upset that he hadn't done it yet? Or was this how she was coping with seeing a man die in front of her?

He was still mulling over Cecelia when he reached the office he shared with Marco and the other assistants. A high, feminine laugh floated into the hallway, stopping Gilbert dead in his tracks, and he suddenly knew the reason for Cecelia's attitude.

Mother Mary, give me strength, he prayed, and stepped through the door.

Marco sat at his own desk, leaning forward, elbow on his knees, listening intently. Gilbert's sister, Lizzie, sat in Gilbert's chair, hands a blur as she told some sort of story. Perched on the edge of Gilbert's spotless desk, legs crossed at the knee, feet dangling, was Edie Shippen.

Gilbert's world narrowed to the heavy silence that cloaked the air just before an explosion—when all he could hear was the steady, constant beating of his heart, echoing through his body like a drumbeat.

Her gray eyes twinkled, and her generous mouth—painted a deep red—broke into a wide, dazzling smile.

"Hullo, Gil," she said.

"Edie," he said, once he remembered how to breathe. "What are you doing here?"

"Hello to you too," Lizzie said, from his chair. "Nice to see my favorite brother."

He gave her an impatient wave. "I saw you three hours ago, Liz." Even as he spoke, his gaze didn't leave Edie's face, shadowed beneath the brim of her gray hat. "What are you doing here?" he repeated.

"Maybe I've come to see you," Edie said. "It's been a while."

Gilbert raised his eyebrows.

"Fine. Two things," Edie said. "One personal, one professional."

"Miss Edie has her first client," Lizzie said from her chair.

Edie beamed from her perch on the desk. Pride swelled in his chest in response. He'd made a joke about her sleuthing, but she'd saved him—and Penelope too. He'd given her those business cards as a measure of his faith in her. As a token of thanks.

"A client?" he asked before he could stop himself.

"Yes, in fact. A Mrs. Patterson of Tower Street, in Manayunk," Edie said. "Sound familiar?"

"Why?" Gilbert asked, and at the same time Marco said, "Yes."

Edie grinned.

"My client believes that her neighbor was murdered by his wife. We're just here to see if either of you might be able to help us."

"We can't comment," Gilbert said. He glared at Marco, who held his hands up, as if to say he was innocent. "Dr. Knight would have our heads."

"I told you it was no use," Lizzie said, standing. "We should have gone straight to Finn Pyle. He'll help us."

"Now hold on," Gilbert said quickly. "How do you know that Pyle knows anything about this?"

"My client gave a very convincing description of the officers at the scene. And the coroners," Edie added, giving him a pointed look. "Two terribly handsome young men: one pale and dark-haired; the other Italian, carrying a camera.

Said the detective was short and round, with a face like a bulldog."

"That could be anyone," Gilbert said. "I can think of at least three detectives she could be describing."

"She called us handsome," Marco pointed out. "Was she one of the neighbor ladies on the porch? That blonde?"

"So he *was* murdered." Edie leaned forward. "That's why you were there?"

Gilbert was going to have to strangle Marco later, in private. "We don't just investigate murders. The coroner's office is called anytime there's a death, natural or otherwise. We're very busy."

"Clearly." Her lips twitched, and Gilbert got the distinct impression she was trying not to laugh at him. "Anyway, you don't need to tell us anything officially. I just promised Mrs. Patterson that I'd look into the matter. She's convinced that Mrs. Byrne, the widow, had something to do with it."

"I think that sounds like police business," Gilbert said. "Nothing we can help you with."

"I see." Edie's shoulders slumped ever so slightly, and Gilbert hated himself with every inch they fell. But he couldn't afford to step out of line—Knight had just warned him of leaving the investigating to the police, and his antics with Edie in the spring had nearly cost him everything.

"I'm sorry," Gil said, softening his voice. "I can't risk my job, Edie. Not over this."

"I understand." She didn't look like she did. She picked a piece of nonexistent lint off her skirt. "Not to worry. I'll see what Detective Pyle can tell me."

"Edie." Gilbert put a note of warning into his voice—then remembered he had no right to tell her what to do. No right to stop her, to tell her that she shouldn't meddle in murder.

"Gil," she replied. Her shoulders were tense, like she could sense his disapproval. Like she was gearing up for a fight.

"Be careful," he said instead.

Her face lit up, just enough that Gilbert knew he'd done the right thing. "Oh, you know me," she said, hopping from the desk with a little laugh.

And that was exactly the problem.

"What was the other thing?" Marco asked suddenly. "You said you were here for two reasons. What was the other?"

"Oh, that." When Edie lifted her gaze again, and some of the twinkle had come back into her eyes. "What are you doing Saturday night, Gil?"

Chapter 4

Finnegan Pyle was all too eager to talk.

Edie had suspected he would be—she'd taken a liking to the long-faced detective during the events of the previous spring, and the feeling was mutual. Pyle had sat with her during the taut hours of Gilbert's emergency surgery, when the doctors had worked to remove a bullet from his liver. He'd also been crucial in keeping her involvement out of the papers and the official police report.

They met in the manicured park in Rittenhouse Square, beside a large bronze lion snarling at a snake beneath its paws. Edie wore a walking suit in a navy wool; the jacket belted smartly at the waist, and the sleeves and hem were embroidered with flowers the same brilliant scarlet as her hat and gloves. The day was seasonally cool, dappled with late-September sunshine.

"I was surprised to get your invitation, Miss Shippen," Pyle said. "Lizzie said you've set yourself up as some sort of private investigator?"

"I have," Edie replied. "I intend to be discreet and to help women who might otherwise be ignored because of who they are or who they are afraid of. We both know that happens more than it should."

He made a small grunt of agreement. And he didn't immediately take his leave, so Edie decided to press her questions.

"My client is concerned about an investigation involving her neighbor. I promised to look into the matter myself. I did assure her that I thought you'd be doing all that you could to make sure justice was served."

At this, Pyle gave her a long look. "You did, huh?"

"Was Homer Byrne murdered, Detective?"

Pyle stopped short. "Christ on a cracker," he muttered, and patted his jacket pocket. He pulled out a cigarette, lit it, and took a long drag. "That's police business, Miss Shippen."

"Which is what I told my client," Edie assured him. She reached out and laid a hand on his arm. "She's devastated by his death—she's known him since he was a child, you see. And she's worried that something will be overlooked. I told her of course that wouldn't happen—not with you and Gilbert on the case. And you know how Gil is—he'd never think about putting a toe out of line. He won't breathe a word to me. But you've been such a help to me before, Detective, and I knew you'd want to put her worries to rest."

"You did, did you?" Pyle asked around his cigarette, and Edie wondered if she'd pressed too hard. But Finnegan Pyle didn't look upset—in fact, he was looking down at her with a sort of concern she'd seen a million times before. *"Poor little thing,"* he seemed to be saying. *"Let me take care of you."*

So she pasted on a look she'd used on her father numerous times in her adolescence: wide-eyed, soft-lipped. She blinked up at him through her lashes.

The picture of innocence. Of helplessness.

Pyle fell for it. He took the cigarette from his mouth and pinched it between his thumb and index fingers. He squinted at the statue, then spoke.

"It's too early to tell if he was murdered, but the lab found traces of cyanide in his system."

A thrill shot through Edie. "Someone poisoned him."

"Not necessarily," Pyle cautioned. "It could have been self-inflicted. Or accidental. Stranger things have happened."

"I see." Edie mulled this over. "Thank you, Detective. I know my client will be very relieved to know you're giving this matter your full attention."

Spots of color bloomed in Pyle's cheeks. "Don't mention it," he said, voice gruff. "Did she happen to say if there would be anyone who would want Mr. Byrne dead?"

"She did," Edie said carefully. "But I don't want to accuse anyone innocent."

"You're not accusing anyone," Pyle said. "You're just giving information that would aid in an official police investigation."

And he *had* just helped Edie immensely. She owed him this much.

"His wife," she said simply. "Isn't it always the wife?"

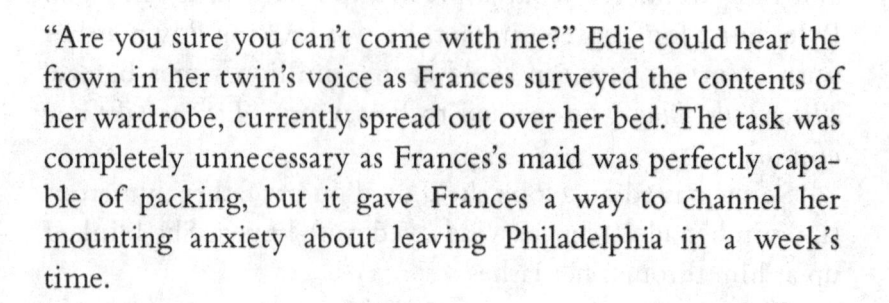

◆ ─────── ◆◆◆ ─────── ◆

"Are you sure you can't come with me?" Edie could hear the frown in her twin's voice as Frances surveyed the contents of her wardrobe, currently spread out over her bed. The task was completely unnecessary as Frances's maid was perfectly capable of packing, but it gave Frances a way to channel her mounting anxiety about leaving Philadelphia in a week's time.

"I've only just started the agency," Edie said again. "I couldn't possibly drop it all and abscond to Paris for the next year."

"It's not a year," Frances corrected as she set aside a soft white sweater. Unlike Edie, she still wore her hair long, though today it was tucked up under itself in a false bob.

"Nine months is most of a year," Edie replied. She understood why her sister was leaving. At times, she'd even considered joining Frances in her trip abroad. It'd be easy to drown her memories and regrets in the gin joints in Paris—to slip into yet another new life, far from the ghosts that haunted every inch of the family's big house in Chestnut Hill. But Frances deserved a fresh start, a chance to live her own life. Edie didn't know if her twin could do that if she tagged along. "I have a case. A client. Colleen Spencer's aunt, actually."

"I know," Frances said. She looked up at her sister. "I ran into Colleen at the gallery, and she caught me up to speed. Do you really think you're prepared to solve a murder? That's serious business."

"I think I can advocate for my client and make sure the police hear my concerns," Edie said, voice tart. "I've been in contact with the police, and they're grateful for my assistance."

"Are they now?" Frances tilted her head, studying her sister. "Well, I'm sure you'll keep yourself busy while I'm away."

Edie needed to change the subject. She had hoped Frances would be supportive of her desire to help women find justice, given the events of the previous spring. But perhaps she was asking for too much. Wanting too much. That wouldn't be anything new.

Edie checked her watch. She'd wanted to catch the next train into Center City, to be gone from the big house before her grandmother returned from her weekly Thursday luncheon at the Cricket Club. She timed these visits precisely to avoid Grandmama. "I should be off," she said.

"Already?" Frances closed the lid to the trunk. "What about dinner on Friday? Daddy's taking us to the Palm Room. I think the Thayers will be there."

Mrs. Thayer had been a friend of Edie's mother and was an interesting sort of woman. She and her son, Jack, had survived the sinking of the *Titanic* nearly a decade earlier. Jack, was a quiet, serious sort. His wife, Lois Cassat, had been close friends with Sarah Pepper. Edie wondered idly if she had also abandoned Sarah after her scandalous marriage to Gilbert, the way the rest of society had. Jack and Lois's eldest child was of an age with Penelope—if Sarah had lived, would all their lives be different?

Edie knew without a doubt that hers would.

"I have plans already," Edie said, "but what about lunch later this weekend?"

They worked out the details. She bade farewell to Frances with a quick kiss on the cheek and dashed out of the house and down the lane to the St. Martin's train station before her sister could press for more details. Her relationship with Frances had improved over the summer months. Frances had slowly come back to herself, stepping out of her shell. She still carried a tremendous amount of guilt about the young women who had died the previous spring—each of them connected to Edie and, by extension, Frances. The weeks they'd spent down the shore in Atlantic City had done them both well. Sunshine and sea air tended to do that. As a result, their relationship was not as strained as it had been when Edie had first returned from California, but she didn't know if they'd ever again be as close as they'd been as girls.

She boarded the train, settling on one of the wooden seats in the front car, and pulled her notebook from her purse. As the train swayed beneath her, she looked over her notes from the meeting with Mrs. Patterson, her thoughts drifting to her conversation with Finnegan Pyle. Homer Byrne had died by poisoning. Pyle had said it was too early to call it a murder, but given Mrs. Patterson's insistence that it was, Edie thought it might be worth visiting the widow. She knew, almost better than anyone, that a murderer could operate in plain sight, with no one around them any the wiser.

The train belched smoke as it pulled into Broad Street Station, elevated across from City Hall at 15th and Market. She cut through City Hall, ducking into the tall, arched corridor that split the building into quarters, and exited on the opposite side of Penn Square. Mrs. Patterson had said that Mrs. Byrne worked as a shopgirl at the stationary store in Wanamaker's, the grand department store directly adjacent to City Hall—and one of Edie's favorite places to shop. She'd pop in, see if Mrs. Byrne was working, and then head upstairs to check on whether her new dress was ready. She almost wished Lizzie were with her so she could tell her assistant that shopping could be a productive use of her time.

"Welcome to Wanamaker's," the door attendant said. Edie nodded at him, stepping briskly over the mosaiced floor into the interior courtyard of the department store. She always got a little thrill coming in here—the ceiling soared over a hundred feet high, surrounded by arched balconies on two sides. The famous golden pipe organ dominated the south side of the courtyard, to her right as she walked through tablewares. She wanted to linger over the ribbons and laces near the center of the floor, but she reminded herself that she was there for business, not pleasure. She passed the bronze eagle, letting her fingers trail along the pedestal.

Hello, Mrs. Byrne, she practiced silently, staring up at the eagle. *I'm a private investigator, and my client believes you murdered your husband. What do you have to say for yourself?*

No, no. That wouldn't do at all. That was akin to rushing in, guns blazing. She needed a softer, gentler approach, even with a suspected murderess.

She was still mulling over the details of what she'd say when she approached the stationer, which was tucked in an alcove beside the millinery. Her attention wavered. Hats of every shape, size, and state of finishing were displayed on wooden hat stands on the shelves.

"Questions first, hat later," she told herself firmly, and turned away from the bits and bobs and put her attention on the fine paper goods . . . and on the girl working the counter. She was about Edie's own age, with a sandy bob parted down the middle and crimped in perfect waves. Her lipstick was bright and her smile wide; this was no widow in mourning.

"Excuse me," Edie said. She leaned forward on the counter, pressing up on her toes. "I'm looking for a girl named Lily? My friend said she's the best."

The woman's brows in surprise. "Lily isn't here, miss. But I'm happy to help you. Are you looking for something in particular?"

"Wedding invitations," Edie said, the words leaving her mouth before she could stop herself. Probably the wrong thing to say, based on the way the woman's gaze dropped to Edie's left hand and the lack of an engagement ring, but it was too late now. She was committed.

"I'm getting married," Edie lied. "I'm here to look at invitations."

"Of course. Miss . . . ?"

"Lawless," Edie replied automatically. *In for a penny . . .* "My fiancé would be here, but he's stuck at work, so it's up to me. Men."

The girl pursed her lips.

Edie barreled on. "My friend said that Lily was the girl to see. The best taste of any stationer in Philadelphia. You're sure she's not available?"

"I'm sure. But I promise you, I will take good care of you," she said. Her voice was surprisingly soft, tinged with only the barest hint of an accent. Italian, if Edie had to guess. Mrs. Patterson had said that Lily Byrne was Italian too. "I will show you the book of samples. Are you interested in printed invitations or calligraphed?"

"Printed," Edie said. "We don't have much money."

Another raised eyebrow—this time accompanied by a sweeping glance at Edie's outfit. She'd dressed simply, today: a long-sleeved dress with a scalloped hem, heeled oxfords, and a navy cloche. But the fabric was expensive—too expensive for her to be pleading poverty at the Wanamaker's counter. "My parents don't approve," Edie said quickly. "They want nothing to do with me or him. So we're on our own. You know how it goes."

The woman's face softened. "I do," she said. She pulled a fat book of samples from one of the shelves behind her and set it on the counter. The spine creaked as she opened it, flipping quickly through a sea of cream- and ecru-colored pages, each with only the slightest variation in texture. "Are you looking for something in particular? What would your Romeo like?"

Edie shook her head. "I don't even know yet," she said, forcing a laugh. "It's all been very sudden, to be honest. A whirlwind. I'm supposed to pick all these things out, and I'm not even sure what he'll like. Isn't that silly?"

The woman gave a surprised laugh. "It's funny you ask about Lily. You sound just like her."

"Is she happy?" Edie asked, making her eyes to go round, but knowing the truth: Lily's husband was dead. "My parents said I'm setting myself up for a lifetime of misery, but I told them it's impossible to be miserable if you're in love."

The girl winced. "No. He died recently. That's why she's not here."

Edie put on a shocked face, bringing a hand to her mouth. "Oh, how awful. What happened?"

The girl glanced back over her shoulder, then leaned close. "No one will tell me for sure, but it was sudden. It just happened a few days ago."

"How awful," Edie repeated.

The girl nodded. "But enough sad things. Tell me about your wedding. Will you be having bridesmaids? Are they wearing a certain color?"

"Our sisters," Edie said. "They'll both be wearing green." She'd always wanted her bridesmaids in green. "It's a winter wedding."

"Oh, I have just the thing," the shopgirl said. She flipped a few more pages, to a sample of a cream invitation with a border of embossed holly leaves.

"It's lovely," Edie said idly. She still had no indication of whether this woman's coworker was a murderess or not, and these questions were getting her nowhere. How did the police do it? She needed something either to reassure Mrs. Patterson that the widow was innocent, or to take to the police to cause them to investigate further. "I just worry that my fiancé won't like it. He can get so terribly cross with me when things don't go his way." She dropped her voice, leaning close.

The girl pressed her lips together. "They expect us to read their minds, and then get angry when we cannot." She cast a quick glance back over her shoulder. "I know . . . I have known men like that. Are you sure you love him?"

"I'm sure."

The girl stared at her a moment more. "I will help you if you help me. You buy this invitation"—she tapped at the page in front of her—"and I will send you to someone who can help make him less angry. A woman from my country. A wise woman—she helped Lily. She can help you too."

She pulled a small white card from the table beside her and scrawled out an address on South Broad Street. "You see her, you ask about la futura. You tell her Nina sent you."

Edie smiled at the girl as she placed the card in her pocketbook and paid a deposit on the invitations. She promised to be back next week with her fiancé for final approval. She wouldn't, of course, but Nina would get the commission on the deposit regardless. And it was a small price to pay for a clue.

Homer Byrne had been an angry man. Angry enough that his wife had sought out a mysterious woman on South Street for help.

Maybe even angry enough to cause his wife to commit murder.

A migraine struck Edie that evening, consigning her to a dark room for the next day. She emerged on Saturday morning as weak-kneed as a newborn colt and ravenously hungry. Her spells were unpredictable things, brought on by too much sun, too little food, loud noises, or a change in the weather. Her only relief had come, in recent months, in the tincture made of chloral and belladonna that she'd started taking in the spring and that the Shippen's family doctor and city coroner, William Knight, insisted she continue. But even the bitter drops failed to keep the vertigo and sharp pains at bay every time. She'd learned long ago to rest when she needed it.

Lizzie arrived a little after noon, carrying a pair of black garment bags in her arms. Aphrodite yipped a greeting, running circles around Lizzie's ankles as she hung the bags on the valet stand beside Edie's armoire. "Glad to see you up and about, miss. Are you feeling well enough to go?"

"I think so," Edie said. Her vision hadn't cleared completely, but she was able to stand without the world feeling topsy-turvy, which was victory enough on its own. "Is that the dress?"

"It is! Just arrived from Wanamaker's."

Lizzie opened the bag, pulling the dress free. A thrill shot through Edie, as it had when she'd ordered it and during her fitting on Thursday. It was without a doubt the most perfect thing Edie had ever seen—a dazzling concoction of silk and sparkling beads. She could hardly wait to wear it.

"My brother's going to die when he sees you in that," Lizzie said.

"We're going as friends," Edie said. She and Gilbert had made a good team. At one point, Edie had thought that their unorthodox friendship might lead to something more, but Gilbert had erected walls between them in the months since, his interactions tinged with a coldness that left Edie feeling unsure and exposed. Edie understood—she'd put his daughter in danger, an unforgivable sin. But she hoped against all hope that friendship between them would still be possible.

Lizzie seemed unconvinced. She pursed her lips and shook her head.

"What?"

"As the person who spends the most time with the two of you, between living with him and working for you—I have thoughts."

"By all means, share them."

"Oh no," Lizzie said. "I'm not getting involved. Not with this."

Edie let it go.

"Speaking of work," Edie said, "any news from Finnegan Pyle? Has he followed up with the address I gave him?"

"Nothing yet, but he's been busy. I've assured Mrs. Patterson that we're working closely with the authorities, and they're taking her concerns seriously. She's grateful."

"Good." Edie had worried about her client while she was bedridden—she hadn't wanted the poor woman to feel ignored or abandoned.

"About that, miss. She also inquired about payment. Should I draw up an invoice? How much are we charging? We've never discussed it."

Edie waved her off and pulled open her jewelry box, on the hunt for the perfect accessories to wear to Ava's party. "Oh, we won't charge her a thing," she said. "Tell her not to worry about it."

Lizzie stared at her, mouth agape. "You can't be serious."

"Whyever not?" Edie asked as she pulled out a thin, golden chain and held it up in the mirror. *Perfect.*

"The whole point of a business is to make money, Miss Edie. You can't keep paying me if you're not—"

"I have more money than I could spend in ten lifetimes, Lizzie," Edie said. "I won't charge these women. It'd be unethical. They need help, and I'm happy to help them. To be their voice."

"She won't like it, miss." Lizzie said. "You'll have to charge her something. Women like Mrs. Patterson—they're proud. They won't be happy with the idea of accepting charity."

"It's not charity."

"That's how they'll see it. Trust me."

"Then a sliding fee," Edie said. "Based on whatever they can afford. We'll start at a dollar and work up from there. Whoever is able to pay will pay. And we can set up some sort of fund to cover those who can't pay anything."

"A dollar is reasonable," Lizzie said slowly, as if she wasn't quite convinced. "I'll handle that this afternoon."

"Excellent," Edie said. And she meant it.

Chapter 5

The door to the Shippen's elegant mansion on Rittenhouse Square opened before Gilbert could even knock. The last time he'd been here, it had been Edie's birthday. He'd been home from the hospital only a few days, and he'd needed to see her with a deep ache that terrified him.

He shouldn't need anything that much. Shouldn't want anything that much—not when he had a daughter to think of. A family.

And yet here he was, thanking O'Mara, the butler, and handing the man his hat and coat while letting Lizzie sweep him inside and up the stairs to a bedroom on the left side of the second floor. The room itself was bigger than the entire top floor of his parent's row house in Manayunk. Penny would be able to roller-skate in circles.

"I know," Lizzie said, reading his mind. "It's a whole different world, hmm? Bath is through the far door, and I'll bring your clothes up in a moment. Mr. Shippen's valet, Johnny, will help you."

"I can dress myself," Gilbert insisted, but Lizzie was already gone. He crossed to the window and looked out. The sun was setting over the western edge of the city, painting the street block below in vibrant oranges and pinks.

He never should have agreed to this. He'd felt badly about denying Edie help with her investigation—after it was his own damn fault she'd started this business in the first place. She'd risked so much to help him find Lizzie in the spring. The least he could do was to agree to go to a party with her this evening. And let her dress him.

The last bit filled him with dread. At least it wasn't a costume party; between Edie and his sister, he was half certain he'd be dressed as the Adam to Edie's Eve, consigned to a loincloth of fig leaves for the evening. His heart skipped, and his fingers tightened on the windowsill.

Breathe.

His hands stayed steady. Slowly, he relaxed, breathing deeply and evenly until his heart resumed normal beating.

A soft knock at the door caused him to turn. A young man—Johnny, presumably, stood holding a black garment bag aloft, trailed by two other men, one carrying a steaming bowl of hot water; and the other, a stack of towels. "Excuse me, sir. I have your clothes."

"Thank you. I can handle it," Gilbert said, but Johnny was already moving, hanging the bag on the valet stand and unearthing a black tuxedo, crisp white shirt, and satin bow tie.

Sweet Mother Mary. A bolt of anger surged through him.

She'd bought the damn tuxedo.

The anger turned to amusement. *Of course* she had. He'd thought, when they left the tailor that day, that she'd let it go. But Edie never let things go.

It was a gift. He'd accept it for what it was, for tonight. He'd wear her clothes, spin her around the dance floor, and at midnight turn back into the pumpkin he was. So he let Johnny guide him to the chair in the corner, and tried to relax as the valet shaved him with a firm, practiced hand and a wickedly sharp blade. He didn't complain, not once, as he donned the tuxedo and Johnny fiddled with the hem and the bow tie.

"Look at you," Lizzie said from the doorway as the valet arranged Gilbert's street clothes into tidy piles. She gave a low whistle, and heat spread up Gil's neck.

"It's too much, isn't it?"

"Not at all," Lizzie said. "You'll be with movie stars tonight. You have to look the part."

"I'm not sure about this, Liz."

"Too late now. Come on—we'll wait for her in the library. She's almost done."

Gil followed his sister down the dark-paneled hallway. Pretty landscapes and more modern abstracts hung along the walls. He recognized a few from the gallery shows that the Philadelphia Twelve, a collective of women artists, had held over the last few months. Three of their number had met their ends at the hands of the Schuylkill Slasher. Absently, he rubbed his middle, where the bullet had passed through him, mere centimeters from fatal injury.

Lizzie showed him into the library. The room was larger than the entirety of his parents' home, two stories tall. They entered on the upper level, and took a winding staircase down to the main level. An elegant writing desk was pushed beneath one of the tall windows looking out over the small, manicured courtyard at the back of the house. A set of green curved chairs faced in toward each other. On the other side of the room, a low sofa sat before a jade-tiled fireplace. A tray sat on the coffee table, piled high with sandwiches and a pot of tea with two empty cups.

"Hungry?" Lizzie asked, but she didn't wait for him to answer before she busied herself pouring them each a cup of tea. He took his, the cup clattering against the saucer briefly before he set it down, clenching his hands into fists.

Christ. His nerves were strung as tightly as barbed wire. *It's just Edie,* he reminded himself, even though he was certain that was the problem.

It was Edie.

Lizzie pressed her lips together, as perceptive as ever. "All right?" she asked.

He looked at her then, really looked at her. The events of the previous spring had changed her too, but she'd bloomed in the summer since—her cheeks were full, and her eyes were lively. She'd changed her hair as well—gone was her tidy bun, ready for service work. Instead, she wore it cropped in the modern style, a pair of barrettes pinning back her bob from her face. Even her clothes had changed—she'd traded in her uniform and handmade clothes for a fashionable yet serviceable tweed skirt and sweater set. Gone was the sticky-fingered little girl from their childhood, or the awkward teenager, or the harried young house maid. Lizzie had become a young woman with a career, seemingly overnight.

God. How much longer until he looked at Penelope and had the same thought? How much had he missed already? She'd be in school this time a year from now. He'd blink, and it'd be high school—hopefully at the Philadelphia High School for Girls, like Cecelia. Then college, if he had his way.

He leaned forward, elbows on his knees. "I think we should move out."

She blinked at him. "Pardon?"

"You, me, and Penelope," he said, his voice leaving in a rush. "Mam and Da deserve a break, yeah? We can't all live in that house together. I have some savings. What if we found a place for the three of us to live? Not for forever—you'll get married and have a family of your own someday—but for now?"

"That's a big step, Gil." Lizzie set her tea down. "You've barely recovered, and your fits . . ."

"Are under control. I've been taking care of myself." He looked down at his hands "I can do this."

She didn't answer, not for a long moment. "I'll think about it," she said. "Penelope deserves her da, Gil. But she also deserves stability. She's never lived without Mam, and what if it doesn't work out? What if you get sick again, and . . ."

"I'm fine." His traitorous hands jumped again, and he rolled his shoulders. "I'm doing better. My memories are back, and I've weaned myself off the morphine." That itself had been a slow, torturous process, overseen by Dr. Knight. He'd decreased his doses gradually since leaving the hospital, and hadn't had any in a month. He ached for it—for the oblivion, the peace—but he couldn't—*wouldn't*—go back to the place where he had been the previous spring.

Nearly dying had reminded him of all his reasons to live.

"I'm her da, Liz. I want her with me. But I can't do it alone. Not with my hours. I'd need your help."

"I have a job too," Lizzie said, rearing back. "I work here, for Miss Edie."

"I know. Next year, when she's in school, it'll be doable. For the both of us." He'd already thought of this. He'd need more time to save money, to put together a proper down payment. To find a house somewhere with trees, and a neighborhood with other children, free from the cramped streets and belching smoke of the mills. "Just think about it."

"I think it's a splendid idea." Edie's voice floated down from above, startling them both from their conversation. Gilbert stood, craning his neck, and froze, transfixed.

Edie stood at the top of the spiral stairs, one hand on each of the railings, posed like a girl in a magazine, glittering from the golden headband tucked into her dark hair, to the toes of her turquoise pumps. Her peacock-blue dress shimmered as she turned down the stairs.

"Well, what do you think?" she asked as she reached the bottom of the stairs. She turned in a circle, showing off the elaborate beading on the dress.

"Jesus, Mary, and Joseph," Gilbert whispered, his mouth dry. He didn't even know where to look—the top layer of the dress was cut wide on her shoulders and gaped open at the front before hugging the curve of her waist. Beneath it, a bodice of thin blue silk dipped low over her breasts. The whole thing sparkled with hundreds of tiny green and gold beads.

"I think my idiot of a brother means to say you look gorgeous," Lizzie said. She rushed to Edie's side, moving the skirt this way and that. "Kate did a lovely job with your hair, miss. You look amazing."

"Thank you, Lizzie," Edie said, but she didn't take her eyes off Gilbert. Something almost feline appeared in the curve of her wine-colored lips. "I think I forgot my handbag in my room. Would you mind fetching it?"

"Of course." Lizzie dashed up the stairs, and then Edie and Gil were alone for the first time in months.

He couldn't move, his feet rooted to the carpet, his hands fisted at his sides. He wanted nothing more than to cross the room in three strides and take her in his arms, but he couldn't.

Wouldn't.

But it didn't matter, because she was moving to him, her strides sure as her heels clicked across the floor. She stopped a few inches from him, her gaze sweeping up his body, tilting her chin up to look him in the eye.

"Hi, Gil," she said. She'd lined her eyes with black, turning her gray irises stormy. "Thanks for coming with me."

"Will you be cold in that?" he asked, even though he meant to say *Hello*, or *You're welcome*, or *We're going strictly as friends*.

Color bloomed along her cheekbones and her collarbones, he noticed, even though he kept telling himself to focus on her face, and not the smooth expanse of skin beneath her collarbone.

"I can think of a few ways to stay warm," she said, and it was his turn to blush. She arched an eyebrow. "I have a wrap," she added, amused. "But I am open to whatever it is you're thinking of."

"I was going to offer you my coat," he said. "Or, I should say, *your* coat. Since you paid an obscene amount of money for it."

"Nonsense." She waved a hand. "Of course I bought it. I couldn't have wasted Monsieur Jacques's time like that, Gil. The man is an artist. Turn around." She twirled her finger in the air.

He did, aware of her gaze on every inch of him as he spun slowly. When he faced her again, she looked a little dazed.

"An artist," she repeated, almost to herself. Then she shook her head, as if clearing her mind. "Well. Shall we?"

The Bellevue was only a half mile from the Shippen's city house, but rich people didn't walk even that short a distance—certainly not at night, dressed the way they were. Gil opened the door before Grover, the pimply young driver, could make his way around the car, and reached inside to help Edie out.

She smiled up at him, grateful, and took his hand in hers. She didn't let go either, after she'd straightened to her feet or once Grover had shut the door behind them.

"I'll call when we're ready to come home," Edie said to the driver, though she didn't look at him. Her gaze stayed fixed on Gil's, and his heart did a funny little somersault behind his ribs.

Friends. He reminded himself. *Penny needs a mother. This can never work.*

But she doesn't need a mother tonight, another voice whispered. *One night won't hurt.*

He didn't know if he could limit himself to one night. They'd tried that, in the spring—a night of slow kisses that left him with an aching heart and a fierce wanting.

"Gil?" Edie whispered. "Should we go in?"

He came back to himself then and offered her his arm. She took it, and they crossed beneath the cast-iron overhang lit by a score of brilliant electric lights. Climbing the small flight of white marble steps, they passed through the wide bronze doors. Gilbert almost stumbled when they reached the grand lobby, with its marble floor and walls and four elevators. The clerks smiled at them from behind their mahogany desk, but Gilbert wasn't seeing them. He was seeing himself, at twenty-one years old, in the winter of 1915, when he'd marched through the grand lobby alone, in a borrowed suit, and taken the elevator to the eighteenth floor, where Sarah Pepper was in the middle of her debutante ball, eighteen years old and newly pregnant. He'd taken her hand, and they'd run away together. By dawn, they had eloped to Elkton, Maryland. They'd lost that baby and the one that followed. The third baby, their sweet Penelope, had survived and thrived, but Sarah's body had grown weak, and she'd hemorrhaged during the birth. He'd buried her in 1917, an infant in his arms. Would he have turned back on that winter night if he'd known what would happen to her? If he'd known what loving her would do?

He thought of his daughter, of her cherubic face and mess of red curls.

He thought of Sarah's hand on the curve of his back, her breath against his skin.

He knew, deep in his soul, that Penelope had been Sarah's last gift to him, and he couldn't imagine a world in which he'd have been lucky enough to keep them both.

Edie squeezed her fingers around the curve in his bicep, bringing him back to the present. Of course she knew what he was thinking—she'd known Sarah, had grown up hearing stories about that night.

"She'd be so proud of you," Edie said softly, and Gilbert nearly kissed her right then and there.

He settled instead for covering her fingers with his free hand and letting her lead the way to the elevator. "Eighteenth floor," she told the attendant, and as the doors closed behind them, Gilbert remembered what it felt like to be young and reckless. Because tonight he'd choose himself, and damn the consequences.

Chapter 6

Almost a decade earlier, the historic Bellevue-Stratford Hotel on Broad Street had been renovated to include an opulent trio of ballrooms on its glass-enclosed rooftop. The central room, called the Rose Garden, had since served as a constant in almost all the major events in Edie's life: her debutante ball, her mother's funeral reception, society weddings. During the early days of American involvement in the Great War, Edie and Frances and their cousins had sat with society ladies and rolled thousands of yards of bandages for the Red Cross to send to the boys "Over There."

Edie kept her fingers on Gilbert's arm as the elevator climbed the floors from the lobby. She hadn't missed the way his arm trembled beneath hers or the way his gaze had lingered on the edges of her costume, on her exposed skin, as if she were as dangerous as a live wire.

The doors opened.

"Eighteenth floor," the elevator attendant said, holding out his hand for a tip from Gilbert, but Edie was already ready with a coin, pressing it into the boy's sweaty palm. "Have a good night, miss."

They crossed the decadently furnished reception room, heading toward the ballroom, which sat in the center of the building, directly across a narrow hall from a library, and between two of the indoor gardens. The party was already in full swing. A trio of young women swayed together in the center of the dance floor, giggling. Edie recognized Isabelle Bateson, one of the Philadelphia Twelve, on the arm of her beau, near one of the tall windows overlooking City Hall. Another couple hovered near the bar, drinks in hand. A band played from the orchestra balcony, high above them, and waiters in white coats moved between it all, carrying trays loaded with canapes, over a floor of real grass, even this late into October.

"All right?" Gilbert asked her. She realized she'd stopped moving, her chest rising and falling in rapid breaths as she searched the crowd for Ava's blond bob.

"Copacetic," Edie said quickly. She gave him a dazzling smile. "Your tie is crooked."

He looked down, dropping her arm. "Is it?"

"Let me," Edie said, stepping close. She fiddled with it a little longer than necessary, breathing in the peppermint scent that seemed to follow him wherever he went.

"There," she said. "Now you're dapper."

"Edie Shippen!" Ava appeared at her arm, squealing, as she pulled Edie into her arms and swung her away from Gilbert, her fingers firm against the curve of Edie's waist, and her lips brushed the corners of Edie's mouth as she pressed a kiss to each cheek. "You look positively edible, my dear."

Edie could say the same of the movie star. Ava wore a smooth column of silver silk that clung to every curve. She was going to say something—say anything—when Ava's gaze swept to Gilbert. She practically purred out her appreciation for the figure he cut in his tuxedo, from the broad slope of his shoulders to the solid length of his legs. Edie was suddenly very, very glad she'd paid for Monsieur Jacques's handiwork, if only to watch the way Ava looked at Gilbert.

"And who is this, pet?" Ava kept her fingers on Edie's waist.

Gilbert's eyes found Edie's, and Edie couldn't breathe, not caught between the two of them as she was.

Thankfully, Gilbert did a little bow, saving Edie from having to answer. "Gilbert Lawless, ma'am."

"Dr. Lawless is a close friend of mine," Edie said. "He was kind enough to be my date tonight."

"Irish *and* a doctor! Oh, Edie, you've been keeping secrets from me," Ava said. She pulled her hand away from Edie's waist and held it out to Gil, fingers pointing toward the floor. "Ava Sylvester. I'm a friend of Edie's from California. And I have plenty of secrets of my own, I promise." She gave an exaggerated wink.

Edie came back to herself. She stepped away from Ava, tucking herself back at Gil's side as he bent over Ava's hand. She noticed, with some sense of triumph, that he didn't kiss Ava's fingers, and when he straightened, his arm slipped around Edie's shoulders possessively.

Copacetic, Edie repeated to herself. Out loud, she said, "Ava's an actress. She's shooting a movie at Norwood Studios. She's playing Juliet."

"I thought I was too old for the part, but Harry insisted," Ava said with false modesty. "He's a visionary. Let's go say hello." She reached out and took each of their hands, pulling them both across the dance floor.

Gil let out a little huff of surprise, and Edie sent him an apologetic look. Ava was over the top in the best of times; tonight, her energy bordered on the frenetic as she led them toward a table beneath a dripping spray of roses, where two gentlemen sat close together, talking in low voices. One was young and dark-haired, and one looked to be about fifty, with close-cropped blond hair, beginning to gray, and a thick mustache. Beside them, pouting into a plate of caviar, was a platinum-blond girl of about sixteen or so, wearing a bright red gown. A dark-haired woman sitting to the left of the blond-haired man took a sip of her drink, made a face, and set it on the table.

"Ah, there she is," the older man said. The younger man turned, and Edie almost gasped when she caught sight of his long nose, high cheekbones, and glittering dark eyes.

"Why, you two could be brothers!" Edie exclaimed, looking to Gilbert.

Gilbert and the man exchanged a skeptical glance. The other man's face was slightly rounder, his jaw a bit weaker, and he was undoubtedly more muscular, but to Edie the resemblance was uncanny.

Ava laughed in delight, pressing her hands to her chest. "Oh my—Duncan, she's right!"

Duncan rose from his chair. "Duncan Carroll. Pleasure to meet you."

"This is my friend, Miss Edie Shippen, and her date, Dr. Gilbert Lawless. Duncan is playing my Romeo."

Duncan Carroll. Edie knew that name. He'd been a stage actor for some years before vanishing in some sort of scandal that Edie couldn't remember much about. Apparently, his career had recovered enough for him to take the lead in the film. He shook their hands enthusiastically, and Ava turned her attention to the others at the table.

"Edie, this is Miss Della O'Malley and her mother, Mrs. Helena O'Malley. And of course, I want to introduce you to Mr. Harold Fox, the owner of Norwood Studios and the director of the film. Mr. Fox, this is my dear friend Edie Shippen. Her late great-aunt was Mae Elkins."

The man sprang to his feet, pressing his hand to his heart. "Mae's backdrops were the stuff of *legend*, Miss Shippen. Her loss is so keenly felt." Edie offered her hand, and the man bent low, brushing a kiss across her knuckles. "I believe your father is Councilman Shippen? We were classmates at Penn. Please tell him I say hello."

"He'll be delighted, I'm sure," Edie said. She should have expected the mention of Mae, but she'd left her grief over her great-aunt on the sunny coast of California—she'd had enough to grieve once she'd arrived back in Philadelphia. She blinked away a sudden onslaught of tears.

"Thank you for having us," Gilbert said, his brogue smooth, rescuing her from herself. The warm weight of his hand on her back kept her tethered to the ground, kept her from dissolving into a million little pieces. "I've seen a handful of your films, Mr. Fox. I can hardly believe you shoot in the city."

"All over," Fox said. "We do some of our scenes from a rooftop in Brewerytown; the lighting is fantastic. The rest we shoot out near the Andorra meadow—have you been to the main studio?"

Gilbert shook his head, and Fox's face fell the slightest bit. "Oh, what a shame. You'll have to come out—both you and Miss Shippen—as my guests. Perhaps tomorrow? We'll be shooting a very famous scene."

"It's the biggest studio on the East Coast," Duncan cut in. "Fox here is a real visionary."

Mr. Fox waved him off. "I'm a businessman, nothing more," he demurred. "Now that's enough chattering. You young people should be dancing. I paid a fortune for this band."

Ava raised a slim shoulder, as if to say, *"What else do you expect?"*

"It was swell to meet you, Mr. Fox and Mr. Carroll. And you too, Mrs. O'Malley, Miss O'Malley. You look gorgeous in that dress." Edie found her voice again, and Della blushed prettily, streaks of pink climbing up her cheekbones.

Edie and Gilbert had just made their way toward the dance floor when Leo Salvatore, Marco's eldest brother and the gangster known as the Butcher of Broad Street, appeared from the crush. "Dr. Lawless, Miss Shippen. I heard my favorite sleuth was here."

"Hello, Leo," Edie said. She presented her hand, and the gangster bent low over it, his lips brushing the back of her hand. "What are you doing here?"

"Business," he said, his canines flashing in a predatory smile. "Business, as always."

"Don't work too hard," Edie said.

Leo laughed. "Have a nice night, Miss Shippen."

They found the center of the dance floor. The band was playing a lively tune, something familiar and full of trumpet, and all around the couples jumped and swayed, kicking up their heels. The singer, a woman, crooned into the microphone about stolen loves, her familiar voice hitching up an octave as Gilbert's hands circled Edie's waist.

"Look up," he said softly, his breath hot against her ear. Then he spun her out, away from him, and Edie looked to the stage, to where a familiar dark-haired woman cradled a microphone in her hands, dressed head to toe in black, from the feather of her velvet turban to the yards of velvet enveloping her body. Even her fingernails were painted black, stark against her pale white skin.

Celeste DuPont, also known as Madame Midnight, had proven a frustration during the previous spring. She'd claimed to be a medium and used her position in the metaphysical circles of Philadelphia's elite to connect young women in desperate situations—like Edie's doomed cousin Rebecca—with doctors willing to help. She'd also helped hide Lizzie when Lizzie feared that Edie's father, Ned Shippen, had been the killer targeting Rebecca and her friends, but didn't think the police would take the word of a girl in service against a city councilman.

"She's everywhere," Edie said when she came back to Gilbert, her hands flat on his chest, which was rising and falling rapidly. She'd tried to forget how much fun she had dancing with Gilbert, how easily they moved together, communicating without words.

Words always complicated things between them.

She spun again. This time her gaze fell on Ava, who was frowning at her castmates. She pointed at Duncan, who threw up his hands, his face a mask of disdain.

Harold Fox grabbed his arm, whispering something in his ear, but the actor shook off the older man's grip and stalked from the room. Della gave a soft cry and bolted after him. Ava rolled her eyes and followed.

Fox seemed to come back to himself. He said something to Leo Salvatore, who clapped him on the back and signaled to the stage. The band switched to playing something soft and classical. Celeste had vanished from sight.

"What do you think is going on?" she asked Gilbert, who shrugged. A waiter in a white coat passed by, handing out tall glasses of sparkling champagne. Gil snagged two, and Edie accepted hers gratefully, taking a sip before the waiter was even gone.

"That's bad luck," Gilbert said, his laugh rumbling out from his chest, "to sip before the toast."

"I didn't think you were superstitious," Edie teased.

"I'm not superstitious. I'm Irish," he said. He kept his glass firmly in hand. "I need all the luck I can get."

Edie took another sip, feeling the bright bubbles burst on her tongue. "I don't believe in luck," she said airily, though a movement to the side of the room caught her attention. Della slipped back into the ballroom, her back pressed against one of the ivy-covered columns, clutching a glass of her own. She stared up at the stage, her expression unreadable.

Edie followed her gaze. Ava and Duncan had appeared on the balcony, with Harold between them. He stepped up to the microphone, holding a bottle of uncorked champagne in his free hand.

"Good evening," he said, and the microphone squealed with feedback, cutting sharply through the air. Edie winced, stepping backward into Gilbert, who steadied her with a hand on her waist. "Good evening," Fox said again. "Welcome to our little party. We at Norwood Studios are so glad you're all here to celebrate with us."

A smattering of applause broke through the ballroom. Fox cleared his throat. "You're probably wondering what we're celebrating. You see, Ava here wanted things to be a surprise! Didn't you, dear?"

Ava nodded but stood stiffly, a smile pasted across her face. On Fox's other side, Duncan Carroll wore the face of a man heading to the gallows.

What on earth is happening? Edie thought. *Something about the film?* Ava had said they were almost finished—perhaps this was to celebrate the end of their work together?

"These two," Harold said, his words drowning out Edie's thoughts. "These two. When they told me the news, I could hardly believe it. But who am I to stand in the way of true love?"

Love? Edie looked up at Ava, wide-eyed. The Ava she knew wasn't interested in love—with flirting, sure. A kiss or a pet. But *love?* Edie's pulse thundered in her ears. Ava hadn't said a word about this. And she would have, Edie knew. She *would* have.

"I have plenty of secrets of my own," Ava had said.

"But Duncan said to me, 'We just couldn't wait, Harry!' And I thought, could we at least have waited until we wrapped the film? What better way to celebrate a wedding than with a film premiere? But these two hopped on down to Elkton without so much as a by your leave."

Elkton. That meant . . .

Duncan shouldered Harold out of the way, snatching champagne glasses from Ava's hand and the bottle from Harold's. He poured sloppily, sending liquid splashing onto the floor below. "What Harry is trying to say is, you're all here with us to celebrate our wedding. Now drink up."

He handed the bottle back to Ava and tipped his glass back, draining it in one long swallow. Ava and Harold stared at him.

"To the happy couple!" someone shouted.

"To the happy couple," Harold repeated, his voice shaking.

Ava looked like she was going to vomit. Edie had the sudden urge to rush to her friend, to wrap the other woman in her arms and comfort her. To demand to know what was going on.

Blood rushed in her ears. She stumbled again, and Gilbert tightened his hand on her hip, his face creased with concern.

"Edie?" he asked. "Are you all right?"

"I'm suddenly feeling faint," she lied, pressing a hand to her head. "Take me home, please."

Chapter 7

They didn't speak as they rode the elevator down to the lobby, nor as the clerk at the desk hailed them a cab. Gilbert helped Edie into the backseat, their hands still joined, and Edie gave the cabbie her address. Some of the sparkle had left her—she folded in on herself as they drove the few blocks back to Rittenhouse Square, streetlights casting her face into shadow.

"Wait here," Gilbert told the driver when they arrived. Edie looked at him, surprised, but Gil shook his head as he walked her up the front steps to her door.

"Do you want to come in?" she asked. "I don't know about you, but I could use a drink right about now."

She looked so hopeful and sad all at once in the lamplight—her big gray eyes, soft; her dark painted lips, parted. Tempting. *Yes,* Gilbert wanted to say. *I want to come in.*

He reached up and brushed his hand over her cheek, swallowing hard. His thumb grazed the corner of her warm, soft mouth, and Edie's eyes fluttered closed. Gilbert found himself leaning in, his heart thundering in his ears.

But then he blinked, and he was back in that crypt, standing over the small, still form of his daughter.

He dropped his hand and stepped back. Edie's eyes snapped open, hurt flooding her gaze.

"Thank you for the invitation. And for the tuxedo," he said, motioning down his body. "I'll have Lizzie bring my things home so they won't be in your way."

"Gil." Edie reached for him. "Gil, wait—"

"Goodnight, Miss Shippen." He was already down the steps, back toward the car. He had to get home, had to put some distance between Edie and himself. Had to remember that whatever spark there was between them must be stamped out, because he couldn't—wouldn't—let himself be distracted again.

His family was his focus. Penelope, Lizzie. His family.

Not Edie.

"Gil!" Edie was starting down the steps after him, her voice raised.

He was a goddamned coward.

"Manor Street, Manayunk," Gilbert told the driver as he climbed into the back seat and closed the door.

The man looked back over his shoulder. "You're sure, bud? That's some dame you've got there."

Gilbert glared at him, clutching his knees. He needed to move, needed to run, but he couldn't, not in this damned tuxedo, not at this hour. The man shrugged and pulled away from the curb.

Gil didn't let himself look back. Not even once.

<hr />

Gilbert bent at the waist, drawing in a deep, ragged breath. Monday's morning air had been cool outside, but inside the boxing gym it was stale with the scent of sweat and the heat of moving bodies.

"Again." The small young man in front of Gil bounced on his toes, one hand on either side of a large punching bag. Jack McConnell had beaten Gilbert every time they'd boxed in the last three months, when Gilbert had started training with him. Three months since he'd weaned off the morphine, under Dr. Knight's care; three months since Tommy Fletcher had dropped him off at this nondescript building near the morgue.

"I can't," Gilbert gasped. Every inch of his body ached, both from the exertion and the blows Jack had been able to land.

Jack kept bouncing, his eyes crinkling in a smile. "Aw, c'mon, Doc. You will. A few more minutes. And then I'll let you go early so you can get yourself pretty."

One more. Gilbert could do one more. He straightened, pushing himself to stand. His own gloves were heavy on his hands, but he lifted them, readying himself.

His limbs were steady. He took a breath in and let it out.

And then his fists flew, each hitting the bag with a vicious *thwack thwack* that sent Jack back on his heels.

"Good. Keep going. Two more minutes."

Boxing had been Tommy's idea. Dr. Knight had instructed Gilbert to find a physical outlet for his difficulties. He'd suggested running or rowing. Gilbert had been too weak to run more than a block, and he had been too polite to remind his boss that he lacked access to the rowing clubs and crew teams dominated by the city's wealthy. Gilbert had been skeptical, at first. He didn't think that fighting—boxing—would bring his mind out of the trenches or keep him from craving the sweet heat of the morphine he'd relied on for years. But it was more than trying to pummel Jack into a pulp—not that Gilbert ever could. Jack was a vicious fighter but a surprisingly patient teacher. They'd spent whole mornings working on Gilbert's balance, on his coordination, his speed. With each day that passed, Gilbert grew stronger and more aware of his body than he'd ever remembered being before. His episodes had decreased too. For the first time in a long time, Gilbert felt like he had rejoined the land of the living.

"That's time." Jack stepped back, clapping Gilbert on the shoulder. "Good job, Doc."

"Thanks." Gilbert stripped off his gloves and untucked his shirt, using the hem to wipe the sweat from his eyes. He knew he stank to high heaven. He'd shower at the morgue and change into fresh clothes, then start his day.

Jack waved him off. He never accepted thanks for his time or money for payment. Tommy had explained quietly that Jack worked for him, leading one of the street gangs of youths who served as the Cresson Street Crew's eyes and ears. He was doing this as a favor; it would be beneficial for a kid like Jack to be owed a favor from a gangster like Tommy Fletcher.

Gilbert remained uneasy with the arrangement. He hadn't liked accepting help from Tommy, but he hadn't had much of a choice. His own mother had been the one to invite the gangster to visit Gilbert in his hospital bed, worried that Gilbert would die before the former best friends could reconcile. Tommy had sworn that he was only trying to help Mrs. Lawless—that he was doing this because they were friends—but Gilbert didn't trust him. Tommy Fletcher would demand his pound of flesh eventually.

"Wait a second, Doc." Jack, usually the picture of confidence, looked unsure. He rubbed his nose. "I got a question for you."

Gilbert paused. "What's that?"

"You're a real doctor, right? Even though you deal mostly with all those dead bodies and stuff?" Jack was staring at Gilbert's face, his dark eyes unreadable. He looked so awfully young; Gilbert kept forgetting that he was more boy than man, eighteen or twenty at the most.

"I went to medical school, yes," Gilbert said slowly. "And I served as a medic in the war. Why? Do you need something? Are you ill?"

"Not me," Jack said quickly. "It's actually for a friend. I was just wondering. I read about this place in Germany where they can take a person who was born a fella and make him into a girl. Or even . . . I've heard it could even be the other way around. Do you know about that?"

Gilbert frowned, thinking. "Gender reassignment? I don't know much of anything about it. I know it's happened, of course—there was a rather famous case of it out west a few years ago." He watched the young man's face carefully as he spoke. He had his suspicions about Jack McConnell, but he understood the need to keep certain aspects of oneself a secret. "It's rare, but not impossible. There might be someone at Hahnemann or Penn who would know more. I'd have your friend start there."

Jack's face fell, but only slightly. "That sounds expensive."

"It probably is," Gilbert said. "Unfortunately, these things usually are."

Jack nodded, almost to himself. "All right." He rubbed his nose again. "One more question, Doc."

"I'm all ears."

"The boss wants to know whether you know anything about a guy who died at Reading Terminal Market the other day. Says its important."

Gilbert stilled. He'd known that Tommy would call to collect on his generosity at some point. He hadn't thought it would be so soon. "Tell Tommy if he has information about a body, he can come down to the morgue himself. I'll be there all day."

And then he left. He had to get to work, get cleaned up.

Had to see what Tommy Fletcher knew.

◆◆◆

Gilbert spent the rest of his morning bracing himself for Tommy Fletcher to step through his office door, but every time he looked up, he was relieved to see it was only Marco. He finished up the paperwork on the Byrne case, undisturbed, and dropped it off at Cecelia's desk on his way to lunch.

Two men killed by cyanide in the same week. Both, according to Jack, with a connection to Tommy's Cresson Street Crew. Dead gangsters were nothing new to Gilbert. He'd seen men—and some women—from every gang in the city come across his table at some point, each meeting their fate in a violent end. Stabbings, shootings, garrotings. Car accidents and house fires. Mostly young—too young; lives snuffed out chasing money or power or even a bit of fun. Poisonings were rarer. Poison had a reputation as a woman's weapon, or a coward's, administered from a distance and with a smaller margin of error. The tool of jealous lovers and scorned heirs.

Cecelia took the file from his hand and slipped it atop the stack in her inbox that never seemed to get any smaller. She and the other girls in the office worked so hard, day after day, typing and answering phones and making sure there was always fresh coffee for the army of coroner's assistants. She did it gracefully and never sighed or rolled her eyes when he dropped off a report. Did she like her job, or was she just good-natured? He should ask her. He'd worked beside her for years and didn't even know what neighborhood she lived in or why she worked at the morgue at all. She took such good care of everyone around her—did she like children? Would she be a good mother? Penelope had Gil's own mother and Lizzie, but Mam was tired, and Lizzie needed to live her own life.

"Did you need something else?" she asked. She cocked her head to the side, her blue eyes meeting his.

"Actually, yes," he said, gathering his courage. He leaned close, propping his elbows on the counter. From here, he could smell her perfume—something sweet and overly floral. "I was wondering what you're doing tonight after work. To make up for the ice cream."

There, he'd said it. Finally. He'd worked up the courage and asked her on a date. Now all he needed was for her to say yes.

Her face fell slightly. "I can't tonight. It's my twelve-hour shift, so I'm here 'til midnight," she said. As if sensing his disappointment, she added, "But what about tomorrow? It's my day off, and there's a great band at Club Rouge. We could go dancing?"

Unbidden, an image of Edie shimmying in a black dress flashed before his eyes, quickly replaced with a vision of her in that dress the night before.

"No," Gilbert said curtly. "Not there."

"Oh." Cecelia chewed on her lip, and Gilbert knew he'd been too brusque. He opened his mouth to apologize, but

Cecelia brightened and said, "That's all right. We can go somewhere else. What about Dante and Luigi's? I'm always in the mood for pasta."

"It's a date," he said, and he wondered why he didn't feel happier that she'd agreed to it.

Chapter 8

Norwood Studios, Harold Fox's shining jewel, sat at the very edge of the city, on the edge of the Andorra meadow, just across the Wissahickon Creek from the Chestnut Hill neighborhood where Edie had grown up. Lizzie practically vibrated from excitement in the front seat beside Grover. In the back, Edie and Frances were more subdued, even as they took the big hill down Bell's Mill Road and crossed a stone bridge spanning the creek. A short time later, they slowed as they approached the gates to Fox's property. Edie checked her watch—a few minutes before two on Monday afternoon. Exactly on time.

She almost hadn't opened Ava's invitation when it had arrived the previous morning. She'd taken to her bed in a fit of pique. Between Gilbert's rejection and Ava's elopement, she was feeling sullen. But Lizzie insisted and shrieked with joy when she found out that Edie (and guests) had been invited to see a few scenes filmed at Norwood Studios. Which is how Edie found herself tucked into the car with her assistant and sister.

"Did you know this was here?" Edie asked her sister as Grover presented Ava's invitation to the guard at the gate.

"I'd heard about it," Frances said. "I mean, everyone has. I didn't realize it was so big, though."

And it was. They drove through the gate, then through a copse of trees, winding downhill. A large brick building stood in the distance. The trees thinned as they approached, and the bumpy drive widened into a proper street—or at least a proper street in the old West. A series of low buildings faced one another: a red-painted schoolhouse, a general store, even a saloon with swinging doors.

"Almost like a ghost town," Frances said. She gave a little shiver. "I heard that the cast and crew all live out here while they're filming. But that can't be true. It's empty."

"Perhaps they're inside?" Edie asked. "Ava's invitation said to go to Studio A. They can't film outside all the time, can they?"

Frances shrugged. She had reluctantly agreed to join Edie and Lizzie, and only after Edie had pressed. Edie had hoped this could be a treat for them all. She'd wanted to do something nice for her sister, but instead, she was left feeling as if she'd forced Frances into something she didn't want to do.

If she didn't want to be here, she would have stayed home, Edie reminded herself. She'd almost requested Lizzie to ask Gilbert to join them instead, but she was on unsteady footing with him after what had happened the other night. They'd shared something special, all those months ago, and then Edie had put his daughter in danger. It was hard to recover from something like that.

She understood.

But that didn't make it hurt any less.

Edie adjusted the brim of her hat and allowed Grover to help her out of the car. She straightened her skirt and jacket while he circled to assist Frances. The older woman from the party, Mrs. O'Malley, appeared at the door, dressed in black, her brown hair cut into a sharp bob at her chin.

"Miss Shippen? Right on time," the woman said, her voice clipped. She turned on her heel, barely waiting for the group to coalesce behind her. "I'm to show you and your guests to the studio."

"Thank you," Edie said, hurrying to keep up. She exchanged a glance with Lizzie, who responded with a grin.

"This is so exciting, miss," Lizzie said. "Can you believe it? We're going to watch a movie be made!"

Edie's excitement mirrored Lizzie's, glowing in her chest and wrapping her middle in warmth. Ava had worked so hard for this, for so long. She could scarcely believe that her friend's dreams had come to fruition.

If the outside of the studio property was deserted, the inside was bustling. A man ran by, his arms full of boxes. To the left, a woman wove through the chaos, a small herd of shaggy dogs trotting obediently at her feet. A trio of girls giggled in the corner, dressed in long gowns and pointed hats.

"Miss Sylvester is filming on our interior set today," Mrs. O'Malley explained. "It's an important scene, crucial to the entire film. It's paramount that she is not distracted. I'll show you where to sit."

"Of course." Some of Edie's warmth dimmed a bit. They weren't here to distract Ava—they were here to watch her work. "You won't even know we're here. We'll be as quiet as little mice."

"Mice are disgusting creatures." Mrs. O'Malley gave a sniff and ushered them through a door on the left side of the corridor. The room inside was cavernous, with a soaring ceiling crossed with catwalks and strung with lights. She pointed to a row of chairs beside the platform in the center of the room. "You'll sit here and stay out of the way."

"Thank you," Lizzie said softly as they took their seats. The platform in front of them was a set designed to look like a crypt, and a stone table sat in the center, surrounded by hanging lanterns. The walls were painted to look like stone too—to the naked eye, they were clearly false, but Edie had seen enough films to know how a camera could trick a person into thinking something was real. Her great-aunt Mae had spent her career painting backdrops like this, first for stage productions before transitioning to film. It was how she'd ended up in California in the first place, with a big house in the Los Angeles hills. She'd mostly retired by the time Edie arrived, but Edie had marveled at her great-aunt's work. She was the only woman in Edie's family who'd ever held any sort of job, and the freedom Mae had out West was shocking compared to the life Edie had been prepared for in Philadelphia. She'd shown Edie that a different sort of future was possible, and Edie was determined to follow in her footsteps.

Another door opened on the opposite side of the room, throwing a square of light into the dim space. Footsteps echoed across the floor, and then Ava was hurrying across the set, her arms wide. "Edie! Oh, you came!"

Ava squeezed Edie into a hug, brushing a kiss on both of Edie's cheeks. Edie stiffened and stepped back. Hurt flashed across Ava's face, gone as quickly as it appeared, and then she moved on, wrapping Lizzie in an equally enthusiastic embrace. "Miss Lawless! I'm so glad you're here. And you must be Frances!" Edie's twin, too, was hugged and kissed. "How wonderful."

Mrs. O'Malley's face remained stern. "You're supposed to be in makeup, Miss Sylvester."

Miss Sylvester. Not Mrs. Carroll. Had they really done it? Really eloped? Or was it all for show?

"Oh, I'll just be a moment. I had to say hello!" She stopped in front of Grover, who was staring at Ava with a slack jaw and wide eyes. "Who's this, Edie?"

"This is Grover, my driver," Edie said. Grover seemed to startle at his name, his entire face flushing scarlet.

"Hello, Grover," Ava said. She leaned forward and kissed his cheek. Edie bit back a laugh—Grover nearly swooned.

"H-h-hello," he finally managed.

"Makeup, Miss Sylvester," Mrs. O'Malley said. "Now."

A shadow passed over Ava's face, but then it was gone as quickly as it appeared. "Oh, all right," she said. She squeezed Edie's elbow, her fingers trailing down to Edie's wrist. "I'll be back in two shakes of a lamb's tail. Sit tight!"

Mrs. O'Malley watched her go, her lips pressed into a thin line, then turned back to the four of them. "As I was saying," she said, "we are on a tight schedule and cannot afford any delays or distractions. *Especially* distractions," she emphasized, her gaze lingering on Edie in a way that made Edie's spine stiffen. She wasn't a distraction. She was a friend. She almost opened her mouth to argue the point, but Mrs. O'Malley was already barreling on.

"In a few moments, Mr. Fox will enter the studio. No one is to speak with him. He is a very busy man with a very important job. Then the crew will arrive. Last will be the actors. In this scene, Miss Sylvester and Mr. Carroll will be joined by Mr. Oliver, who is playing Friar Laurence. It's a very important scene. We must get it right."

The assembled group nodded solemnly, and with one last suspicious glance at Edie, the woman retreated.

"This is so exciting," Lizzie said. "The two lovers of fair Verona! She mentioned Friar Laurence. Do you think it means . . ." She trailed off, her eyes wide.

"Ava did say they were nearly finished," Edie replied. "I wonder if this is dear Romeo's death scene."

"Don't you think Duncan Carroll is a bit old to be playing Romeo?" Frances asked. "He must be close to thirty. And Romeo is barely more than a child, isn't he?"

"Sixteen," Grover piped up. "And Juliet is thirteen. It's a little young, if you ask me. But I don't know how they did things back then."

The three women turned in their seats to look at the driver, who blushed furiously beneath his pimples. "English was my favorite subject in school," he muttered. "And I liked Shakespeare the best. There's all sorts of murder afoot."

"His best works are rather bloody," Edie agreed. "*Hamlet*, of course. And my favorite is *MacBeth*."

Behind Edie, Mrs. O'Malley drew in a sharp gasp. In two steps she was back, her face pale. "Miss Shippen," she said, nearly breathless, "never mention the name of that play in a theater. It's simply . . . it isn't done."

"Why not?" Edie asked, genuinely perplexed.

"Because," Mrs. O'Malley replied, her gaze serious, "it's bad luck."

Frances covered her mouth with her hand. To everyone else, Edie knew her twin looked composed, but Edie knew that Franny was holding back a laugh. This woman didn't seem like one to be superstitious. Thankfully, the arrival of the crew distracted them all. Suddenly the room seemed to be crawling with people and echoing with a cacophony of voices—men shouting as they scrambled on the catwalks above them. The lights clicked on with a hum. Other crew members swarmed onto the set in front of them, adjusting the ivy hanging on the faux walls, repositioning a pile of rocks on the floor. Not one person spared Edie or her group a second glance, until Harold Fox arrived on set. He spotted them instantly, his graying eyebrows raising. He walked over.

"I see we have an audience today."

"Miss Sylvester insisted," Mrs. O'Malley said, stepping between them. "I'm sure you remember Miss Edith Shippen from the party, Harold. And this is her sister, Miss Frances Shippen, and their associates. Ladies, this is my brother, Mr. Harold Fox."

"How do you do?" Frances said, but Edie was still caught on *brother*. There was not the slightest family resemblance. The woman's sharp bob was dark, as were her eyes and brows. Harold Fox was fair, from his pale blond hair, gently streaked with white, to his watery blue eyes. His mustache, which was waxed at the ends, was a sparkling white.

"Mr. Fox went to school with Daddy," Edie explained to Frances.

"For a time. Expelled my sophomore year, I'm afraid," he said. His entire demeanor changed—his shoulders relaxed, and his face softened. "Tell your father I say hello."

"Of course," Frances said. "I'm having dinner with him tomorrow evening at the Palm Room. I'm sure he'll be delighted to hear from you."

"And be sure to tell him how impressed you are with the film," Fox added. "They said it couldn't be done—Shakespeare on film! But old Fox will prove them wrong."

Edie gave a polite nod. She didn't know to whom Fox was referring—but it didn't matter, because he was already moving on, turning his attention to his sister. "Where's that girl of yours? We're about to get started."

"I'm here, Uncle Harry!" Della appeared beside them. She carried a black slate board, which she promptly presented to her uncle. A small brown monkey sat on her shoulder, its tail curled down the girl's back. "Sorry we were late. Jade caused some mischief."

"That creature is a menace," Harold said. He looked down at the slate and frowned. He rubbed at the black surface, then pulled a chalk from his pocket and scribbled something on the line.

"Della. Act five, scene three," he said as he wrote. "I thought I told you that over breakfast."

Della's cheeks flushed. "I must have forgotten," she said. "So sorry."

Harold's reply was lost as a second rush of people entered. Two men, dressed in hose and doublets, talked quietly as they walked. Ava returned, her costume changed to a medieval-styled gown with a slashed overdress and puffed sleeves. Her bob was hidden beneath an elaborate wig of long curls cascading halfway down her back. Flat, pale makeup caked her skin, turning her face a ghastly white, and her eyes were ringed exaggeratedly in black liner. Red rouge painted her cheekbones and lined her mouth—Edie knew that on film, she'd look beautiful. But in person, the effect was unsettling, like a life-size china doll.

Duncan wore a similar amount of makeup. He walked confidently, striding across the stage like he owned it. He bounced on his toes, rolling his shoulders. He peered down over his long nose at a script in his hand, his dark eyes intense, his mouth pressed into a line.

"That's Duncan Carroll!" Lizzie hissed from her seat beside Edie. "He's so tall in real life! And handsome!"

"That's funny, since his resemblance to Gilbert was the talk of the party," Edie teased.

Lizzie let out a scandalized huff. "He does *not*. He's gorgeous, and Gilbert is my brother."

"He does, doesn't he?" Frances said, ignoring Lizzie's protests. "Look at the cut of his shoulders. Are you sure your brother isn't moonlighting as a movie star?"

"He's safe in the morgue, where he belongs," Lizzie muttered. Her cheeks had flushed. "And he looks nothing like Duncan Carroll."

"Shh," Mrs. O'Malley admonished them. Chastened like a trio of schoolgirls, Edie, Frances, and Lizzie smothered their giggles and settled back in their seats.

"All right, places," Harold Fox called out. Ava and Duncan and the rest of the cast settled into their positions—Ava, lying motionless on the stone slab; one of the other men, on the floor beside her; and Duncan, posed in the doorway. On the opposite side of the stage, the actor playing Friar Laurence stood off to the side with the man playing Balthasar. Della stood in the middle of the set, the slate in her hand. Harold crossed to a tall metal camera on a wooden tripod, fitted with a variety of round lenses. He peered through the viewfinder on the side, slid the camera slightly to the left, and spun the lenses until he was satisfied. With a nod to the man beside him, he stepped back and did the same to the camera on the other side of the set. Both cameramen took their positions, hands on the camera's cranks.

"Roll film," Harold announced.

Della counted to five and then hurried from the shot. As soon as she was clear, Harold yelled, "Action!"

Edie leaned forward, rapt. Ava remained motionless on the slab, her chest barely rising and falling. Duncan, as Romeo, burst into the crypt, sword in hand. He took two steps, his face twisting into an expression of anguish. "Oh, my love! My wife!" he cried, voice breaking.

Edie's own chest hitched. He delivered his famous monologue, line for line, as beautifully as if he were on stage in front of an audience of thousands, not captured on film for people who would read it on dialogue cards, never able to hear the grief etched in each note.

Were they really in love?

It seemed impossible.

He leaned over Ava, the sword clattering to the ground beside her. He traced the lines of her face with shaking hands and wept. "'Eyes, look your last! Arms, take your last embrace! And lips'"—he pressed his face to hers, dropping kisses over her cheeks, her nose—"'oh you the doors of breath, seal with a righteous kiss a dateless bargain to engrossing death!'"

He pulled a vial from his pocket. The glass glinted ruby red beneath the stage lights, a swirling liquid inside. He held it up, turning it slowly in his hand. "'Come, bitter conduct, come, unsavory guide, Thou desperate pilot, now at once run on the dashing rocks thy sea-sick weary bark! Here's to my love.'" He uncapped the vial, tears running down his face, his expression full of anguish. He tipped it to his mouth, his Adam's apple bobbing in his throat as he swallowed. "'Thy drugs are quick. Thus with a kiss, I die.'"

He slumped forward, his body cocooning Ava's on the slab.

"Cut!" Harold yelled. He climbed down from his chair, frowning.

Duncan and Ava both sat up. Harold crossed the set, his hand rubbing at the back of his neck. He conferred briefly with his actors, then pointed to Della, who handed him the slate. He scribbled on it and handed it back.

"From the top!" he shouted. "Let's do this again."

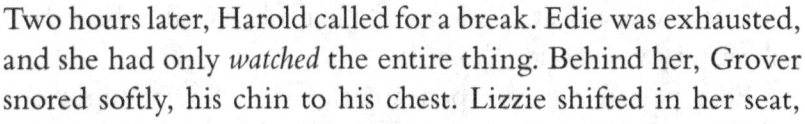

Two hours later, Harold called for a break. Edie was exhausted, and she had only *watched* the entire thing. Behind her, Grover snored softly, his chin to his chest. Lizzie shifted in her seat, stretching her legs. Finally, Ava approached, her face glistening with sweat and cake makeup, hot from the lights above. She hugged Edie, pressing a kiss to each cheek.

"I hope you're having a nice time," Ava said. "Harold's a genius, isn't he?"

Edie wasn't so sure about that. The man had seemed to spend a lot of his time growling and frowning, snapping at his niece and the actors, stalking between the cameras and calling, *"Cut"* for something as simple as a leaf out of place. Ava took it in stride, but Edie had noticed the way Duncan stormed from the stage, the line of his shoulders tightening with every step. They'd be back at it in fifteen minutes—just enough time for the cast and crew to grab a quick drink of water and freshen up their makeup. Edie also took the chance to use the restroom. She slipped from the set and into the corridor, smiling at those she passed. The ladies' room was clearly marked, on the left. It was small and clean, with a sharp antiseptic smell and tiled floors. There were two stalls—one, occupied.

Edie took the open stall. She locked the door and hung up her handbag.

The woman in the next door let out a little, hiccupping sob.

Edie froze. "Are you all right over there?" she asked.

"I'm fine," the woman said, though Edie could hear the tears in her voice. "I just—I'm all right. It's just my time of the month and—"

"Do you need a Kotex?" Edie was already digging in her bag for the slim blue cardboard box. "I've got an extra."

There was a beat of silence. "That'd be swell," the woman's watery voice said. "Thanks."

Edie passed the box beneath the stall. She thought the tears went beyond menstruation, but she also wasn't going to press a stranger for information in the bathroom. She was washing her hands when the other stall opened and Della, Harold's young niece, emerged, her eyes red and downcast. She stopped short when she realized Edie was still there.

"Oh," she said. "You're Miss Sylvester's friend."

"Edie Shippen," Edie said. "You work for the studio?"

"Not really. Uncle Harry's in charge, and I help out where I can. I'm Della." The girl washed her hands, avoiding Edie's gaze. "He said when I'm older, I'll get to act, but I have to work my way up first."

Della's tears had tracked mascara down her full cheeks. She rubbed at them, smearing the black makeup deeper under her eyes.

"Here." Edie fished a tissue from her handbag and passed it to the girl. "We can't have you go out there looking like that."

"Thanks." The girl seemed surprised. She wet the tissue and cleaned her face. "You're nicer than Miss Sylvester."

Edie gave a little laugh. "She can be prickly, but she's a real kitten underneath," she said. "Don't let her fool you."

Della seemed doubtful. "If you say so," she said. "I'd better be getting back. Uncle Harry doesn't like to be kept waiting."

Edie checked her watch—the break was already nearly over. She returned to her seat in the darkened studio room. Grover was still asleep, and Frances and Lizzie were deep in conversation, but looked up when Edie appeared.

"Ava said they're doing one last take, and then they'll break for the day," Frances said.

"Places, everyone!" Harold called out, signaling the end of the break. "From the kiss, Duncan, please."

The actors arranged themselves on the stage. Ava reclined, a bouquet of flowers clasped over her breast. The actor playing Tybalt sprawled on the floor at Duncan's feet.

"Action!"

"'Come, bitter conduct, come, unsavory guide.'" Duncan wept as he pulled the vial from his pocket once again. This time, the glass vial was green; the shape, bulbous. "Thou desperate pilot, now at once run on the dashing rocks thy seasick weary bark! Here's to my love.'" He tipped it to his mouth, grimacing against the taste. He gave a little cough, breath rasping, committed to the part, his voice wavering over the words. "Thy drugs are quick." He rubbed at his throat, his eyes bulging slightly. He drew in an unsteady breath, his hands shaking. The vial hit the ground at his feet and rolled, and the sword clattered beside it. He lurched forward, gasping. "'Thus with a kiss, I die.'"

He collapsed on top of Ava, his body convulsing grotesquely. He twitched once, twice, three times, then stilled.

"Cut!" Harold yelled. He leaped from his seat, clapping his hands. "Bravo, bravo. What a performance! The show of your life, dear boy."

Edie climbed to her feet. A trickle of dread worked its way down her back—Duncan still hadn't moved. Something was wrong.

Ava let out a soul-shattering scream, and Edie's dread morphed to fear. She broke into a run, desperate to help her friend, even though she knew it would make no difference.

Because Duncan Carroll was dead.

Chapter 9

Gilbert and Marco arrived at Norwood Studios just behind Finnegan Pyle. The uniformed officers had already cleared the scene, gathering a small number of witnesses in the lobby of Studio A. Gilbert recognized Harold Fox, the studio owner, sitting on a chair near the door, his hands clasped, staring off into the distance. Beside him, the blond girl from the night before wailed into a crumpled handkerchief. Ava paced the floor, her face a mask of fury beneath her caked makeup.

The girl let out another sob, and Ava shrieked with rage. She crossed the lobby in three quick steps. "Enough, Della," she practically spat, shaking the girl hard. "Get. A. Grip."

"I won't!" Della wailed. "He's . . . he's . . ."

"Dead," Ava said again. "He's dead."

"Gil!"

Gilbert's head snapped to the other side of the lobby at the sound of his name. His sister rushed at him, pale beneath her freckles. Edie and her sister, Frances, sat on chairs on the opposite side of the lobby with their driver, Grover. Gilbert barely had time to process the fact that Lizzie and the rest were here, at this crime scene, before she barreled into him, wrapping her arms tight around his chest. He dropped his bag on the tiled floor and held her, his hands stroking her back.

"Liz? What are you doing here?"

"We were invited to see today's shoot," Edie said. There was something urgent in her voice. "They were filming Romeo's death scene. Only—"

Pyle appeared beside them. "Scene's in here, lover boy," he said. "Leave the questions to me."

Gilbert ignored him. "Are you all right?" he asked his sister, and only when she gave a nod did Gilbert release her shoulders and pick up his kit. "I'll be right back," he said.

The studio itself was a cavernous room. He and Marco walked quickly, their footsteps echoing in the big, empty space. The stage in the center was dressed to resemble the Capulets' tomb. Duncan Carroll was on his back beside the stone table, head lolling to one side, his skin a bright cherry red. A fencing foil was beside him, as well as a woman's slipper—Ava's, most likely.

For a moment, Gilbert stared down at the dark-haired actor. It was hard to believe that just a few nights prior, they'd been introduced at the party at the Bellevue, and now here they were: one living, one dead. A shiver worked over Gilbert—the only one he allowed himself. He shook his head, clearing his mind. Duncan Carroll was dead, a corpse like any other, and Gilbert had a job to do.

He knelt down, opening his bag, and fell into the same easy rhythm that he and Marco had perfected over the years. Gilbert made his notes on the body—the position it was in; the condition of the skin, teeth, eyes; and any evidence of trauma visible to the naked eye. Marco moved around him, camera flashing, capturing every detail of the scene. Pyle appeared, watching from the side of the set for a moment, then approached.

"Romeo, dear Romeo," Pyle said. He ran a hand over his face and shook his head. "I have to say, this is a first."

"All signs point to cyanide poisoning," Gilbert said. "We'll know more once we get him in the lab."

"Quite the busy week for Dr. Harrison," Marco said. "I can't remember the last time we saw three poisonings in such a short time."

Gilbert couldn't either. Poisoning—whether intentional or accidental—was a common enough death. But he'd never dealt with three men, so close together, all dead of the same symptoms. Usually there was a variety: rat poison, mixing cleaning chemicals, or a contamination in the water supply.

If Jack McConnell was right, the other two men knew each other. Duncan Carroll—a man of wealth and means, even before his star rose in cinema—was the outlier.

"Heard there was some party the other night. Romeo and his Juliet made quite the splash," Pyle said. "The papers said they had a row right before Fox announced their elopement."

"No offense, Detective, but you never struck me as the type of fella to read the celebrity pages," Marco said.

"I'll have you know, I read the entire paper, front to back," Pyle said. "I'm more than just a pretty face."

Gilbert snorted. He put away his notebook and stood, brushing his hands on his trousers. "No one ever accused you of being just a pretty face."

"Oh, shut up," Pyle said. "I was just trying to say, this should be easy enough. Open and shut."

"You think he did it to himself?" Marco asked. He stowed his camera and helped Gilbert lay out the canvas body bag that they'd use to take Duncan Carroll's corpse to the morgue.

"Nah," Pyle said. "Someone told me recently it's always the wife."

Gilbert had almost forgotten about Tommy Fletcher by the time he made it home that evening. He climbed out of the car as the sky faded into purples and blues over the side of the hill, and froze when he saw the gangster sitting on the Lawless family's front stoop, his long limbs sprawled as he smoked a cigarette. Tommy leaned back, his elbows on the steps behind him, and Gilbert's young daughter, Penelope, played at the gangster's feet. She was bent over a basket, talking softly to something inside. Gilbert caught a flash of gray fur and swore to himself.

A kitten. Tommy Fletcher had bought Penelope a kitten.

"Hey there, Bertie boy," Tommy said. He pulled the cigarette from his mouth and smiled at his childhood friend. "I was on your block, and I thought I'd stop by."

"Da!" Penelope ran to greet Gilbert as he climbed out of the car. "Mr. Fletcher brought me a kitten. I've named him Reginald."

"Or Regina. We're having a bit of a disagreement on whether it's a he or a she," Tommy said.

"You shouldn't have," Gilbert said.

"Don't I know it." Tommy stubbed the cigarette out on the step beside him and stood. "Penny, sweetheart, why don't you run inside to your gran? Your da and I have some grown-up business to discuss."

Penny looked to her father for confirmation, and Gilbert gave a reluctant nod. He didn't like the idea of Tommy anywhere near his family, but like it or not, he'd ended up in the gangster's debt.

"I heard you might have a name for me," Gilbert said once Penelope was safely inside the house, kitten in tow. He'd let his mother deal with the cat—what did one need to even take care of a kitten? Images of milk-filled saucers and tinned sardines filled his mind. Damn Tommy. The last thing he needed was one more thing to take care of.

"Oh, you know it doesn't work like that," Tommy said. "Tell me what you know about this business with Homer Byrne. Pyle said he suspected poison."

"And you know *this* doesn't work like that," Gilbert snapped back. "I can't comment on an ongoing investigation."

Tommy gave him a long look. "Two of my boys ended up on your table, Bertie. I need to know if it's something I need to worry about."

Gilbert shook his head. "Poison doesn't seem like something that happens in your line of work. Seems a little subtle, doesn't it?"

"That's what I thought when I heard about Byrne," Tommy admitted. "I thought maybe his old lady did him in—she's Italian, you know. A bit of a temper. But now . . ."

"*It's always the wife.*" Pyle's voice echoed in Gilbert's head, and he hesitated. He wasn't sure how much information to give Tommy—especially when information was the only shred of power he wielded over his former friend. "You heard I was there, right? When it happened?"

Tommy nodded. "Having an ice cream with the youngest Salvatore brother," he said, snorting. "I wondered about that."

"Marco had nothing to do with it. There wasn't a thing any of us could have done," Gilbert replied. "The autopsy confirmed it."

This seemed to mollify Tommy. "His name was Frank Burkhart. He grew up in Pennsport and moved out here with his folks a few years ago. His parents run the hardware store on Manayunk Avenue. Dropped out of school, went to New York, got into trouble—the usual. He got out of Sing Sing and came home, so I gave him a chance."

"Burkhart." The name didn't sound familiar to Gilbert. Then again, he'd been away from the neighborhood for a long time. He'd kept his distance for good reason. "What sort of chance?"

"Delivery boy," Tommy said. "He'd ride along with the drivers, make sure the product got where it needed to go."

Muscle. Burkhart had been hired muscle, then. Even more unlikely that he'd met his end via cyanide instead of a more violent death. "Byrne was a teamster."

"They worked together." Tommy's face darkened. "They'd just started a new route, actually. Running rum to Leo Salvatore's bar. Byrne's wife's brother was one of Salvatore's guys, and they set the whole thing up. A real Romeo-and-Juliet situation."

Gilbert stopped short at that. "What did you say?"

"Homer and his old lady. Two worlds colliding. Leo and I could have handled it differently, but we decided it was to our advantage to work together. Homer was happy to help."

Two worlds colliding and two dead gangsters to show for it. Two links in the chain between Tommy's Cresson Street Crew and Leo Salvatore, the Butcher of Broad Street. This new truce between the two gangs was delicate.

Murder could very well rip it apart.

Gilbert's parents took the kitten in stride, much like everything else in life, and insisted that Tommy Fletcher stay for supper. Gilbert stayed quiet through the meal, watching the gangster flirt with his mother and make jokes with his father. They still thought of Tommy as the skinned-knee little boy from the house behind them, not a ruthless criminal who regularly sent men to their deaths without a second thought. Gilbert knew better.

Tommy wiped his mouth with his napkin and sat back in his chair. "Mrs. Lawless, once again, you have outdone yourself," he said. "Don't tell my mam, but I think you're the best cook in Manayunk."

Aoife Lawless, Gilbert's mother, beamed. "You're a flatterer, Tommy. Stop all of that."

"He's right, and you know it," Bert, Gilbert's father and namesake, mirrored the gangster's pose. "It's not flattery if it's true."

"May I be excused?" Penelope asked. She still had half of her meal—boiled cabbage and pork—on her plate.

"If you have two more bites," Gilbert said.

"Gran?" Penelope looked to Aoife, and Gilbert had to press down a surge of irritation. He was Penelope's father, but here she was, looking to her grandmother for direction. He pressed his lips together. He'd been absent for so much of his daughter's life, and it was no one's fault but his own.

Aoife met her son's eye. "Your da is right," she said. "Two bites."

"But . . ."

"Two bites," Aoife repeated.

"Fine." Penelope picked up her fork and made two quick nibbles, then slid from the table, beelining for the kitten, asleep in its basket near the stove. She scooped it up and let herself into the back garden. Gilbert watched her go, and his mother watched him.

"She can't get into trouble out there," Aoife reminded him, and she was right. It was a small yard—a perfect square, fenced on two sides and a solid stone wall at the back. He'd been much bigger when they'd moved into this house: a boy of twelve, full of anger and drive. He'd climbed that wall without a second thought, right up into Tommy's yard above, and gotten himself into years of trouble.

Tommy caught his eye, like he knew exactly what Gilbert was thinking, and gave a little half smirk. "I should be off," he said, standing. "No rest for the wicked. Bertie, a moment, before I go?"

Gilbert was all too happy to see the back of Tommy Fletcher. He rose too. Once on the street, Tommy lit another cigarette. "She's a sweet thing, that little girl of yours," he said.

The hair on the back of Gilbert's neck rose. "Stay away from her," he said slowly, carefully, so that every word was clear. "I swear to you, Tommy, if you touch a hair on her head, I will do everything in my power to destroy you."

Tommy held up his hands in mock surrender. "Easy there, Da. I meant nothing by it." His voice was easy, but his eyes were hard. "Can't an old friend give a compliment?"

Gilbert stared at him. "I already told you what I knew about your associates. I don't have anything else to share."

"But your sister might," Tommy said. "Pyle said Lizzie's working for that girl you brought around in the spring. Said she's some sort of investigator now. Said they're looking into Byrne's death."

"I don't know anything about Miss Shippen's investigations," Gilbert said. He couldn't follow what Tommy was getting at. Was he threatening Edie or Lizzie or Penelope? All three? None of them? "Just tell me what you want, Tommy. I won't play games with you."

"Just tell them to be careful," Tommy said. "I think Lizzie's a good girl. It's in her interest too, that this deal with Salvatore works out. She's still stepping out with him, isn't she?"

Gilbert closed his eyes. Lizzie's on-again, off-again relationship with the gangster had lasted through the summer, ever since Leo had helped her hide the previous spring. He'd warned her that it was a bad idea, but Lizzie was not the type of sister to listen to brotherly advice. She'd thrown it in his face that everyone had warned him from pursuing Sarah, his late wife, as well, and he'd reminded her that Sarah had died because of his involvement with her, and they hadn't spoken for nearly a week.

"Leave her out of this."

"Just tell them to be careful," Tommy repeated. "I wouldn't want them to get hurt."

Gilbert stayed on the sidewalk long after Tommy left, his hands fisted at his sides. This was all his fault, entirely. He'd encouraged her with those damn business cards: *Edie Shippen, Lady Detective.* He'd thought he'd give her a new direction—she'd been so good at tracking down clues the previous spring. He'd imagined she'd busy herself with missing watches or lost dogs. Maybe a cheating husband. Nothing that would put her back in the type of danger they'd found themselves in last spring. Nothing that would put his family—his sister, his daughter—back in harm's way.

The sound of the front door opening behind him had him straightening. His father stood in the vestibule, coat on, pipe in hand. He took one look at Gilbert and said, "Walk with me."

The tone of his voice brokered no argument. It was a tone etched deep in Gilbert's bones, one that made him unclench his fists and fall into step beside his father. They walked slowly, down past the church and onto the street that ran parallel to the hill—more slowly than they used to. The senior Lawless had his cap pulled down over his balding head. He still refused a cane, though his steps were less steady than they'd been even a year ago.

Gilbert knew that his father was waiting for him to talk. To say something. So he did—he told his father about the poisoned men, their connection to Tommy, and to Lizzie and Edie's first case.

"Whatever Tommy Fletcher wants you to do, you do," Bert said finally. He didn't stop walking and didn't look over at Gilbert when he said it. He tipped his hat at the woman washing her windows across the street. "You're a proud man. I know that. Lord knows, I know it," he said. "But I've watched what he's done in this neighborhood. He's not a man you cross."

"I could lose my job," Gilbert said. "How can I provide for Penny—for all of you—if I feed him information? I'm already on thin ice with Knight after what happened with Lizzie. I promised him I'd toe the line."

"You could lose more than your job if you don't," Bert said sharply. "You're not a daft lad. You know what sort of things he's capable of. Your history has protected you for now, but it won't forever. It won't protect Pen."

Gilbert's blood went cold. "He won't touch her."

His father's face softened. "No. I don't think even he would harm the lass, but he could hurt you or Lizzie. Or your mam or me."

Their pace slowed. They stood in front of a shell of a row house—the windows were blown out; the interior, demolished. The bricks in the front were scorched and black. Gilbert remembered the family that had lived here. They'd come from Galway, the same as the Lawless family, a man and a woman with two sons. They'd kept mostly to themselves. The boys had gone to school at St. John the Baptist, a few years behind Gilbert. He'd owned a shoe shop on Cresson Street—a large corner spot with a basement and a subbasement. Gilbert's heart sank.

"Liam was a proud man too," Bert said finally. "A good man. We'd gone to school together, you know. He'd known Tommy's da too. I think that's why he thought he could say no to Tommy when the time came. Tommy didn't see it that way. He saw Liam's refusal as a betrayal. As an act of defiance. As something to be punished."

Gilbert looked back at the burned house. In his memories, he saw a round-faced blond woman smiling at him from the window.

He remembered now what had happened. It had been in the early days after his return from Europe. He'd barely been able to leave his bed, trapped in a waking nightmare, one relieved only by the morphine Dr. Knight gave him with every visit. There had been a fire in the middle of the day. An explosion in the kitchen at the back of the house. The boys had been at school; the man of the house, at work.

The woman had burned to death, trapped inside. Less than a month later, the shoe shop had sold, and the newly widowed man and his sons had left the city entirely.

He'd spent the last few years thinking it was a tragic accident.

"You do what Tommy Fletcher tells you to do, son," Bert Lawless said. He clapped his hand on Gilbert's back, squeezing tight. "Understand?"

Gilbert understood.

Chapter 10

"Miss Shippen, you have a caller." O'Mara, the butler, stopped in the doorway to Edie's room. She'd only just returned and had already stripped off her gloves and hat. She hung her coat on the hook beside her door and rubbed at her temples—at least she was still wearing her shoes. She had no idea who would be calling at this hour—the October sky had faded to purple, and after everything that had happened on set, Edie was exhausted. She wanted nothing more than to curl up in bed with a hot cup of peppermint tea, a novel, and her dog. Maybe then she could forget the way Ava's screams echoed through the studio, the way Duncan had gasped as he died.

The way they'd all watched it happen, thinking he was acting.

"Who is it, O'Mara?" she asked sharply.

"Dr. Lawless, miss. He said it was important."

Edie stilled in front of the mirror, halfway to tucking her hair behind her ear. "Gilbert's here?"

He was the last person Edie expected to have at her door. She had hoped to see him when Grover dropped Lizzie off at their home in Manayunk barely an hour ago, but he had been absent. At work, probably.

"He's in the front parlor. Unless you want me to ask him to leave . . . ?"

"No, no, don't do that," Edie said. She fixed her hair and gave O'Mara a bright smile. "It's a surprise, is all. Is there any of that apple cake left from last night? Have Cook send some of that up with a pot of tea. No, coffee," Edie amended. "Actually, just send both."

O'Mara, who had known Edie since birth, raised both of his white eyebrows. "Anything else?"

"That's all. Thank you," she added as O'Mara headed in the opposite direction, toward the service stairs at the back of the house. She took a deep breath and finished adjusting her hair. Gilbert wouldn't be here without good reason. He'd made that clear as crystal the other night. So, she just had to see what he wanted, and then send him on his way.

Gilbert stood with his back to the door, his hands on his hips as he stared at the oil painting over the fireplace. It was one of Ophelia Van Pelt's last paintings, begun on a spring day in a sunny courtyard, the edges unfinished. The model had her face turned away from the painter, her hair falling in long dark waves over her nude torso, a bouquet of sunny flowers dangling from her hand, and a soft scarf draped over her lap. The lines were soft and hazy, the colors muted, almost dreamlike.

That day felt like a dream to Edie, when she thought about it.

"My father doesn't know that's me," Edie said, stepping into the room. "He'd be mortified to find out, don't you think?"

Gilbert startled, turning. "It's lovely," he said, then seemed to realize what he said, a pink flush spreading over his cheeks and up to the tips of his ears. He turned back to the portrait. "When was it painted?"

"The day we met, actually," Edie said. She touched the place on her forehead where he'd bandaged her—only a slim, slivery scar remained beneath her bangs, a reminder of the mugging that seemed to have changed everything. "It was Ophelia's. I bought it at the art show on my birthday. It seemed like the least I could do. I can't help thinking she'd still be here if it wasn't for me." The words left her so easily—she'd barely been able to speak about the murders in the spring to anyone else. But Gilbert had been with her when they found Ophelia's apartment. He'd been called to the scene where Ophelia's body was found. He understood in a way no one else did.

Gilbert didn't say anything. He reached his hand out and took hers gently. "It wasn't your fault," he said. "Not then. And not today either."

Edie didn't think that needed a reply. She turned her gaze away from the painting and looked at him instead.

He opened his mouth. "Edie—"

"Here's the cake you asked for, miss," O'Mara announced, setting a tray on the coffee table beside the sofa. Edie stepped back quickly, pulling away from Gilbert's touch and throwing the butler a grateful smile.

"Thank you, O'Mara. I'll take it from here."

The butler nodded and departed while Edie busied herself with cutting two slices of the apple cake. "Coffee?" she asked Gilbert.

"Please," he said. He rubbed his hand along the back of his neck and took the cup she offered. She inclined her head toward the chair across the coffee table—the one at a safe distance from her seat on the sofa—and he sat.

Edie poured her own tea—peppermint, brewed to perfection—from the pot and spent an extra minute fussing over the cup.

"I'm a little surprised you're here," she said at last.

"It wasn't planned," Gilbert said. "But I had to see you. I had to speak to you."

"Oh." Edie's heart fluttered. Maybe—maybe he'd changed his mind, then. "Well, then. What's going on?"

"I had a visit from Tommy Fletcher this evening." His eyes stayed on her face as he spoke. "He was very interested in your case. Too interested."

"My investigation into Lily Byrne?" Edie put her teacup down with a clatter. *This* was even more unexpected than whatever notion she'd had of Gilbert suddenly deciding to forgive her for putting Penelope in danger. "Why would he care?"

"Homer Byrne worked for him. The Cresson Street Crew has been supplying the Salvatore Brothers with booze. Byrne and a second man were the ones who served as go-betweens. And now they're both dead."

"My client thinks Mrs. Byrne had something to do with her husband's death. She didn't say anything about anyone else," Edie said. Her mind was whirling—she still hadn't heard anything from Pyle concerning the lead she'd given him from Wanamaker's. She wondered if he'd follow up at all, now that he was overseeing the investigation into

Duncan's death. She leaned forward. "I thought you weren't going to help me."

Gilbert had both hands wrapped around his coffee cup. "Tommy Fletcher is dangerous. Especially when he thinks he's been wronged."

Edie realized what Gilbert was saying. "He thinks Leo Salvatore knows something. And he thinks that, because of Lizzie's involvement with Leo, I'm likely to protect him instead of revealing the truth." She frowned, offended. "I would never."

"I know that," Gilbert said gently. He swallowed, staring down at the coffee. "He was waiting at my house when I came home from work today. He was with Penelope."

Cold horror washed over Edie. To threaten Lizzie was one thing, but Penelope? Gilbert's daughter was only four. A child.

A child Edie had herself endangered once before.

"I'll tell you what I know," Edie said. "It isn't much." She summarized her conversation with Lily Byrne's coworker at Wanamaker's, then added, "But Pyle already knows this, and we know he's in Tommy's pocket."

"We only have Tommy's word that the dead men were on his payroll," Gilbert pointed out. "But I believe him. One poisoned man is unremarkable. Two? Who worked so closely together? That points to something bigger."

"It doesn't make sense," Edie said. She picked up her tea and sipped at it, hoping the bracing freshness of the mint would help her focus. "What would Leo Salvatore gain by sabotaging his own deal? And what does Lily Byrne have to with it? Unless . . ." Edie looked up sharply, an idea forming in her mind. "Lily is Italian. Mrs. Patterson mentioned it, and so did her friend from the shop. Could someone else be looking to move in on Leo's territory? Who would benefit most from this deal falling through?"

"I don't know," Gilbert admitted. He looked so defeated. "None of it makes sense."

"I don't know either. But I know someone who might." Edie took another sip of tea, then stood. "Did you drive here?"

Gilbert stood too, putting his coffee down on the tray, the cake forgotten. "I did. Why?"

"Good," Edie said. "I'll go get my coat. I'll be right back."

"Are you going somewhere?" Gilbert asked, seeming genuinely confused. Edie sighed, trying not to be impatient with him.

"We're going to South Philly," Edie said. "If Pyle won't follow up on that address, we'll do it ourselves."

Edie read the address for the fourth time, just to be sure, squinting beneath the yellow light from the gas lamps overhead. "This is it," she said.

The building in front of them was nondescript, a narrow row house identical to every other one that stretched down this block and the next. Despite being a little over a block from the hustle and bustle of South Street, the narrow street was still, and the address Nina had given Edie was eerily quiet. No lights were on inside despite the deepening twilight. A pile of unopened newspapers sat on the front step, and a spiderweb stretched across the doorframe.

"It looks abandoned," Gilbert said. He stepped over the newspapers and knocked against the wooden door, the sharp raps echoing down the street. "Are you sure she wasn't pulling your leg?"

"She seemed sincere," Edie said, even though the possibility that the shopgirl had lied to her seemed more likely with every passing second. "She said this was the place to come if I was having trouble with my fiancé. She said this was where she sent Lily Byrne for something called la futura. I looked it up—it just means 'the future.' Do you think it's a code?"

"I think it's a dead end." Gilbert hurried back down the steps to join her on the sidewalk. "No wonder Pyle wasn't giving you any updates."

Edie kicked at a stone on the sidewalk, frustrated. This was her first case, and already she'd botched it. "I should give Mrs. Patterson her retainer back," she said. "I'm not cut out for this."

Gilbert didn't answer. That irked her even more, anger sparking in her chest. She whirled on him, hands fisted on her hips. "Gee, thanks, Gil, for the support."

"Shh." Gilbert held his finger to his lips. He stepped close, slipping his arms around her waist, pulling her close. He dropped his face down toward hers, and Edie's heart flipped. "Someone's watching us. Don't move," he said, his grip tightening on her waist, and the fluttering in her chest turned to bolts of fear.

"Who?"

"I don't know. They're on the corner across the street. Beside the car." His gaze flicked up, then back down to her. "Could be nothing."

"What do we do?" Edie could barely think, this close to him. He still smelled the same—coffee and peppermint.

"We're going to see if they follow us," Gil said. "There's a pasta spot not about a block and a half from here, at 10th and Catharine streets. It's always packed; we should be safe there."

"What about the car?" Edie risked a glance over Gil's shoulder. She didn't see anyone, but then again, the street was dark, with long shadows stretching between the streetlights.

"We'll come back for it," Gil said. He reached down and laced his fingers with hers. "Walk slowly. Naturally."

Every inch of Edie's body screamed at her to run, but she did as he said, falling into step beside him. Their pace was measured—a pair of lovers out for a twilight stroll.

The unmistakable sound of footsteps echoed down the street behind them. Edie tensed, and Gilbert's grip on her hand tightened. "Stay calm," he said. "But when I say *go*, you run. Do you hear me?"

The next block was even more abandoned. The tall, hulking shape of a school rose on one side, empty for the evening. A cemetery stretched along the other side of the street, the graves crooked and overgrown.

"The restaurant is just around the corner from the school," Gil said. "Whatever happens, get there."

"I'm not leaving you," she hissed. "You'll run with me."

"Edie." His tone brokered no argument, but she honestly didn't give a fig about what he wanted. She hadn't left him in that crypt all those months ago, and she'd be damned if she'd leave him now.

The footsteps grew closer. Edie bit her lip.

"Hey! Mister! You dropped something," a voice called out from behind them. It was young, and singsong. "Wait up."

A young man, tall and broad, materialized out of the darkness ahead of them. "You two sure are in a hurry," he said. Something glinted in his hand.

Gilbert stopped, tugging Edie's hand hard. He stepped in front of her. "We don't want any trouble," he said. "We're just on our way to dinner."

"That's pretty funny," a kid behind them said. Edie whirled, pressing her back to Gilbert's. He was barely more than a boy—short and gangly and snub-nosed, with his cap pulled down over his eyes. "Since there's nowhere to eat on this block," he finished.

"Yeah, but there's plenty of parking," Gil said, his voice artificially light. "You know how that can be around here."

"You knocked on the strega's door." The boy in front of them stepped closer. "What do you want from the old witch?"

Edie decided that honesty might be a better approach. "Help," she said simply. "We were hoping for her help. Do you know where she is?"

The boys exchanged glances. "She's long gone from here," the taller one said. "But she said if anyone was looking for her, to tell them to find Madame Midnight. She'll know how to get in touch."

"Madame Midnight? You mean Celeste DuPont?" Edie tugged free of Gilbert's hand. "Who said that?"

"The strega." The shorter boy looked at her like she'd gone mad; maybe she had. "Now pay up." He held out his palm.

"Gilbert, pay the boy," Edie said, her mind whirling. Celeste DuPont, a fraudulent medium and jazz singer who went by the name Madame Midnight, performed nightly at Club Rouge.

The same club owned by Leo Salvatore.

Chapter 11

"Close on Monday." Edie stared at the misspelled sign on the door of the new location of Club Rogue, in a swanky section of Locust Street. It was a bold move for the gangster—one made possible by his new arrangement with Tommy Fletcher. They were moving in on territory owned by other, more established gangs. The notorious Piccadilly Club and the rowdy 21 Club, both owned by Max Hoff, were each barely a block away. "What do you think that means? 'Close'? On Monday? It's Monday, and I certainly don't feel close to anything."

"Closed, I think," Gilbert said. "They're closed."

"Well, that's ridiculous," Edie huffed.

"Everyone needs a night off," Gilbert said, as she shuffled through her purse, pulling out a tube of lipstick. "What are you doing?"

"Fixing their grammar," Edie said. She leaned forward, neatly adding a *d* to the end of the sign. "There. Now it makes sense."

He could only stare at her as she returned the lipstick to her purse, satisfaction on her face. She was the most ridiculous creature Gilbert had ever met. She looked up at him, a smile tugging the edges of her lips.

"I guess we should call it a night. We'll find Celeste another day."

He couldn't say he was too broken up about it; he was exhausted. They could follow up with Celeste after a good night's sleep—the damned woman seemed to be everywhere they turned, anyway. She'd been both a help and hindrance to them the previous spring. She'd shown up at the Norwood Studios party just this week and was somehow connected to Lily Byrne.

Wait.

She'd been at the studio party, performing. That wasn't unusual—she was one of the most sought-after singers in the city—but could it be a coincidence that she had been there just a few nights before Duncan Carroll died?

"Does Ava know Celeste?" Gilbert asked once he'd gotten the car started. They rumbled along down Locust toward Rittenhouse.

"I don't think so. Why?" Edie turned toward him. "You don't think Duncan's death is related to the others, do you?"

"Three men are dead," Gilbert said carefully. "It bears thinking about."

"Two gangsters and an actor who have no connection to one another," Edie pointed out. "Unless you think Duncan has some connection to Tommy Fletcher?"

"Or Leo Salvatore," Gilbert said. It felt unlikely, even as the words left his mouth. "Do you think he'd talk to us?"

"I can think of someone he'd talk to," Edie said. "The question is, will she talk to *him*? I think they've been on the outs lately."

Gilbert had never approved of his sister's on-again, off-again relationship with Leo Salvatore, the gangster known as the Butcher of Broad Street. Sure, Leo had kept her safe from a deranged killer the previous spring—Gilbert would always be grateful to him for that—but the man was a ruthless killer. A criminal.

And for some reason, madly in love with Lizzie.

"We can ask Marco?" Edie suggested.

"Marco stays out of his brothers' business," Gilbert said. "It's tidier that way."

"Well, then I guess it's up to us," Edie said. She yawned, pressing her hand against her mouth. "But I don't think we'll find anything out at this hour. Do you?"

No, he didn't. He saw her home safely, watching as she climbed the steps up to the arched stone doorway. She slipped inside, and Gilbert counted to ten, then pulled away from the curb.

He should go home. Give his daughter a kiss on the forehead and get a good night's sleep. But instead, he put the car into gear and headed to the one place where he knew he'd find answers.

"I thought you went home hours ago," Cecelia said. The lamp on her desk gave off a warm pull of light. "Everything all right?"

"I figured if I couldn't sleep, I might as well work," Gilbert replied. "How's it here?"

Cecelia waved her hand toward the switchboard. "Surprisingly quiet. How was the scene out at Norwood Studios? Was it anyone famous?"

"Duncan Carroll," Gilbert said.

Cecelia gasped. "No. I just read about him in the paper today—he just got married! What happened?"

"That's what I'm going to find out," Gil said. "Is anyone else here?"

"Harrison's the one on call tonight," she replied. "He's down in his lab, as usual."

That was excellent news. Gilbert respected most of his fellow assistants. He wasn't particularly close with any of them save Marco, but he genuinely liked Isaiah Harrison. And if it was as slow a night as Cecelia said it was, the other doctor would have enough time on his hands to help him. He picked up a clipboard from the rack and headed back to the bullpen, where he hung up his hat and swapped his jacket for his lab coat.

He found Isaiah right where Cecelia had said he would, in the lab in the basement, awash in artificial lighting. He rapped his knuckles against the door. The other man looked up from his paperwork and broke into a smile.

"Gil. I didn't know you were working tonight."

"Couldn't sleep," Gilbert said. "How's it been here?"

"Slower than usual, which is a good thing," Harrison said. "I heard you and Marco were called out to the movie studio. Bet that was quite the scene."

"Same as any other, really," Gil said. "I wanted to check with you about that. Has anyone opened him up yet?"

Harrison shook his head. "Knight said he could wait 'til morning. But I did get a blood sample. Figured I might as well run it while I was here."

"Let me guess. Cyanide."

"Luck of the Irish," Harrison said with a laugh, but Gilbert didn't smile. He had been correct—Duncan Carroll had been poisoned. But by whom?

"Is there any way to tell the type of cyanide used to poison someone?"

Harrison shook his head. "No. Well, very technically—yes. Cyanide appears in different forms. It can be inhaled—we see that a lot with fire victims."

Gilbert thought about this. "What about chlorine gas?"

"That's right," Harrison said. "It's ugly stuff. Used a lot during the war, but we don't see a lot of it here, thank God. Mostly, it's ingested, like with the Byrne case. Usually accidentally. It can be injected, though that's less common. I've even seen cases where the liquid form is absorbed through the skin or the eyes during an accident." He gave a quick shudder. "But that sort of thing doesn't show up in the lab tests. That's where you all come in."

Gilbert knew this. All of the evidence had to work together to point to cause of death. In Homer Byrne's case, the cyanide found in his system explained the physical symptoms Gilbert was able to observe through autopsy: high oxygenation of the blood, constricted blood vessels. Cardiac events. Easily mistaken for a heart attack or a blood clot in the lungs. Not every cyanide victim turned the telltale cherry red or was found in the vicinity of the poisonous substance. Not everyone could smell the famed bitter almond scent either.

He thanked Isaiah and headed back upstairs. Duncan Carroll's body was already in cold storage in one of the autopsy rooms. He turned on the lights, washed his hands, and set out his instruments.

It was time to see what sort of secrets Duncan Carroll would reveal in death.

The autopsy disclosed nothing surprising. Duncan Carroll had been a healthy man of about thirty years of age, his blood and organs showing signs of acute cyanide poisoning. Gilbert was just finishing his paperwork when Dr. Knight arrived the next morning. He stopped in the doorway to the assistant's office, starting at the sight of Gilbert already at his desk. "Good Lord, son, have you slept at all? I thought Harrison was on call last night?"

Gilbert raised his head. His normally spotless desk was approaching messy—a cup of coffee, cold, sat at his elbow, and stacks of files surrounded him. "I had work to do," he said, rubbing at his forehead. He almost told Dr. Knight about his suspicions concerning the last three cases—that Byrne, Burkhart, and Carroll were somehow connected in death—but stopped himself. Knight hadn't entertained the idea of Gilbert investigating on his own in the spring, and he had made it clear upon Gilbert's return that any deviation from the status quo could cost him his job. The police were in charge of solving murders, not coroners.

Knight stepped closer, his face softening. "Have your spells returned?"

Gilbert shook his head, his hand going automatically to the breast pocket where his morphine had lived for so long. That, at least, he could be honest about. "No, sir. I'm feeling better. Stronger. You were right about the physical activity."

"Glad to hear it," Knight said. "Stay the course. We need you healthy in both mind and body."

Gilbert heard the underlying message: stay clean and sane, and stay employed. The slasher case the previous spring had put a new sort of press scrutiny on the coroner's office. In order to retain the trust of the public, their work had to be unimpeachable. Perfect. They couldn't have trembling cowards collecting evidence—especially ones who lost hours of their lives to waking memories.

Gilbert knew, of course, that he was one of the lucky ones. He'd seen some of the others when he was in the hospital during the war, shaking and drooling. Some spent days staring into the distance, trapped in battles long since ended, forced to endure electric shock therapy, cold water therapy, or worse. And even they were more fortunate than others; they had a roof over their heads, food to eat, and a bed to sleep in. So many others were consigned to the streets by families ashamed of their cowardice, painted as pariahs by those who had no idea of the horrors they'd faced. By the men who had stayed safe on the home front while Gilbert and his brothers in arms had bled and died in muddy trenches across France and Belgium, especially in the early days, before the AEF dug trenches of their own. They'd learned the hard way that the American troops were significantly taller than their French and English counterparts. Their helmeted heads rose above the trenches, providing easy targets for German snipers. The months Gilbert had spent at war had been hell.

But he was home now. He'd been home these last four years, and he'd worn out the patience of those around him. He was expected to be better. To close the door on that chapter of his life and get on with it.

To be healthy, as Knight had put it.

He was trying. He really, really was.

"Yes, sir," Gilbert said, closing his fists to hide the tremor in his fingers.

"Now go home. Get some rest," Knight said. His sharp gaze landed on Gilbert's hands, then swept back up to his face. "We can't have you falling asleep at your desk, can we?"

Gilbert knew that Dr. Knight was right. He stood, organizing the piles on his desk, and dumped his cold coffee down the sink. He'd drive home, get a few hours of rest, and keep searching for Celeste Dupont.

His family depended on it.

Chapter 12

Edie didn't sleep. She paced the halls of the house like the mad wife in a gothic novel. Aphrodite kept up with her for a little while but had given up sometime around three, curling up in her fluffy bed beside Edie's own.

Edie's father, who was staying at the city house during election season, startled when he opened his door the next morning, and found Edie, still in her nightdress and wrapper, rearranging the art in the hallway. "You're up early," Councilman Ned Shippen said to his daughter, pulling his own dressing robe tighter around his rounded middle. "I don't think I've seen you awake at this hour since you were in school."

Edie straightened the frame of the painting in front of her and gave her father a long look. "Couldn't sleep. It was a long night."

"Another spell?" Ned's hand flew to his temple, his shorthand for Edie's migraines. She shook her head, and he relaxed slightly. "Bad day yesterday?"

"You can say that." Edie chewed on her lip. The painting, an abstract in shades of blues and golds, was still crooked. She reached out and pushed it slightly to the left—*there*. Perfect. "What do you know about Norwood Studios?"

Ned blinked. "Harry Fox's film studio?"

"The very one. Mr. Fox sends his regards, by the way. You went to school together?"

"Penn." Ned frowned. "He was always cutting class to play with his damned camera. How is he doing?"

"Not well," Edie said. "His leading man dropped dead in the middle of filming."

"Dear God." Ned stared at his daughter. "What happened? Are you all right?"

"I'm fine. I'm just—well, I can't stop thinking about it. It keeps playing over and over in my head. He was fine one moment—delivering his lines perfectly—and then boom! Dead the next. Gilbert said there was nothing to be done, but—"

"The Irish coroner?" Ned's eyes were close to bugging out of his head. "He was there?"

"Dr. Lawless, yes," Edie said. "The *war hero* who helped me catch Rebecca's killer. Keep up, Daddy. He came later, with the police."

Ned pressed his lips together but didn't say anything. "I bet Harry took it hard," he said, returning to the subject of the party. "The leading man—that's got to be a huge setback on top of all his other troubles." He sighed. "But Harry always lands on his feet, dear girl. Don't worry too much about him."

"Other troubles?" Edie turned to his father. "Like what?"

"The studio's been in financial trouble ever since the war," Ned said. "It's funny that we're talking about him now, actually. I haven't thought about him in years, and now he's brought up twice in the space of a week. First, he shows up at my office, and now this." Edie's father tightened the belt of his robe.

"He came to see you?" Strange that he hadn't mentioned it either time that Edie had spoken with him. She frowned.

"He wanted a loan for this movie of his," Ned said. His face fell. "I had to say no, of course—it didn't look like a smart financial move for the family. He's a nice fellow, but I have you girls to think of. I can't invest in risky ventures. Now, since you're up, how about we both get dressed and go out for breakfast? Give Cook a little break."

Edie gave him a grateful smile. "Sure thing," she said, pressing a kiss to his cheek. "I'll be ready in a flash."

She dressed quickly in a simple shift dress, with a matching long coat in hunter green, and selected a coordinating cloche hat from her closet. A quick swipe of lipstick later, she bounded down the stairs to the foyer, where Mr. O'Mara, the city house butler, was bringing in the newspaper.

"Can I see that?" she asked.

"Of course, Miss Shippen," he said. He handed it over without blinking, and Edie tore into it, expecting Duncan Carroll's death to be front-page news. There was speculation about who would win tonight's World Series game between the Giants and Yankees now that Babe Ruth was barred from the game on doctor's orders, and news about the Irish delegation en route to London. But there wasn't a mention of Duncan Carroll above the fold of the *Philadelphia Inquirer*, or below it, for that matter. Not a single word about it in the local news section or even in the culture section. Even the police blotter was scrubbed of any mention of a disturbance at Norwood Studios the previous day.

"Huh." Edie dropped the paper on the table beside her as her father appeared. He accepted his hat from the butler and gave his daughter a quizzical look.

"What's wrong?"

"Why wouldn't the tragic death of a famous film star be splashed across every newspaper in this city?" Edie already knew the answer, but she wanted—no, *needed*, to hear her father say it.

But then there was a knock on the door, and she didn't get to say anything. Not when Ava Sylvester stood on her doorstep, clutching a simple black coat around her shoulders, shivering in the cool morning air.

"Edie," she said, her voice shaking over the syllables. "I need your help."

◆―――◆◆◆―――◆

It took a little while to get the details out of Ava. She accepted a cup of coffee and a cigarette, which she smoked while the coffee went cold. She sat in the green barrel chair across from Edie in the library, her knees drawn up beneath her chin, like a child. Ava didn't say anything for a while. She smoked, staring off into the distance. Edie waited—Ava could be like this, sometimes: moody, prone to melancholy, even without reason. This time, she had a reason, and Edie knew that her friend would talk when she was ready. Finally, she sighed, stubbed the remnants of the cigarette in the ashtray, and looked up at Edie with her big blue eyes.

"They think I did it," she managed to say.

Edie's stomach swooped. This was bad. "Who does?" she asked, even though she didn't need to.

"The cops. Who else? I didn't do it," Ava said. "I couldn't hurt anyone—you know that. Not even—" Her words broke off in a sharp sob, and Edie wanted to rush to her, to wrap Ava in her arms and promise that everything would be all right, that no one could believe that Ava was capable of murder.

Edie had learned the hard way that anyone could be a killer.

She pressed her hands together, careful to keep them on her lap. "Why do they think you did it?" she asked, keeping her voice even.

Ava kept jabbing the cigarette at the ashtray, even though it was out, smearing the ash around the silver surface. "The wife always does it," she said dully. "And that second-rate detective on the case has already decided that since I'm the *wife*, I'm clearly guilty."

Wife. Edie's words to Finnegan Pyle about a completely different wife echoed back at her, and she winced.

"Did you love him, Ava?"

Ava snorted. She looked up at Edie, and her gaze was flat, defeated. "Darling, do you really have to ask me that?"

"Tell me the truth, Ava."

Ava dropped her gaze, her cheeks flushing. "I've never lied to you."

"And yet you've never been entirely honest with me either." Edie stood and circled her desk. She leaned against it and crossed her arms over her chest. "Why didn't you tell me you'd gotten married when I saw you last week? Isn't that something you'd tell a friend? If you loved him, why keep him a secret?"

Ava stared up at her. "Edie."

"Did you really love him?"

"Of course not," Ava snapped. "He was a brute. I could never love someone like him."

"Did you hate him?" Edie asked instead.

"I barely gave two shits about him," Ava said sharply. She dropped the cigarette stub and stood too, mirroring Edie's stance. "He was a drunk and a cheat and a damned good actor. The best I'd ever worked with. So no. I didn't hate him. I didn't love him. But I respected him. He was my ticket into the big time, and now he's dead, and they'll see that I fry for it."

Ava still wasn't crying. She stared at Edie, defiant, and that was all Edie needed to see to believe her.

"All right," Edie said. "I believe you."

"Just like that?" Ava said. "I yell at you, and you believe me?"

"If you were trying to fool me, you would have cried," Edie said. "I've seen you work those tears a million times." She stepped close, grabbing the other woman's hand. When she looked up, Ava's eyes *were* rimmed with tears—but not ones of desolation. Tears of hope.

"I didn't kill him," Ava said again. Her fingers squeezed Edie's, and Edie's heart somersaulted in her chest. She could do this—she could help Ava. She was an investigator, wasn't she? A sleuth? She'd set out to help women who couldn't advocate for themselves. What better way to do that than to prove her friend wasn't a murderer?

"I believe you," Edie said. "And I'm going to help you prove it."

Chapter 13

A few hours of sleep did nothing to ease the swirling questions in Gilbert's mind, or suddenly clear up the connections between the dead men. The answers seemed more opaque than ever. Three men: two connected to Tommy Fletcher and Leo Salvatore, and one famous actor. All dead by cyanide.

But why?

He finished his breakfast right as Lizzie came downstairs. She looked as tired as he felt, with dark circles ringing her brown eyes. The day before had been trying for her.

"Do you want to talk about it?" he asked, keeping his voice low. Penelope was playing with the kitten, Reginald, in the back garden. His mother had already left for her daily Mass, and their father read the paper in the front parlor.

Lizzie glanced at Penelope through the back door. "I just feel terrible about the entire thing. He was dying, and none of us knew it. We thought it was part of the act. He carried on, even though . . ." her voice hitched. She put her toast back on the table. "Never mind, I'm not hungry. Will you drive me to work? I'm sure Miss Edie's wondering where I am."

Gilbert wasn't sure that Edie would be up and about at this hour, given their search for Celeste DuPont the night before. He should have explained to Lizzie what was going on—the way Tommy had taken an interest in their investigation, and the implied threat he'd made. But she was already moving. She cut up the toast and set it aside—they'd soak it in milk and put it out for the kitten later. He said goodbye to Penelope and his father and met Lizzie at the car.

The drive from Manayunk to Rittenhouse Square took longer than usual at this time of day; construction on the new Parkway off East River Drive slowed them considerably. By the time they pulled onto Walnut Street, Lizzie was fussing about being late, and Gilbert still hadn't found a way to tell her about Tommy's threats or his new involvement with Edie's case. He parked the car on the curb and cut the engine.

It was now or never.

Lizzie looked surprised. "What are you doing?"

"I'm coming in," he said. "I . . . I need to tell you something." He explained the situation with Tommy Fletcher quickly. Lizzie's face darkened with every word; by the end, she was furious.

"That utter bastard," she said. "He's worried about me going on dates with Leo, is he? Maybe he should look in his own house first. His own sister's been with the Salvatores for *months*, but suddenly I'm the problem? I'll show him a problem."

"We'll give him the information he wants, and he'll leave you alone." Gilbert said. "It's even more of a reason for us to find a new place to live. We'll bring Mam and Da with us. Somewhere out of Tommy's reach."

"This whole city's in Tommy's reach," Lizzie pointed out. "Are you willing to do that? Willing to leave everything? Your job, your friends? Your home?"

Gilbert didn't have many friends, not anymore. Not outside of Marco, anyway. "I can find a new job," he said. "I would, if it meant seeing you all safe."

"Well, speak for yourself," Lizzie said. She flung open the car door. "I like my job and my friends. I'm not going anywhere."

"Liz!"

It was too late—she'd already slammed the door. Gilbert rubbed his hands over his face, frustrated, and followed her.

"Will you wait just a second?" he called after her as she hurried up the steps. She unlocked the door and stormed inside. He caught the door as she moved to slam it. "Please. Wait."

"Family squabble?" Edie stood at the top of the stairs, her hat in her hand. She looked mildly amused, which only made Gilbert more irritated. "Whatever it is, it needs to wait. We have a new client."

"A new client?" Lizzie asked. She had her back turned on her brother, like she couldn't even bear to look at him. It was completely unfair—Gilbert was only trying to help. To keep her safe. "Who?"

Edie stepped aside, revealing Ava Sylvester, a pale wraith wrapped in a black coat, on the landing behind her.

"We're going to prove that Ava didn't murder Duncan Carroll."

Edie and Ava were on their way out to speak with Harold Fox. Gilbert decided to drive, while Lizzie would stay close to the phone. O'Mara, Edie's butler, was under orders to bring Lizzie a copy of every newspaper he could get his hands on. She'd scour the pages for any mention of Duncan or stories reporting any other mysterious deaths.

Ava passed the drive in melancholy silence, punctuated here and there by heaving sighs. Edie seemed sure that her friend was innocent, but Gilbert couldn't help stealing glances back at the actress as they drove. She'd seemed so unhappy with Duncan at the party—the complete opposite of a blushing bride. But had she been unhappy enough to kill him?

Edie had raised those same questions about Lily Byrne. It would have been easy enough to point fingers at the two women—to write them off as jealous lovers, and to chalk the deaths up to coincidence. Except for the addition of Frank Burkhart.

Ava directed them toward the back of the studio's property. They drove through the tiny town at the center of the lot, as bustling as any main street. Children played there, and men were hard at work, hammering and painting a new building while a group of women rolled a pair of garment racks down a wooden ramp.

"It's something, isn't it?" Ava remarked from the backseat while Edie and Gilbert took it all in.

"How many people work here?" he asked.

"Close to five hundred," Ava said. "They live here too. Mostly employees and their families. Harry has four to five films shooting at a given time, and each has its cast and crews, plus the makeup people and the wardrobe departments, the artists. There's also the kitchen staff, the cleaners, and the doctor and nurses in the infirmary, plus a school for the children. I've got to hand it to Harry. It's a whole self-contained operation. He even has a hundred head of longhorn cattle."

"What are the cattle for?" Edie asked.

"The Westerns, mostly," Ava explained as Gilbert drove past the building for Studio A, where Duncan had filmed his fateful scene the day before. "But also for beef, to stock the kitchens and to sell for profit. He also has several hundred acres of farmland in Montgomery County."

"How'd he get the money for all this? It's got to be expensive to keep a place like this operating," Gilbert asked.

"There's a lot of money in films, Doctor," Ava said primly. "And lots of people eager to invest when they see the kind of genius Harry is."

"My father said he comes from money," Edie cut in before Gilbert could fire back a smart remark. "He's from New York, isn't he? One of the four hundred?"

"He and Duncan both," Ava said. "They bonded over it, both the black sheep of their families. But I don't hold it against him—or against you, darling," she added, patting Edie's shoulder. "Not everyone can be self-made."

Gilbert made a small snort in the back of his throat.

Edie flashed him a look, then asked, "So everyone lives on set?"

"There's a small tract of houses for the families on the other side of the warehouse," Ava explained. "The single girls all live in the rooms above the shops, with an assigned house mother in each building. The single men have a dormitory on the other side of the set, near the rail station. It's all very much on the up-and-up."

"The actors too?" Edie asked. "Duncan lived over there?"

"Oh no," Ava said with a little laugh. "We have our own quarters in Harry's house, over that hill. Apparently a British General once lived there during the battle of Germantown, and it's been added on to over the years, so it's huge. He likes to keep a close eye on his talent," she added with a waggle of her eyebrows. "Turn left here."

Gilbert obliged, and they wound down a narrow country lane in the cut between two rolling hills. A sprawling whitewashed stone farmhouse sat in the little valley, backing down to a creek. It had a large circular drive lined with trees, and a vast green lawn, as lush as any English country estate. A glass-walled greenhouse sat down the hill about a hundred yards from the main house, and from the car, a red clay tennis court was barely visible.

A stout, dark-haired man appeared at the door when Gilbert parked. His suspicion turned to relief when he saw Ava climb from the car. "Señorita Ava," he called. "¿Dónde has estado? ¡Nos tenías preocupados!"

Ava replied in rapid-fire Spanish, her hands moving quickly. The man seemed mollified and turned his attention to Gilbert and Edie.

"Hola, welcome. My name is Martinez, Mr. Fox's butler. Welcome to Norwood House. Mr. Fox is currently in a meeting, but you are welcome to wait for him with Señorita Ava."

"There's no need for that, Martinez." Harold Fox appeared in the large, wood-paneled foyer, Finnegan Pyle beside him. "The detective was just leaving."

"Bertie." Pyle's long face was haggard, his eyes rimmed in red and dusted in shadows, his suit rumpled. Harold Fox, beside him, looked even worse. Fox startled slightly, his eyes going wide at the sight of Gilbert.

"Hello, Finn," Gilbert said. "Working hard?"

"Something like that." Pyle jerked his thumb at Harold Fox, who was still staring at Gilbert, his mouth pursed. "You remember Mr. Fox?"

"Of course. Hello, sir," Gilbert said. "Gilbert Lawless."

"The Irish doctor, of course," the man said. "And Miss Shippen too. Thank you both for bringing dear Ava home. We were worried sick about her all night." He turned his attention to Ava. "What were you thinking, vanishing like that?"

Ava stared at the ground, looking more like a sullen teenager being scolded by her father than an actress on the precipice of fame. "I needed air," she said finally.

Pyle was staring hard at Ava. "On second thought," he said. "I think I'll stay. I should probably talk to Miss Shippen again, and I have a few more questions for you too, Miss Sylvester."

"I'm sure you do," Ava said.

"Why don't we all step into my office," Harold Fox suggested.

"I'll bring a tray of lemonade," Martinez offered.

"Perfect. This way." Harold said. His office was just beyond the serviceable stairs. Gilbert could tell right away that much of the original farmhouse had been preserved during renovations: a center hall with a room front and back on either side. The house sprawled out from there, of course, but Harold had kept the back left room for his office.

It reminded Gilbert of Dr. Knight's office—tall bookshelves lined the walls, filled with matching leatherbound volumes, their spines pristine. A blue and white vase that sat on a side table, filled with willow branches, probably cost more than Gilbert's car.

Edie was the first to speak.

"Are you going to tell us why there isn't any news about Mr. Carroll's death in the papers this morning, Detective?"

Ava let out a little squeak of surprise. Harold's face flushed, but Pyle only smiled down at Edie.

"Can't get anything past you, can we? We wanted to get a head start on the investigation. Thankfully, Mr. Fox agreed. He spoke with his people, and we will release the information when we deem it necessary."

"So you're lying to the public."

"We're buying ourselves time to conduct a thorough investigation. One I'd appreciate you cooperating with."

"Of course." Edie stood, smoothing out her skirt. She sent a reassuring smile to Ava, then turned her focus to Pyle, eyes narrowed. "How is the investigation, Detective? Any suspects?"

Pyle sighed, his own gaze bouncing between the two women. "Why don't we speak privately, Miss Shippen? I have a few more questions for you."

"You're welcome to the patio," Harold said, motioning to a set of French doors on the back wall. "It's quiet out there. No one will hear you."

They stepped outside just as a soft knock on the door announced the arrival of the lemonade. Martinez set the tray down on the table in front of the sofa. He flipped over the glasses with an expert hand and moved to pour, but Ava reached out, stilling him. "Gracias," she said softly. "I've got it from here."

"Of course, Señorita Ava," Martinez said. He ducked his head and left as quickly and quietly as he'd arrived. Once the door was closed, Ava busied herself pouring the lemonade into crystal glasses. Gilbert accepted one, sipping at the sweet, tart drink.

"Sit," Harold commanded, pointing to one of two chairs arranged opposite the sofa.

Gilbert moved to where he was directed. Harold took the other chair when he had his own glass of lemonade. Once Ava lowered herself onto the sofa, both men sat.

Harold stared down at his glass, not drinking. He heaved a heavy sigh. "Dr. Lawless, I'm sorry we aren't in better spirits this morning," he said.

"Don't apologize, Harry. Everyone knows how devastated we are." Ava didn't sound particularly devastated. "Poor Della was sobbing all evening. I could hear her through the wall," she added. "I couldn't take it anymore. I had to leave."

Gilbert understood. He'd spent many sleepless nights after Sarah's death, wandering the streets until the sun rose over the horizon. He drank his lemonade slowly, unsure of how to respond to that. He had never been one for small talk; he didn't see much point in it, and he had always been comfortable with silence. Ava seemed determined to fill the space with chatter.

"It is really remarkable, isn't it?" she said to Harold. "I know we teased them both about it the other night, but the resemblance between Dr. Lawless and Duncan is really uncanny."

"I've been thinking the same thing," Harold said. He stared at Gilbert, lips thin, then nodded. "With a little makeup, and a long camera angle? No one could tell the difference."

Ava tilted her head and stared at Gilbert too.

He shifted, uncomfortable under their scrutiny. "What will happen with the film? Will you recast?" he asked.

"It depends on several things," Harold said. "The first is whether we'll be allowed to resume work. Your detective friend made it quite clear that we are all suspects in Duncan's death. Of course, it also depends on how long we can keep the news from the press. And . . ." Harold sipped his coffee. "Well, quite frankly, son, it depends on you."

Gilbert wasn't sure he'd heard Harold Fox correctly. "Pardon?" he asked. "I thought you said me."

"I'd like to hire you to finish the scenes we have remaining in the film."

"You want *me* to do it?" Gilbert nearly jumped from his skin. "Surely you're joking. Surely."

"I don't see another option," Harold said. "We can't finish the film without a Romeo. We can't reshoot at this point, and the resemblance between you—well, it really is amazing."

"So don't finish the film."

"Dr. Lawless, I assure you, if we don't finish this film, no one in my employ—and I mean *no one*, from the actors all the way down to the girls who feed us every meal and the fellas who haul the firewood, will get paid. There are hundreds of people depending on Norwood Studios for their livelihoods. Would you take that away from them?"

Gilbert looked to Ava. The starlet watched him expectantly.

Gilbert set his glass down on the table. He stood, right as Pyle and Edie stepped back into the room, closing the door to the patio behind them. Edie tilted her head, frowning.

"What's wrong?"

"I've just offered Dr. Lawless a job," Harold Fox said calmly. "Please help him come to his senses and accept it."

"A job?"

"They want me to finish the bloody film in Duncan's place," Gilbert nearly growled.

"That's a wonderful idea," Edie said. Her eyes sparkled. She was probably imagining Gilbert in some ridiculous costume, beneath layers of makeup. "Oh, how exciting, Gil. Congratulations!"

This was madness. Of course she'd think it was a good idea—that was precisely why he couldn't do it. Gilbert turned to Pyle. "Finn. Please. Help me talk some sense into them."

Pyle rubbed his chin. He hitched his thumb back toward the patio, where he and Edie had just emerged from. "We'll be right back, Mr. Fox." To Gilbert, he said, "Let's chat."

Gilbert followed Pyle out to the patio. Edie stepped out after them. The space was private—it backed against the addition on one side, and the other three were surrounded by a six-foot hedge. A fountain in the center of the patio bubbled merrily.

Gilbert pinched the bridge of his nose. "I can't do this. I have a family to think of—I have a job. Dr. Knight has been patient with me, but this? This is madness."

Edie and Pyle exchanged a conspiratorial glance, and Gilbert's heart dropped. "What?" he demanded.

"You need to do it." Pyle said.

"Absolutely not," Gil said. "Out of the question."

"Gil," Edie said softly, "it could help the investigation."

"Your girl has a point, Bertie," Pyle said. "It'll give us time to investigate. It's most likely that the wife offed him—"

"She did not," Edie interrupted.

"—but this would be helpful for the investigation, either to prove—"

"—or disprove," Edie said.

"Or disprove her guilt," Pyle added sourly. "Something strange is going on, Bertie. I can feel it in my bones. We still haven't been able to find the vial he drank from—all the witnesses said it was green glass. There are a million little bottles at that place—none of them green."

"You think the killer took it?" Gilbert stopped short at this. "You're sure it's gone?"

"It's somewhere," Pyle said grimly. "You doing this will give us time to find it."

"So I'm to . . . what? Live the life of a dead man for however long it takes to shoot this film?"

"Ava said they were mostly finished," Edie said. "It shouldn't be more than a few days' worth of work."

"And what if she didn't kill him?" This he addressed to Pyle. "If it wasn't Ava, and the killer's plan was to sabotage the film, what's to stop him from trying again? This is madness. I'm supposed to put myself in danger for this? I have a daughter, Pyle. I can't." Penelope had already lost so much, and she'd come so close to losing him as well. He had been reckless with his life in the past; he couldn't do that again. She deserved better. "I won't."

Pyle leaned forward, resting his arms on the balcony railing. He gave a deep sigh. "Bertie, old buddy, old pal," he said, "just hear him out. For my sake."

Which is how Gilbert found himself sitting on the sofa in Harold Fox's office, listening as the director explained the job. They had only a few scenes left to film—mostly filler and reshoots. They could coordinate around his work schedule.

It didn't sound unreasonable. Except for the fact that someone had poisoned Duncan Carroll, and someone could very well try to poison Gilbert.

"If it would make you feel better, Dr. Lawless, I am prepared to compensate you fairly for your time," Mr. Fox said quickly, interjecting before Gilbert could voice the rude thoughts swirling through his brain. "Half of Mr. Carroll's contracted rate would be appropriate, I think. So one thousand two hundred and fifty dollars?"

"For a week's wages?" Gilbert froze. That amount of money was more than he'd make in two months as a coroner's assistant. An extra two months' wages, all for a week of work? He'd spoken with Lizzie about moving out, about giving his parents a break. This would put him closer to that reality. Months closer. "You can't be serious."

Mr. Fox laughed, his mustache twitching in delight. "I wouldn't joke about money, my dear boy," he said. "Duncan was contracted for twenty-five hundred dollars per week, plus food, lodging, transportation, and medical benefits. Half of that would be twelve fifty, with everything else included. And the housing and food allowance would extend to you as well, Detective, and any of your staff you bring to set. Of course."

"That's very generous," Pyle said. Even his eyes were wide—an entire family in their neighborhood of Manayunk could live for months on less than a thousand dollars, earned from backbreaking labor in the textile mills along the canal. And yet film stars were earning that much—and more—in a single week?

Who are you to accept that much? a voice in the back of Gilbert's head said. *Who do you think you are?*

Think of all you'd be able to do for Penelope, another voice whispered. *For your parents. For Liz. For yourself.*

Gilbert looked down at his hands, already so much softer than the scarred and calloused hands of his father, who'd spent decades working dangerous machines on factory floors. Softer even still than his grandfather's, who'd worked as a tenant farmer in Ireland, beneath the boots of the English.

This amount of money would be life-changing. For himself, for his daughter.

Pyle met Gilbert's gaze and gave a little nod of encouragement. Gilbert had seen that nod a dozen times before—the dare to *"Do it"* before he dropped a toad down the back of Tommy Fletcher's shirt, before they plunged into the Devil's Pool in the Wissahickon, before they rolled up their sleeves for a fight.

"All right, Mr. Fox," Gilbert said, holding out his hand. "You've got yourself a deal."

Chapter 14

"Lizzie, if you don't close your mouth, your face is likely to freeze like that," Edie said. They were walking briskly down Chestnut Street; or at least they had been until Lizzie asked her about Ava, and Edie shared Gilbert's news. Then Lizzie froze on the sidewalk, her hand pressed to her chest.

"I'm sorry, Miss Edie. I thought you said that my brother was going to be in a movie." Lizzie let out a hysterical little sort of laugh that caused the man walking past to give her an even wider berth. "I must have misheard you."

"You didn't," Edie said. Aphrodite strained at her leash, pulling Edie slightly to the side. "He's not too happy about it either."

Once Gilbert had agreed to the role, things seemed to move quickly. Detective Pyle had promised to call Dr. Knight to have Gilbert loaned to the police department for the duration of the investigation. Gilbert had been sent home to pack his things, and the studio had arranged for a car to bring Edie home.

"No, he wouldn't be," Lizzie said. She'd started walking again, keeping pace with Edie and the dog. "Why? How?"

Edie explained the entire situation, and Lizzie listened, her frown deepening with every word. "So you're either going to prove Ava innocent and catch the real killer by using my brother as bait, or find out she really killed him?"

"Or someone else at the studio," Edie said. "My father said Harold is having money troubles. Money can cause people to act irrationally. Or perhaps it was another actor, driven mad with jealousy over Duncan's role?"

"Maybe." They stepped out of the way to let a man walking a larger dog pass them by. "It also could have been self-inflicted. He seemed in a dark mood at the party."

"He did." Edie didn't know what to think of the whole thing. "And then there's this business with Celeste Dupont. I have to see what she knows about this supposed witch, so we can figure out whether or not Mrs. Byrne actually murdered her husband."

"Leo's convinced Tommy has something to do with it," Lizzie said. "He has no proof, of course. But he thinks Tommy is trying to sabotage their deal."

"According to your brother, Tommy Fletcher thinks the same thing about Leo," Edie said. She rubbed at her temples. "So. We need to make a list of things to do."

"I'm on it, miss," Lizzie said. She held up her palm, ticking imaginary boxes off a list. "One, track down Celeste Dupont. Two, find out who killed Duncan Carroll. Three, stop a gang war. Four, collect photographic evidence of my brother dressed as Romeo. Easy enough."

"You forgot one," Edie said.

Lizzie tilted her head. "I did?"

"Five, dig out our best black dresses. Homer Byrne's funeral is tomorrow morning, and I intend to finally get a look at Mrs. Byrne."

———◆•◆•———

Homer Byrne was to be laid to rest at nine o'clock on Monday morning, in a full Catholic Mass at the parish of Saint John the Baptist in Manayunk, the same parish that Lizzie and Gilbert had grown up attending. Edie, who was Episcopalian, had never attended a Latin service before. They stopped at the Lawlesses' home to procure a veil, which Lizzie insisted was needed. "You'll need to blend in," Lizzie said. "Some women wear hats, but none as fine as yours. Just follow my lead, all right?"

Edie had never been inside the tidy row house on Manor Street—or seen a narrower street. Grover's car seemed to barely fit. She followed Lizzie up the front steps and into the narrow vestibule, which smelled delightfully of fresh bread. A flight of stairs led straight up, and a doorway to the left opened onto a front parlor.

"Mam? Are you here?" Lizzie yelled.

"For the love of God, what have I told you about yer hollering, Elizabeth?" Mr. Lawless appeared in the doorway, rubbing at his ears. He caught sight of Edie and straightened. "Oh. I didn't realize we had a visitor."

"How do you do, Mr. Lawless? I'm Edie Shippen. We met last spring." Edie held out her hand.

Mr. Lawless stared down at it for a moment. He shared Gilbert's dark eyes and his long, straight nose. In his youth, he had probably shared his son's slim frame and tall height, though he'd rounded out with age.

"That's right. At the hospital. It's nice to see you again, dearie. Let's call the wife, so she can get us some cake." He turned to the stairs, and bellowed just as loud as his daughter had, "Aiofe!"

"What in the world is all this noise for?" Lizzie's mother appeared at the top of the stairs, Penelope behind her. "I'm right here, you don't have to—oh! Miss Shippen. Hello!" Aifoe hurried down the stairs. "We weren't expecting you." She said the last part while glaring at her daughter.

"Oh, it was a last-minute thing. I was invited to a funeral today, and it's Catholic, and Lizzie—"

"Say no more." Mrs. Lawless's entire face lit up. "You need a veil, of course. Can't wear a hat like that. Come upstairs. I'll see which one of mine looks best on you."

"What's wrong with my hat?" Edie asked. She'd opted for a drooping musketeer style today, complete with a pheasant feather.

"It's just a bit much for a funeral, dearie," Mrs. Lawless said. "Especially around here."

Mrs. Lawless bustled Edie and Lizzie upstairs. Penelope followed, shyly peeking out from behind her aunt's skirts. The child had Lizzie's bright red curls but her mother's clear blue eyes. Edie smiled at her.

"Hello, Penny. I'm not sure if you remember me."

"You're Da's princess friend," Penny said, as if Edie had offended her. "You took me to the zoo, but Mr. Fletcher bought me a kitten."

"Oh, well. I'm not sure how I can compete with a kitten," Edie said. She crouched down, so she was eye to eye with the girl. "What do you think?"

"Well, you're prettier than Mr. Fletcher," Penny said.

Edie laughed out loud. "That's a relief," she said.

"In here, Miss Shippen," Mrs. Lawless called. She beckoned Edie into the front bedroom. It was small but tidy, with two narrow beds topped with matching white chenille bedspreads. A caned rocking chair sat in the corner, with a bright rag quilt draped over the back. A basket of knitting sat beside it. Edie had the feeling she was being invited into a space that few outside of the family ever saw. The room was a world apart from her own mother's bedroom, and yet something about it felt so achingly familiar that Edie had to swallow past the sudden rise of emotion in her throat.

A mirrored armoire was built into the wall, and Gilbert's mother had it opened. She gently sorted through the contents of her top drawer and emerged with a length of black lace. She draped it over her arm and turned to Edie. "Irish lace. Me mam made it herself."

Edie reached a hand out, tracing the delicate scalloped pattern. "It's beautiful, Mrs. Lawless," she said. "But I couldn't possibly wear that. It's a family heirloom."

"And you'll look pretty as a picture with it in your hair," Mrs. Lawless said. "I insist."

"Don't bother arguing with her," Lizzie said from the doorway. "Mam never loses an argument. Actually," she added, straightening, "come to think of it, neither do you. I might pay money to see which one of you comes out on top."

"Oh, shush," Mrs. Lawless said. "Sit down there, Miss Shippen. I'll get it pinned properly."

Edie perched on the edge of the mattress. Mrs. Lawless stood behind her, hands gentle. She laid the bit of lace over Edie's hair and pinned it into place. It draped over Edie's ears, covering her head completely in the back and brushing her shoulders in the front. Mrs. Lawless stepped to Edie's front, adjusting it just so. She put cool fingers beneath Edie's chin, tilting it up. "There," she said. "You almost look Irish. Black Irish, with that hair, but Irish all the same."

Edie gave her a grateful smile. "Thank you, Mrs. Lawless."

"No thanks necessary, dearie," the older woman said. "You saved our Bertie, Miss Shippen. And our Penelope. You're one of us now."

◆―――――◆―――――◆

Lily Byrne made a beautiful widow.

Edie and Lizzie found seats on the aisle at the back of the church, though there wasn't much of a crowd to compete with. Lily processed in just ahead of the wooden casket. She was older than Edie was expecting—perhaps in her midthirties, with blond hair tucked into a false bob. She wore a fashionable black dress that Edie recognized from Wanamaker's, with a square neck and chiffon sleeves. She held her head high as she took her seat at the front of the church, one row in front of Tommy Fletcher. As if he felt Edie's gaze on him, the gangster turned. His eyes met Edie's, and he tipped his hat. He didn't seem surprised to see her one bit.

"All of the pallbearers are Cresson Street Crew," Lizzie whispered in Edie's ear. "Tommy is really showing up for her."

The organ blared through the church as the cantor began to sing. Near the front, Lily's shoulders shook. Edie, who had focused her language studies on French, not Latin, let her gaze drift over the other assembled mourners.

Nina, the shopgirl from the stationary shop, sat a few rows up with a few other young women—Lily's other coworkers, Edie had to assume. Mrs. Patterson was also in attendance, with her niece beside her. Colleen was a member of the

Philadelphia Twelve, a Marxist, and a tremendous friend. She'd been college roommates with Edie's late cousin Rebecca, and Edie had made it a point to stay in touch.

The service took nearly an hour. Edie knelt when Lizzie knelt, stood when Lizzie stood, and stayed in her seat near the back while the rest of the gathering took communion. Lily only audibly sobbed once—when the priest said the final blessing over her husband's casket, sprinkling the top with holy water. The pall bearers carried the casket out of the church slowly, behind the priest, Lily trailing behind.

"We'll go to the grave next," Lizzie whispered. "Just fall into line with everyone else."

The mourners filed out in reverse order—the front pews first, then the middle, and then finally Edie and Lizzie. Edie kept her head bowed, glancing up through her lashes as the others passed, but Nina didn't seem to recognize her. Colleen, however, did and lingered on the church steps.

"What are you doing here?" she demanded, once she'd crossed herself with water from the small font at the church door.

"Working," Edie said.

"Working . . . *oh*. She didn't." Colleen stared at Edie, her jaw slack. "She really hired you?"

"Well you don't have to sound so surprised about it," Edie whispered back. "I'm very capable."

"That woman did not kill her husband," Colleen said. "I don't know what's gotten into my aunt's head, but you have to stop entertaining her ideas."

"Someone killed him," Edie replied. "She may not be right about Mrs. Byrne's involvement, but she is at least right about that."

"Shush," Lizzie hissed at them. They'd processed around the side of the church, down the hill to the cemetery gate beside it. A train lumbered by on the Cresson Street tracks, drowning out whatever else Lizzie was going to say.

The graveside service was short. The priest said a prayer and shook more holy water on the casket. Mrs. Byrne dropped a handful of dirt atop it. She had pulled her veil down, obscuring her face entirely. Tommy stood beside her, and she clung to the gangster. Once the service concluded, the mourners stopped beside her, one by one, each paying their respects.

"Are you going up?" Lizzie asked as the crowd trickled down. Colleen and her aunt had left without saying a word to the woman. Nina and the other shopgirls stood in a cluster just down the hill.

"I might as well," Edie said.

"What are you going to say to her?"

"I haven't figured that part out yet." Edie slipped into the end of the line, behind a heavyset man in a rough cap. He spoke a few words to Mrs. Byrne and gave her arm a gentle pat, then shook Tommy's hand.

"Miss Shippen," Tommy said when Edie approached. His eyes narrowed.

"Mr. Fletcher, so lovely to see you again, despite the circumstances." She turned to Mrs. Byrne, whose face was unreadable beneath black lace. "Mrs. Byrne, I'm so deeply sorry for your loss."

Mrs. Byrne inclined her head. "Thank you. Did you know Homer?"

Edie shook her head. "No, I didn't. I'm here on behalf of a friend." Her heart kicked up—here she was, in front of her prime suspect. She didn't know when she'd get another chance to speak to the woman, so she blurted out. "She told me to ask about la futura. She said you could help me."

Mrs. Byrne moved so quickly Edie didn't have time to react before the woman's palm cracked across her face. Edie stumbled back, stunned, her hand going to her cheek immediately. "You little bitch," the widow snarled. "Tell that strega she killed my husband. Tell her I'll kill her too!"

Tommy had his arms around Mrs. Byrne, who turned to the gangster, sobbing against his chest. "Get her out of here," he snapped at Lizzie, who had come at once to Edie's aid.

"Come on, miss," Lizzie said. She slipped her arm around Edie's shoulder, guiding her back down the hill, where Grover waited with the car. Edie didn't protest, still stunned into silence.

"Say, are you all right?" Grover asked, jumping out of the car at their approach. He opened the door and helped Edie inside. "What happened to your face?"

"I'm fine," Edie said. And she was, despite the fact that her cheekbone still stung; she was pretty sure she'd have a bruise come morning. But she didn't regret it—not a bit. Because Lily Byrne's reaction confirmed what Edie had suspected— once she found the woman behind la futura, she'd find Byrne's real killer.

Chapter 15

Gilbert's first day on set began with a minor disaster involving a monkey and a lit cigarette.

The monkey was named Jade. It belonged to Della, Harold Fox's niece. The monkey had no role in the film but tore around the big house like a deranged toddler, swinging from the furniture and stealing whatever baubles it liked. Gilbert distrusted the creature immediately upon meeting it at supper the evening before, and the feeling was apparently mutual.

He had, out of ignorance of the monkey's antics, left the transom window atop of his dressing room open, in order to allow ample airflow between the rooms . . . and inadvertently providing easy access for Jade to travel wherever the damnable creature pleased.

He'd slept fitfully all night, dreaming of fire and deep, dark holes in the ground. He'd fallen asleep on the sofa in his dressing room, waiting for the makeup crew to arrive. At first, when the weight of the monkey hit his chest, he only stirred, thinking it was his daughter climbing into his bed after her own bad dream—the poor child had had a stretch of them since the ordeal in the spring. He rolled, stretching out his arm, and said, "'S'all right, mo leanbh. Da's here."

The monkey bit him.

Pain radiated up Gilbert's hand, and he sat bolt upright with a shout. The monkey rolled off the sofa, hissed, and jumped on top of the dresser. It grabbed a glass jar of aftershave as Gilbert leaped up, and in two quick hops it scampered up the wall and out through the open transom into the corridor beyond. Gilbert gave chase, crashing through the door as the monkey flung the bottle at Pyle, who dropped his lit cigarette with a shout. The bottle shattered on the hardwood, and the cigarette ignited with a *whoosh*.

"Shit!" Pyle scrambled backward, and Gilbert stopped, momentarily stunned. He'd just been dreaming about fire, and now . . .

"Move!" Pyle was already past him, grabbing the blanket from the back of the sofa and dropping it on the fire, smothering the flames. The monkey jumped again, climbing up the curtains, where it perched on the brass rod and bared its pointy little teeth at them.

Pyle crossed himself. "Saint Michael, protect us," he muttered. "Is that a demon?"

"Miss O'Malley claims it's a monkey," Gilbert said. He rubbed at his hand—the bite hadn't been deep enough to draw blood, but he had a set of narrow scratches across his skin that were already raised and beginning to itch.

Pyle stared at the creature again as he pulled another cigarette from the silver case in his chest pocket and lit it. "You ready for today, Bertie?" he asked.

"No." Gilbert had no idea how he was supposed to act in a film. "This is never going to work."

"It will." Pyle took a drag of the cigarette. "It's brilliant, really. From all accounts, Carroll was a bit of an odd duck and reclusive, only socializing with Fox and the cast. Very few people ever spoke with him, let alone knew him well. Those who knew him well enough to notice the difference between you two know that you're here as part of the investigation."

"And the people with the most reason to want him dead," Gilbert pointed out.

"Which means they'd have no reason to harm you," Pyle said. "They know you're not him. You're giving me time to prove that someone on this set killed a man, Bertie. And you heard Fox. If they stop production, no one here gets paid. You really wanna be the one responsible for that?"

No. Gilbert didn't. He'd seen the children running down the street of Norwood Studios when he had arrived the day before, round-faced and laughing as they chased one another in some game they were all invested in. He thought of his own child, whom he worked so hard to support, and his parents, who had worked themselves to the bone raising him and Lizzie, and now were looking after Penelope in their twilight years, when they should be resting.

He thought of the deal Fox had struck with him—he'd get paid fairly for his time on set. It was a number that had made his head spin when he'd heard it. It'd be enough to buy a little house somewhere in the city, or even on the Main Line, in a nice neighborhood with leafy sidewalks and a good public school. Far from the smoke of the mills.

Far from the reach of Tommy Fletcher.

A knock at the door interrupted them. It was Mrs. O'Malley, the stern-faced widow who seemed to run the entire operation. "You're needed in costumes, Mr. Lawless."

Gilbert stood. It was now or never. He preferred it to be never, if he was being honest, but now would do.

———◆———◆———◆———

Gilbert had stayed up late the previous evening, reading over the script. He'd read as much Shakespeare as anyone else during high school, and Fox hadn't been lying: they were nearly finished with the production. Most of the big, famous scenes between had already been shot. Instead, his efforts would be on the smaller scenes—the filler, as Fox had explained it, as well as action scenes that would involve little actual acting on his part.

Today's scene was thankfully straightforward. Gilbert clutched the script in his hand as he read over the pages again, and a cheerful, full-hipped woman with ruddy pink skin adjusted the medals on his chest. He felt ridiculous, dressed in tight hose and a close-fitting doublet, and his skin itched. He'd be dueling with the actor playing Paris today. Harold wasn't happy with the choreography in the initial shoot, so Gilbert would be doing it over again.

"Knock, knock," Ava said, poking her head inside. She wasn't involved in today's scenes, so she was dressed casually in a sweater and long skirt.

The costume woman looked up and smiled. "Ah, Ava. Come in. Keep your Romeo here company while I fetch a few more pins." She bustled out, humming to herself, as Ava slipped inside and settled into the seat beside him. She leaned close, and Gilbert caught a whiff of her perfume, which smelled heavily of jasmine. He leaned back, rubbing his nose.

Ava seemed unbothered. "How are you feeling, Dr. Lawless? Nervous?"

"I shouldn't be," Gilbert said, though the tremor in his hand clearly showed he was in fact nervous. He'd stared down German machine guns, for Christ's sake. Confronted a deranged killer in the bowels of a crypt. Performed countless autopsies, cataloged the most gruesome deaths. And yet here he was, shaking like a lamb at the thought of being in front of a camera, of his likeness being shown in nickelodeons all across the country. "It's ridiculous."

"It's natural," Ava assured him. She settled in the chair beside him and plucked the script from his fingers. "I threw up right before my first scene in front of the cameras, you know. I was all set to go, everyone was in place, and—bleh." She mimed vomiting, then grinned. "Shockingly, they hired me for another film after that. It quickly becomes a job just like any other."

"The pay must help," Gilbert said before he could stop himself. He still couldn't believe how much he'd make for a week's worth of wages.

"Oh yes. Can't complain there," Ava said. She was quiet for a moment, then added, "My parents were migrant workers. We picked all sorts of produce, following the seasons, all across Mexico and California. I was working at a farm stand on Huntington Pier when a fellow approached me and handed me a business card. I don't think he knew I was Mexican until I opened my mouth," she added. Her laugh was hollow as she tugged on a blond curl, as if to illustrate her point. "Anyway, I stopped being Eva Sanchez and was given a dialect and elocution coach, and Ava Sylvester started modeling a few weeks later. Now my parents live in a big house overlooking the Pacific. They don't have to work anymore—now I can take care of them."

He looked up at her, surprised by her candor. "I had no idea," he said softly. "I thought you'd grown up like . . . like . . ."

"Like Edie?" She smiled ruefully and shook her head. "Not a chance. I worked for everything I've gotten. And now my parents live next door to the house where her aunt lived. That's how we met."

Footsteps heralded the hairdresser's return, and Gilbert turned his attention back to the script, tapping his foot.

The next few hours were a study in hurry up and wait—not unlike his time in the AEF. Gilbert would stand in place, fencing foil at the ready, while one of Harold's assistants—or even Harold himself—would adjust his pose, moving the angle of his elbow a fraction of an inch higher or lower. Then he and the actor playing Paris would perform a carefully choreographed series of steps, swords ringing together, before Harold yelled, *"Cut,"* and they began all over again.

"How are you finding things?" Della asked him during lunch, once Gilbert had showered and changed back into his own clothes. She fed a slice of cucumber to her monkey, who grabbed it in its tiny hands, hissed at Gilbert, and scampered up onto Della's shoulder to eat.

Gilbert eyed the monkey warily, his own appetite vanishing. He set his sandwich back down on his plate. "Tolerable," he answered.

"It's like being paid to play make-believe, isn't it?" Della said as if he hadn't spoken at all. "I know what happened to Duncan was terrible, but I'm very glad to have you with us,

Dr. Lawless. It makes me feel safer, knowing that the police are investigating and that you're here to keep me—I mean, *us*—safe." She batted her long lashes at him.

"Mm-hmm." Gilbert forced himself to take a bite of the sandwich, the thin-sliced turkey turning to ash in his mouth.

Della scooted closer. "There's just something about you, Dr. Lawless. I can't put my finger on it, but I just . . . I just feel like I can trust you." She put her hand on his arm. "I feel like . . . I know you."

Christ. Was this girl—this *child*—flirting with him? He set down the sandwich and stood, gently disentangling himself from her. "Miss O'Malley," he said, his voice kind, "I understand the last few days have been trying, but—"

To his surprise, the girl's chin wobbled. "Oh, Gil—they've been *awful.*" She let out a big, gulping sob, and a torrent of tears splashed down her face, and her shoulders shook, dislodging the monkey, who leaped to the table and scampered to the fruit tray, where it helped itself to a slice of apple. "I just don't know what to do."

Gil froze, awkwardly standing beside the bench. He patted her shoulder. "There, there," he said, careful to keep a healthy distance between them. "Were you close with Mr. Carroll?"

"I-I-I . . ." Della picked up a napkin and dabbed at her eyes. "I looked up to him, almost like an older brother. This is my first film helping out Uncle Harry, you see, and he wanted to make sure that I was feeling comfortable. He was so kind to me, until—" She broke off, sobbing.

They were alone in the mess tent save for the damned monkey. Gilbert lowered himself slowly to the bench beside Della—she was a child, after all, despite being a dozen years older than his own daughter. He thought of Penelope, and his chest tightened. It would be so easy for someone to take advantage of her here—her mother and uncle were always busy, paying attention to the actors or the million other details needed to make the movie a success. No one seemed to pay much attention to Della.

"Have you been mistreated, Miss O'Malley?" he asked. Something in his tone must have belied the black rage boiling within him at the thought of it, because she flinched, her face turning bright red.

"No, of course not. Nothing like that," she said. "Mr. Carroll never did anything untoward. He was a gentleman. He viewed me as his kid sister." She offered up a watery smile.

"You said he was kind to you, until . . ."

"Until he *died*," Della said firmly. "He was kind to me until he died." Now it was her turn to stand, and she did, summoning the monkey with a snap of her fingers. "Good day, Dr. Lawless."

He stared down at his sandwich and sighed. He'd give anything to be back in the cold quiet of the morgue right now, but here he was, playing pretend for the entire world to see.

Alone for the first time in hours, he ate, then checked his wrist out of habit, though he'd left his watch in his dressing room. Surely Pyle would need help with something; the detective had commandeered an office in the main studio building, just over the hill. He set off, walking briskly, past a group of men in work clothes, tearing down a set. One saluted, and Gilbert waved back.

"Watch it!" The shout came from somewhere over his shoulder, and Gilbert barely had a second to process the word when a bone-rattling crash echoed through the ravine. He dropped flat to his stomach, covering his head with his hands, his face pressed into the gravel path.

"*Incoming!*" another man yelled. When Gilbert lifted his head, the idyllic film set was gone, replaced with the desolate gray and brown of no-man's-land. He scrambled to sitting, careful to avoid the razor wire atop the trenches. His gray trousers faded into muddy olive drab wool, and his breath came in shallow, rapid spurts.

Not real, he told himself. He pressed his fingers against his temples. He closed his eyes and forced himself to breathe steadily, in and out. *Not real.*

One, two, three. He tapped his fingers against his temples, counting in the rhythm while two battles raged around him—one in his mind, and one on the set around the bend. *One, two, three.* His temples, his shoulders, the curve of his elbow, the ground beneath him.

Six months ago, he would have reached for the morphine in his pocket. Three months ago, he raged and wept as Dr. Knight weaned him off it, in the thick of his recovery. One week ago, he'd have high-tailed it to the boxing gym, where he and Jack McConnell would spar until his body and mind were too exhausted to care what was past and what was present.

"Gil?" Warm hands gripped his shoulders. *Edie,* a distant part of his brain whispered. He kept tapping, muttering, as the war in his mind faded. She rubbed a hand over his back in short, firm strokes, the way his mother had when he had been a boy, up with a night terror.

He drew in a deep, shuddering breath. And then another. He forced his eyes open, even though every molecule in his body screamed at him to keep them closed, to hide, to run from the horrors that he knew awaited him beyond that fence.

Except the grass around him was green, and the sky was blue. The ground beneath him was gravel, not mud, and Edie Shippen was on her knees beside him, rubbing his back with a gloved hand, her bottom lip caught between her teeth, and an angry red streak stretching across her cheekbone.

"You're hurt."

Surprise flickered across her face. "There you are."

Shame and relief warred within him. His hands trembled as he turned toward her. Her arms came around him, cradling him, and he sagged against her, his nose nestling in the curve of her neck.

"It's all right," she whispered. "I've got you. You're safe."

Chapter 16

Edie didn't know how long she sat there with Gilbert cradled in her arms. Long enough for his trembling to cease, for the chill from the ground beneath them to settle into her bones. She'd have sat there forever if that's what it took to calm him.

He stirred. Edie helped Gilbert stand, keeping her hand on his elbow, which trembled beneath her touch.

"Gilbert," she said, her voice soft, "what's going on?"

That seemed to jolt him from whatever spell he was under. "I'm fine," he said. "Don't worry about it. I must have overheated."

Edie nodded, even though she knew that he was lying to her. She slid her hand down his arm to link their fingers together, half afraid he'd pull away. But he didn't, even though Edie wasn't sure why.

His fingers flexed around hers. A thrill shot up Edie's arm from where their skin brushed together, and she looked up at him. He reached up and gently traced a finger over her cheek, where Lily had struck her.

"Who did this to you?" he asked, his voice serious.

Edie gave a sheepish smile. "I asked too many questions at Homer Byrne's funeral. His widow didn't like it."

A heartbeat of silence passed between them, and Edie thought for a moment that he would lean down and kiss her. But instead, he dropped his hand and squinted up at the sky.

"I'd appreciate it if you didn't tell anyone about this," he said. "Not Lizzie or Pyle. Or Ava."

"Ava?" She dropped his hand and stepped back. "Why would I say anything to Ava?"

"You seem close with her," Gilbert said. "We're here because the police suspect her of murdering her husband—a man I'm tasked with impersonating."

"She—she didn't kill him." She hated how small her voice sounded. "I thought you'd at least trust me. Ava is my friend."

He fixed her with a flat stare, and she flushed, knowing he was thinking about the events of the previous spring. "Forgive me if I second-guess you as a judge of character. I did that once before, and not only did I end up with a bullet in me, I also almost lost my daughter."

Edie reared back as if he'd struck her. What he said was true. Of course it was, and he had every right to feel the way that he did, but to hear it actually leave his lips . . . Tears welled up in Edie's eyes, and she turned her back on him, pressing her fingers to her mouth.

"Wait." Gilbert stepped forward, putting his hand on her shoulder. "Wait, Edie . . ."

She didn't stick around to listen. She jerked away from him, turning on her heel and darting down the path toward the studio building before he could stop her.

She'd been trying to find Ava in order to ask her a few more questions about Duncan and the film. After the funeral, Edie and Lizzie had decided to split up. Edie would head to the studio while Lizzie would see what else she could find out about the substance called la futura. Martinez, the butler at the big house, had directed Edie down toward the main studio, where Gilbert was filming and Ava was being fitted for one of her final costumes.

"Edie, I'm sorry." Gilbert was right behind her, his footsteps heavy on the path. Edie ignored him and slipped into the main studio building. She didn't want to hear his apologies; he could keep his secrets, the same way that Ava kept hers. The same way that Frances had kept hers.

It's me, Edie said to herself. *I'm the problem.*

Gilbert had been clear about one thing: they could be friends, but nothing more. Of course they wouldn't be anything more—Edie was coming to realize that people didn't view her as the type of girl anyone could depend on. What had Theo called her all those months ago? A butterfly—pretty and delicate, always flitting from one fancy to the next, from one beau to another.

Edie had thought Gilbert had seen her for what she really was—not a butterfly, but a woman, red-blooded and whole and complex, and deserving of love and respect for who she was.

Of course, she'd been wrong.

"Edie," Gilbert said again. "I'm sorry. You caught me at a bad time. All of this"—he gestured down at himself, from the makeup to the costume—"has me in a sour mood. I'm sorry."

"Just forget about it," Edie said, though she doubted she'd be able to. "Just tell me how to get to Ava's dressing room, and we can pretend the whole thing never happened."

Ava's room.

Her name hung heavy in the air between them. Gilbert, graciously, didn't comment on it. He only pointed down a corridor to the left.

"This way." He led her through a warren of back rooms. "Her room is through here."

"Are all the rooms back here?" Edie asked. She stopped, an idea brewing. "Even Duncan's?"

Gilbert nodded. "Mrs. O'Malley gave me a quick tour this morning. We've been told to stay out of it during the investigation, but—"

"But we're part of the investigation," Edie interrupted. "We're here at Pyle's insistence." Technically, *Gilbert* was here at Pyle's behest, but Edie wasn't going to split hairs. "Which one is his?"

Gilbert glanced up and down the hallway. It was empty in either direction. "This way," he said.

The room was toward the center of the corridor. The door was locked, but Edie opened her bag and pulled out a slim container. She adjusted her gloves, then opened it, revealing a set of lockpicks. She made quick work of the lock while Gilbert stared at her, mouth gaping as she stood swinging the door open into the darkened dressing room.

"Where did you learn to do that?" he asked, and Edie blushed. She knew he was thinking of back in the spring, when she'd picked the lock on the trunk beneath his bed and stolen his gun.

"Ava, actually," Edie said. "Her parents kept the liquor locked up in their dining room, and we'd help ourselves whenever they went out, and then refill the bottles with water. We used bobby pins, but I had this made up a few months ago. Just in case."

"The two of you were close, then?" Gilbert asked.

"Very." Edie hesitated. She didn't like speaking of those early months in California, when she had been plagued with endless headaches and swirling despair. "I don't want to talk about Ava. If you don't mind."

The dressing room was dark, especially once Gilbert closed the door behind them. He fumbled around on the wall until he found the chain for the light. It clicked on, filling the room with a soft yellow glow.

"What are you looking for?" he asked.

"I don't know," Edie admitted. She turned in a slow circle, taking it all in. It was a small room—a square of about eight feet on each side, with doors opposite each other. One led into the corridor. Edie wondered where the other led—a closet, perhaps.

"The costume department is through there," Gilbert said, tracking her gaze. "Each room connects to them."

"And anyone could enter through there?"

"I suppose, yes," Gilbert said. "They lock, but the wardrobe folks have keys. That way they can deliver costumes or whatever else. It's supposed to be efficient."

"Especially if you want to kill someone," Edie said. "In and out, with no one the wiser."

A vanity table, topped with a mirror, sat against one wall, with a garment rack beside it, where Duncan's street clothes—a tweed suit—still hung neatly, with a pair of black oxfords on the rack below it. A sofa and a side table were positioned on the opposite wall.

Drawers. Edie would start with the drawers.

She eased the first one out. It was full of nothing remarkable—receipt paper, an earmarked copy of the script, a set of expensive fountain pens. A stack of photographs were in the next drawer—each one of Duncan in various poses, staring at the camera. "Headshots for adoring fans?" Edie asked, handing them to Gilbert, who shrugged.

She moved on to the other drawers. A datebook, which was empty. A package of violet gum with half the sticks remaining. A bottle of gin.

"I'm surprised the police didn't take that," Gilbert said. He bent at the waist to peer at the bottle, which was half full. "It could be poisoned. I should see if Harrison can test it."

"Pyle said they still haven't found the green vial that he drank from on set." Edie cast another look around the room. "That's odd, isn't it?"

"Do you remember what happened?"

Edie closed her eyes. Of course she remembered. Duncan's death was seared into her memory the same way that Theo's was, and her mother's. There were some things a girl couldn't forget.

"He dropped it," she said. "It rolled away—to the left, I think. Beyond that, I couldn't say. Ava started screaming, and everyone rushed to them. I don't think anyone thought to look for it until later."

"If he killed himself, it would still be there," Gilbert pointed out. "Only a person with something to hide would have taken it."

Edie had to agree. She was about to say so when the door to the dressing room next door creaked open, then closed.

She held a gloved finger to her lips.

Two voices, both women's. The first, high and light, was unmistakably Ava's. And then a second voice. Deeper, almost sensuous.

Edie knew that voice.

Celeste Dupont.

Edie's eyes grew wide. Celeste, who knew something about la Futura. She'd been at the party with the rest of the cast at the Bellevue. And now she was here, on set, with Ava.

Doubt settled heavily on Edie's shoulders—Gilbert had accused Edie of trusting too easily. She didn't want to look at him, didn't want to see the confirmation in his eyes. He moved quickly, picking up one of the pair of tumblers on the table beside the sofa. He pressed it to the wall, and Edie did the same, sharpening the hushed voices on the other side.

"Action seems necessary," Celeste was saying.

There was a sharp sniff—was Ava crying? Edie pressed herself closer to the wall, listening. "I don't know if I should," Ava said. "Everyone's watching me. The police, Harry . . . it's like I'm living under a microscope. It seems too big of a risk."

"Would it be a bigger risk to wait?" Celeste asked. There was a rustling on the other side of the door of fabric swishing. Edie could almost picture Celeste pacing Ava's dressing room, probably swathed in black. Her mind filled in the rest: Ava, sitting on a settee, handkerchief clutched between her hands. "Things don't stay buried forever."

"They don't need to stay buried forever," Ava snapped, "as long as they stay buried for now. What else?"

There was a pause. A shuffling—*cards*. And then silence.

And then, Ava's voice, quietly resigned. "Death."

"So it appears," Celeste said.

Edie reared back. She dropped the glass, and it hit the concrete floor, shattering into a thousand glittering shards. Gilbert whipped around, eyes wide, staring at her.

"What was that?" Ava asked. "Is someone in Duncan's room?"

"The door," Edie hissed. "It's unlocked."

He moved quickly, turning the lock as Edie yanked the chain for the light, plunging them both into darkness. She inched across the floor, shoes crunching over the broken glass, until her hands found Gilbert's. He squeezed her fingers.

Footsteps approached. The knob rattled. "Locked," Ava said. "Let's try the other side. Maybe someone from wardrobe is in there."

"Is that door locked?" Gilbert whispered.

Edie had no idea. "Let's go," she hissed, tugging Gilbert toward the door. They only had a matter of seconds to leave before Ava came in from the other side. He unlocked the door and they tumbled out into the corridor, closing the door behind them.

Right into Celeste DuPont.

"Miss Shippen. Dr. Lawless," the medium said, tilting her head. "How lovely to see you."

Ava's dressing room had an identical layout to Duncan's, but while his had been cold and impersonal, Edie could see traces of Ava everywhere she looked—in the fringed scarf draped over the mirror, the framed photo of Ava's family on the side table. She'd covered the concrete floor with a warm rug woven in reds and golds. Her makeup spilled across the vanity table, and a collection of hats hung on hooks on the wall. Even the room smelled like Ava—like vanilla, tobacco, and orange blossoms.

Edie and Gilbert sat on Ava's settee like a pair of chastened children. Ava crossed her arms, staring down at them, disappointment palpable in her frame. Celeste sat at the vanity table, looking amused by the entire situation.

"I can't believe you were spying on me, Edie. I thought you were trying to help me!"

"We weren't spying on you," Edie said. "We were looking through Duncan's room for any clues to clear your name, when we heard you speaking with *her*." Edie flung her hand in Celeste's direction.

"My medium?" Ava blinked. "You know Madame Midnight?"

Gilbert let out a little laugh. "We're acquainted, yes," he said. "And she's not a medium. She's a fraud."

"We heard you talking about death," Edie said. "We have reason to believe that she's been involved in at least two other murders. So I think you two have some explaining to do."

Celeste at least had the good graces to look offended. "I haven't a clue what they're speaking of," she reassured Ava. To Edie and Gilbert, she said, "We were speaking of death as a metaphor. A drastic change. A chance for a new beginning. A spiritual death, if you will. Not a literal death."

"Madam Midnight was reading my tarot cards," Ava explained. She picked up a card from the vanity table and held it out. A skeleton in knight's armor rode a white horse over the prone body of a man, with a priest and a child praying in the corner. "See?"

Tarot cards. "I thought you communicated with spirits. Or have you given that up since the spring?" Edie asked.

"I do what I am called to do," Celeste said airily. She stood, picking up her handbag. "Now. If that's all you have for me . . ."

She couldn't leave. Not now, when she was the one link they had between all three deaths. "Tell us about la futura!" Edie blurted out.

Celeste froze. "What did you say?"

"La futura. What is it?"

The handbag hit the floor. Celeste ignored it, her dark eyes staring intensely into Edie's. "Where did you hear that term?"

"What does it mean?"

Celeste pressed her lips together. Edie could see, for perhaps the first time, that beneath her dark lipstick and turban and fringed wrap, Celeste Dupont was just a woman. A human being like any other.

"It's dangerous," Celeste whispered. "It's not something you play with, Miss Shippen."

"People are dead, Miss Dupont," Gilbert said from beside Edie. "We aren't playing."

Celeste closed her eyes. "There is a woman—and no, before you ask, I don't know her name. She's like me. Gifted. Don't roll your eyes at me," she snapped at Edie. "Just because you don't understand doesn't mean it's not true." She took a deep breath, then continued. "She came to this city with nothing. Less than nothing, if you can believe it. She wanted to help others who found themselves in situations like what she had endured. I believe you can empathize with that, Miss Shippen. Isn't that why you started your little detective agency? To help others?"

Edie crossed her arms. "Who is she?"

Celeste continued as if Edie hadn't spoken. "When she first arrived, she needed help. Money. A roof over her head. Food in her belly. Fate brought her to me—she had heard from a friend of a friend that I might be able to help her. Not in the usual way," Celeste said before Edie could ask. The medium had a network who helped women like Edie's late cousin Rebecca: young, unmarried, and desperate. There were doctors who helped those who wished to return to their normal lives, and others who helped arrange a safe place for the women to spend the duration of their pregnancies. She connected the women with couples unable to have children or with employers willing to take a risk on a young unmarried mother.

"What did you do?" Edie asked.

Celeste stared at her. "I brought her to Leo Salvatore."

Chapter 17

It all came back to the Butcher of Broad Street.

"Do we trust her?" Edie asked Gilbert as they walked back to the big house.

"It's all we have to go on," Gilbert said. "We still don't know what la futura is, or how it connects to anyone but Homer Byrne. It could be a total dead end."

The breeze picked up, sending a cascade of dead leaves swirling around their feet. The air felt heavy, like rain would come soon. "Maybe we're looking at this the wrong way," Edie said. "We've been so focused on la futura and the connections between the dead men. But what if it really was just a series of coincidences? What if whatever la futura was had something to do with Homer Byrne's death, but nothing at all to do with Frank Burkhart's or Duncan's? What do we know about Frank Burkhart anyway?"

"Nothing. We just have Tommy's word to go on that he was hired as a delivery boy on Byrne's route." A sick feeling rose in Gilbert's stomach. "You think Tommy's chasing shadows?"

"It's entirely possible that Frank Burkhart was responsible for Byrne's death and then killed himself later that day in a fit of guilt," Edie said. "Just like it's possible poor Harold murdered Duncan in a pique of rage."

Gilbert stopped in his tracks. "You think Harold killed Duncan?"

"I don't know—I was just talking. Anyone who was there that day could have killed Duncan. Mrs. O'Malley. Frances. Even sweet Della," Edie said, scoffing. "If we have no suspects, that means everyone's a suspect."

"Now hold on just a minute," Gilbert said. His brain had snagged on *Harold*. Harold, who had been so quick to offer Gilbert the role. Harold, who had asked Ned Shippen for money only a few days before his leading man died during filming. Harold, who had forced his two leading actors to elope and announce their marriage. "You're right. There's something odd going on with Harold Fox."

"He's an eccentric. Of course there's something odd about him," Edie said. "I didn't mean anything by it."

"Think about it, Edie." Gilbert wrapped his hand around hers and tugged her to a stop. He'd been such a fool—part of the answer had been right there in front of them the entire time. "Who else did we see at the party that night?"

"Isabelle Bateson. She was wearing the most fabulous purple dress—do you remember it?"

"Not Isabelle. Think."

He watched her face closely—the way her eyes fluttered closed, the lashes kissing the pale skin of her cheeks. The slight dusting of freckles across the bridge of her nose, hidden beneath a layer of powder. The darkening bruise on her cheekbone. The way her eyes snapped open when it hit her—the same way it had hit him—a flash of triumph that lit her from within.

"Leo Salvatore," she said, breathless. "He was there, at the party. He was talking with Harold."

"And Homer Byrne was delivering liquor to his club. With Frank Burkhart."

"So maybe Tommy isn't chasing shadows after all," Edie said. "Maybe Leo is trying to sabotage their deal. But how does Harold fit into this?"

"He needed money. He went to your father, remember? A man he'd barely spoken to in what—twenty years?"

"Closer to thirty," Edie said. "Daddy was . . . what? The class of 1892? '93?"

"How desperate would you have to be to ask someone so distant—practically a stranger—to finance your film?"

They both knew the answer to that question. Harold Fox had been desperate to save his studio.

But had he been desperate enough to kill?

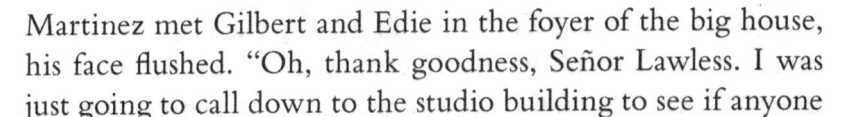

Martinez met Gilbert and Edie in the foyer of the big house, his face flushed. "Oh, thank goodness, Señor Lawless. I was just going to call down to the studio building to see if anyone could find you."

"What is it?" Gilbert asked. His heart kicked up—he knew that Dr. Knight had agreed to temporarily reassign him, but he couldn't help wondering if perhaps they'd found another victim of cyanide poisoning. "Did the coroner's office call?"

"No, no," Martinez said. "It's your family. Your mother—she called."

A void, black and yawning, opened up beneath Gilbert's feet. He could barely hear himself ask, "What's wrong?" over the sound of the blood rushing in his ears. His mother would only call if something was terribly, awfully wrong.

"She only said to call her back as soon as you could," Martinez said. "She said they are with your sister. I assume you know how to reach them?"

"Lizzie should be at my house," Edie said. She tilted her head. "That's odd. What would they all be doing at my house?"

Gilbert didn't know, but he was sure it wasn't for something as joyful as an unplanned dinner party.

"Can I use your telephone, Martinez?" he asked.

"Si, Señor. It's in Mr. Fox's office. You remember the way? He won't mind—he is reviewing film from the other day with Detective Pyle."

Gilbert and Edie hurried through the foyer and into the office, which was empty, just as Martinez had said it would be. Edie shut the door behind her, then pointed to the telephone on the desk. "Call. Do you remember the exchange?"

"Of course I do," Gilbert said. He'd picked up the phone more times than he would like to admit over the last few months, ready to tell the operators to connect him to Shippen House. He'd stopped himself every time.

He sat in the chair behind the desk, his knee bouncing as the operator connected his call. Edie leaned beside him and pressed her hand to his arm, the gentle pressure steadying him. Lizzie answered on the first ring. "Shippen Investigations," she said, breathless. "This is Lizzie speaking."

"It's me," Gil said. "What's going on?"

"Oh, Gil, thank goodness," Lizzie said. "Everyone is fine, and they're with me. That's the important thing."

Her reassurance did nothing to ease him. "Liz."

"Someone broke into the house."

A burglary. If Gilbert hadn't already been sitting down, his knees would have given out. Beside him, Edie's fingers dug into his arm.

He had to keep breathing.

"What did they take?"

Lizzie's voice hitched. "It's too soon to tell. Tommy called me, and Grover and I fetched Mam and Da straight away. We're all safe, but the front window is smashed, and the entire place is ransacked. Tommy said he'd find out who did it—he thinks it was random. He's hopping mad. I'm just worried. I don't know where we'll sleep tonight."

Edie stood up straight at this. "They'll stay with me. Tell her that. They're welcome to stay as long as they need to."

Gilbert stared up at her. "Edie, they can't."

"Why not? The house is massive, and it's just me and Daddy. Grandmama never leaves Chestnut Hill, and Frances is departing for Paris next week." When Gilbert didn't move, Edie gently took the earpiece and the receiver from his hand. "Lizzie? It's me. Is O'Mara there? Yes? Have him make up the nursery for Penelope and put your parents in the yellow room. Let him know what room you'll stay in—take your pick. And you'll all need clothes—have Grover take you all over to Wanamaker's and charge it to the account."

She was quiet for a moment as Lizzie spoke. She cut her gaze to Gilbert, who could only sit and stare at her, open-mouthed. What did she think she was doing? This was too much entirely. He could never repay her.

"Edie," he said quietly.

She held up a finger and said to Lizzie, "Excellent. We'll be home soon." She hung up the earpiece on the receiver, then turned her attention to Gilbert. "Now you can lecture me. Go on."

"This is too much. We can't live with you, Edie. We could never repay—"

"Stop right there." She cut him off, stepping close, crowding his space. She pressed her finger into his chest. "You don't have to repay family, Gil. We nearly died together in that crypt. The least I can do is open my home to you for a few nights. Unless you'd rather your daughter sleep on the street?"

He caught her hand and placed it flat on his chest. Their gazes locked, and suddenly Gilbert couldn't breathe. Not when she was this close, smelling of vanilla, her touch burning through the fabric of his shirt. Not when his heart was threatening to beat right out of his chest.

He shouldn't have been surprised that Edie would open her home to his family without a second thought. She was the same woman who had helped him find Lizzie without hesitating, who had put her life in danger to save his daughter.

To save him.

He'd been such a fool.

Edie's mouth parted. Gil's hand left hers and settled on her waist, pulling her closer. Her eyes drifted shut, and with the gentlest tug she tumbled into his lap. He wrapped his arms close around her as she draped herself over him, her head resting on his shoulder, their chests pressed together, hearts beating in time.

She fit so perfectly in his arms.

"Thank you," he said into her hair.

Edie lifted her head and pressed a kiss to his cheek. "You're welcome," she said. "Now come on. I'm sure you're anxious to see for yourself that they're safe. I—*ouch*." Edie had knocked her ankle against the desk drawer as she stood, and she winced.

Gilbert looked down. She'd kicked the drawer open slightly, the edge of files just visible.

"What do you think those are?" Edie asked. She kicked at the drawer again. "Oops. Clumsy me." It slid open silently, revealing folders organized alphabetically.

Personnel files.

Gilbert glanced up at the door. "We shouldn't," he said.

"He shouldn't leave his desk drawer open," Edie said, shrugging. "Keep an eye out for Martinez, will you?"

"Just hurry," Gilbert whispered.

He didn't need to tell Edie twice—she knelt down, thumbing through the names. "Carroll, Carroll . . . Ah!" Edie sat back on her heels. "Here we are. Webb, Duncan Carroll. Webb?" she looked up at him, brow crinkling. "Why do I know that name?"

A footstep creaked outside the door.

"Edie!" Gilbert hissed. She dropped the file behind Gilbert's back, wound her arms around his neck, and slid the drawer shut with her foot, standing just as Martinez stepped into the office.

"Is everything all right with your family, Señor Lawless? Ah." The butler stopped short, his gaze bouncing between Edie and Gilbert. "I've interrupted. I'm sorry."

"No apologies," Edie said breezily. She gazed down at Gilbert affectionately, and even though Gil knew it was an act put on for the butler's sake, he leaned in. Her fingers tightened on his shoulders. "We've had a bit of a shock—there's an emergency at home, and Gilbert and I must return to the city at once. Please tell Miss Sylvester and Mr. Fox that we'll return first thing in the morning."

"Of course, Miss Shippen," Martinez said. "Do you need me to call a car?"

"I can drive," Gilbert said. He couldn't stand up, not with the damned file behind his back. He shifted in his seat. "I just . . . need a moment." Heat crept up his neck at the implication, but it had its intended effect on Martinez.

The butler flushed. "Of course. Take your time. I will inform Mr. Fox of your plans. Have a nice evening," he added, slowly backing out of the room.

"Smooth," Edie teased as soon as the coast was clear. She picked up the file and slipped it into her bag, hugging it close to her chest with one arm. "Let's go."

"He thinks I was taking advantage of you," Gilbert said. "Are you really all right with that?"

"You did offer to be my scandal once before," Edie said, as they hurried to the car. "But maybe you forgot about that."

Gilbert nearly choked. He reached out, turning her to face him. "I haven't forgotten," he growled.

Edie stared up at him, her stormy eyes flashing. "Could have fooled me."

They were so close now, their faces nearly touching. Gilbert stepped even closer, crowding her until her back pressed against the car. Every moment of that night was seared into his memory in photographic detail. He dropped his forehead to hers, their breaths mingling together. He'd decided in the ensuing months that whatever existed between them was a terrible idea.

At this moment, he didn't really care.

Their first kiss had been gentle. Tender. This kiss was the opposite: fire and frustration, teeth clicking together, months of pent-up anger and longing pouring free from them both. She dropped her bag to the ground and sank her hands into his hair, tugging him closer. She nipped at his bottom lip, teeth sharp, and he gripped her waist like she'd disappear if he let go.

And then, as abruptly as they'd come together, they broke apart, each breathing hard. She raised a trembling hand to her mouth. "Oh" was all she said.

He'd finally done it—he'd struck Edie Shippen speechless. He should throw a parade in triumph, take a victory lap. Instead, he settled for pressing one more kiss against her cheek and stepping back, giving her space. He opened the car door and helped her inside, using the moment he needed to crank the engine, in order to catch his breath. To figure out where they went from here.

Chapter 18

Edie was glad for the extra moment Gilbert took to start the car. She pressed her hands to her face, still stunned, and took a deep breath. She'd kissed Gilbert, and he'd helped her in the car like kissing was a thing they did every day, like that was at the root of their existence: they kissed and caught murderers. Simple as that.

Right. Murderers. She dug into her bag as Gilbert climbed into the driver's seat. Neither of them spoke as he put the car in gear and drove back onto Ridge Avenue from the studio. She read carefully. The first few pages were nothing special—a photograph of Duncan clipped to a short dossier, containing his height, weight, date of birth. A list of roles he'd played and a series of news articles. And then . . .

No. That couldn't be correct. She read the packet again. "How odd," Edie said.

"What is it?" Gilbert asked, glancing over at her.

"It's a life insurance policy on Duncan Carroll Webb," Edie explained. "Daddy has them on all of us. I had to update mine when I came back from California."

"Life insurance." Gilbert rubbed his hand across his middle. "So in the event of Duncan's death, the beneficiaries would receive . . . how much?"

"A hundred thousand dollars."

Gilbert whistled. "Who's the beneficiary?" he asked. "Ava, as his wife?"

Edie flipped the page, scanning for any mention of Ava. There wasn't. But on the last page, there was *something*.

"No," she said. "It's not Ava. It's Harold Fox."

"A hundred grand would solve a lot of problems," Gilbert said. "He'd be able to pay back whatever loans he took out to finance the film. People have killed for less than that."

They lapsed into silence. Edie closed her eyes, mind churning. Where had she heard the name Webb before? She hadn't gone to school with any Webbs and didn't remember anyone with that name in California. No, she'd heard it earlier—as a child.

Her eyes flew open. "I remember where I heard the name Webb before. Have you heard of them?"

Gilbert shook his head. "Should I have?"

Edie closed the file, tucking it back into her purse. "They're old money, the New York kind. I can't believe I never put two and two together. My grandmother went to finishing school with Caroline Webb Mortimer. They absolutely despised each other, by all accounts. Apparently, her nephew, Duncan Webb, caused some sort of scandal and vanished. Grandmama used to tell us all sorts of horrid stories about what could have happened to him—things she'd use to scare us into good behavior."

Gilbert kept his eyes on the road. "So Duncan Carroll is actually Duncan Webb?"

"Duncan Webb's mother was Althea Carroll. Of the Nantucket Carrolls," Edie explained. "He didn't vanish into thin air—he simply took his mother's maiden name and became an actor!"

"But he did disappear. Didn't he?"

"Oh yes." Edie chewed on her lip. "Later, long after Duncan Webb dropped out of society. That would have been . . . when? 1913? '14? I hadn't come out yet. But that's beside the point. Why would a member of New York's four hundred need a life insurance policy? The Webb's fortune is enough to make my family look destitute."

"Maybe his family cut him off. Maybe they disapproved of his choices and decided to teach him a lesson." A storm passed over his face. "Your people always love to use their money to try to bully their children into submission."

Edie knew he was thinking of Sarah and the way his late wife had been treated by her parents. She'd been disowned and cast out, penniless, because she'd chosen to marry Gilbert. To Edie's knowledge, they hadn't even acknowledged Penelope.

And now they were alone in their big house, both children dead and buried.

"It's possible," she said. "It's also possible that he wanted to earn a living on his own merit."

They lapsed into silence again. Edie kept reading as the engine rumbled beneath them. She knew one person who could answer their questions about the Webbs. She was the last person in the world Edie wanted to speak with, but she didn't see a way around it.

"Gil," she said, "can you take me to the Chestnut Hill house? I need to speak with my grandmother."

It was Wednesday, which meant Edie's grandmama would have supper with her friends at the Women's League. She wouldn't want to be late, and the standing dinner date began precisely at five. Which meant Edie had just about an hour to get the information she needed—no more. It also gave her an escape route.

Grandmama was in the upstairs parlor when Edie and Gil arrived at the house. They agreed it would be best for Gilbert to wait in the car. Flora was difficult enough when she was dealing with only Edie. She'd be impossible with Gilbert present.

Edie handed her hat to the butler and made her way down the hall. She'd not set foot in the house since the spring, when she'd had a row with her grandmother after Theo's funeral luncheon. She'd already mostly been living in the city house, and to be quite frank, she couldn't separate the memories of that horrible day from the happier occasions the house had seen. If she closed her eyes, she could still hear her jagged breaths and frantic heart as she ran, gun in hand, trying to escape. Trying to find Gilbert's daughter. Trying to find help.

Edie stopped just before the pocket doors that led into the room that was her grandmother's domain, steadying her hand on her heart. That was all over and done with. In the past. She'd get the information she needed from Grandmama and get back to the car in two shakes of a lamb's tail.

Of course, that depended entirely on her grandmother's cooperation.

Flora Shippen sat at her desk, a stack of letters beside her, her back to the door. She didn't even bother to turn around at

Edie's entrance. "Frances, I didn't expect you home for another hour," she said. "Is everything all right?"

"Oh, she's still out," Edie said lightly, and her grandmother startled, dropping her pen and turning around in her chair. "It's me."

"A polite young lady should not show up unannounced," Grandmama said, recovering enough to coat her voice with ice. "But then again, you did turn your back on the family."

"Turn my back on the family?" Edie felt her own voice rising a pitch, and almost turned on her heel and left before she remembered she was here for a reason, and, as the lady herself had said often to Edie through childhood—she could catch more flies with honey than vinegar. "I'm here to see you."

"You want something." Flora turned back to her writing desk. "Out with it."

"Do you know anything about Duncan Carroll Webb?"

Flora snorted. "That boy caused a lot of trouble. I don't know anything about his recent antics."

"I'm not interested in recent. I want to know where he disappeared to over the summer of 1919."

"You do, do you?" Edie's grandmother fixed her with a shrewd look. "I want my granddaughter to stop her selfish, spoiled behavior and spend her time doing things that befit a young lady of her social standing."

"Grandmama—"

"Frances tells me that you've taken a job." She said the word *job* the way she might say *intestinal issues*. "I told her that she must be mistaken. But then Lavinia Thayer said that her sister's maid is friends with that dreadful red-haired maid of yours, and said the same thing. She was gloating about it over salmon croquettes. I haven't been able to eat fish since. So I checked with George, and he said your trust fund is in fine shape."

"You asked the accountant to look at my trust fund?" Edie asked. "What gives you the right? I'm an adult. I don't need your permission to do a single thing." She was angry now. She could feel her neck heating and knew her skin was turning splotchy and red, the prickly feeling climbing from beneath the neckline of her black dress to her face. "And for your information, I'm not taking a paycheck. I'm using my position to advocate for the less fortunate. Isn't that what you always wanted us to do? Be involved with charity?"

"I want you to put as much attention into finding a husband as you are into making my life difficult." Flora fixed her with a stare. "I'm not getting any younger, you know, and since we lost poor Rebecca, and Frances lost her dear Theo, I've been so worried that none of you girls will know happiness."

"I'm perfectly happy," Edie said. "And Frances is better off." She pinched the bridge of her nose. "This is pointless. I don't know why I even tried. You'd rather sit there and lecture me than answer the one simple question I had for you."

She would find the information another way. She knew a dozen other grand dames of Philadelphia's upper crust. Grandmama had grown up in New York, one of the elite four hundred. Surely there must be another one or two of her classmates still running about. She could send Lizzie to the library and have her search through past issues of the newspapers from that summer, trying her best to find whatever information she could. They'd learn something useful.

Edie turned on her heel. She was halfway to the door when Flora said, "I want dinner."

Edie froze. "Pardon?"

"Once a week. Mondays. You'll be here every Monday at seven sharp for dinner with your father while your sister is in France. She leaves on Friday, so we'll start this coming week."

"And if I do that?" Edie turned around slowly.

Flora Shippen stood in front of her writing desk. She wore a look of determination on her face, and her hand was steady where it gripped the back of her chair.

"Why, child, I'll tell you everything you want to know."

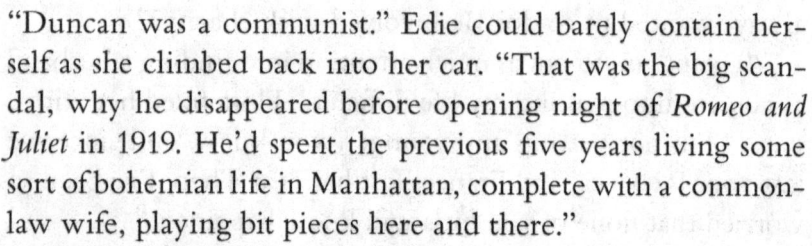

"Duncan was a communist." Edie could barely contain herself as she climbed back into her car. "That was the big scandal, why he disappeared before opening night of *Romeo and Juliet* in 1919. He'd spent the previous five years living some sort of bohemian life in Manhattan, complete with a common-law wife, playing bit pieces here and there."

Gilbert blinked at her. "What?"

"A communist! Well, Bolshevik, technically. He was arrested during the Palmer Raids. Grandmama heard from a cousin who is friends with Duncan's aunt that his aunt was simply *beside* herself, but her husband is in Congress, and they somehow managed to get the charges dropped and the whole thing swept under the rug. But they let the woman rot."

Edie's grandmother had reported the incident with barely contained glee, as if Edie were her coconspirator instead of her adversary. She wondered if that was how Frances had always felt; she wondered if her life would be different if her grandmother hadn't seemed set against her from birth. Apparently, all they needed was a common enemy.

"Is she still in prison?" Gilbert's gaze was sharp. He was thinking exactly what Edie had when Flora had shared the news.

"Grandmama didn't know. But Pyle would be able to find that out, don't you think?"

Duncan Carroll had kept many secrets. And perhaps one of them was the reason someone wanted him dead.

Chapter 19

Gilbert parked at the morgue. Edie had the life insurance document in her purse, and they had the bottle of liquor they'd recovered in Duncan's dressing room. He checked his watch—it was just a few minutes before five. With any luck, Harrison and Marco would still be at work. He and Edie would be able to see if the bottle held traces of cyanide . . . and see if Marco knew anything about the mysterious la futura.

The knot in Gilbert's chest eased as they climbed the steps to his office. He thrived on routine and predictability, and the last few days had been anything but. Simply walking down the familiar corridors restored a sense of order to his world—this was a place where he knew what was expected of him, where he had a sense of control, where he knew he was making a difference. Not on that damned film set, covered in makeup and surrounded by grown adults playing pretend.

"Dr. Lawless." Cecelia stood abruptly when he walked into the office. Her voice was cold; it dropped to an arctic chill when she spotted Edie on his arm. "Miss Shippen."

"Cecelia." *Cecelia.* A sinking feeling filled him. He'd forgotten about Cecelia entirely. The date. He'd asked her to dinner. He'd made plans with her. And then . . .

He'd stood her up. He'd spent the evening chasing la futura with Edie instead.

Her bottom lip trembled. "I waited for an hour for you. I . . . thought something had happened to you."

Edie's eyes grew wide. She slipped her arm from Gilbert's and said, "Excuse me. I'm going to find the ladies' room."

"Stay," Cecelia demanded. "You need to hear this too." She came around from behind the desk, her blue eyes glistening behind her spectacles. She marched right up to Gilbert and shoved her finger in his chest, hard enough that he took a step backward. "I deserved better than that, Gilbert Lawless. I deserve an apology."

She deserved more than an apology, but he didn't have anything else to give her. "I'm sorry, Cecelia," he said softly. "You're right. I have no real excuse, none that matters."

She returned to her desk, not even looking at him. "Good. Now, I have work to do, Dr. Lawless."

He'd been dismissed.

Edie waited until they were in his office to speak. "She seemed upset," she said. "What did you do?"

He winced. "I was thoughtless. She deserved better."

Thankfully, Edie left it at that.

In the few days Gilbert had been gone, Marco had managed to cover both his own desk and Gilbert's with stacks of folders, but the room was empty. None of the other assistants were in their shared bullpen. A few years earlier, Knight had implemented a board at the front of the bullpen, with each of the assistants listed by last name, and a round magnet placed in a column to indicate whether they were off duty, in the field, performing an autopsy, in the lab, or on break. It wasn't a perfect system—there were plenty of times Gilbert had been roused from bed in the middle of the night to head to the field without stopping to move his marker—but it was generally reliable. He scanned down the list until he reached *Harrison, I.* The marker was under "Off duty." Thankfully, the marker beside *Salvatore, M* was placed in "Autopsy."

"I'll start there," Gilbert said, tapping the board. "You stay here. The last thing I need is Dr. Knight finding you in an autopsy room."

"It's fine," Edie said. "I'll call Lizzie to check in. See if she can find out anything about this woman Duncan left in prison."

Marco looked up when Gilbert slipped into the autopsy theater. The cadaver on the table in front of him was a man in midlife, judging by the receded hairline, slight paunch, and jowls. No visible trauma that Gilbert could see.

"Mr. Movie Star," Marco said. He smiled, but it didn't quite reach his eyes. "How's the life of leisure?"

"Not for me," Gilbert said. He shrugged into his white coat and washed his hands at the sink. "You all right?"

"Exhausted." Marco's smile dipped slightly. "It's Harrison's day off, so the lab's backed up. And this fellow and his four friends came in this morning from the drunk tank."

Gilbert looked up sharply. "What happened?"

"Looks like tainted liquor," Marco said. "Someone cut their booze with wood alcohol. Pickled them from the inside out."

Gilbert swore softly. There had been more and more deaths like this in the year since Prohibition had been enacted. Outlawing the sale of liquor hadn't quenched the city's thirst. To the contrary, it seemed to drive more and more otherwise law-abiding citizens into dangerous situations. Criminals, looking to make a quick buck, cut the alcohol with water or, worse, cheap mineral spirits meant for stripping paint, not consumption. But the politicians in Washington didn't know or didn't care, and neither did the teetotaling groups who had legislated their own morality on the rest of the country.

"It's worse than that," Marco said, cutting into Gilbert's thoughts. "It's bad enough they're dead. But all of them were drinking at Club Rouge before they were brought in for public intoxication. The uniform cop on duty thought they'd dry out in the cell. But instead . . ."

Club Rouge.

Gilbert swore again. "Tommy Fletcher is supplying the liquor to Club Rouge. Homer Byrne and Frank Burkhart were the men in charge of delivering it."

Marco leveled him with a look. "Do you think he has something to do with this? If Tommy is undercutting their deal, Leo needs to know."

"Unless Leo is the one sabotaging it." Gilbert hated saying that, but he'd seen the gangster's handiwork come across his table. Leo was a violent, unscrupulous businessman. But even Gilbert had to admit, poisoning his clientele seemed out of character.

Marco stared at him pointedly. "Careful, buddy. That's my brother."

Gilbert held up his hands. "Fine."

"He takes the club seriously. He wouldn't do a thing to put it in jeopardy."

Except selling illegal booze night after night, but Gilbert wasn't going to point that out. "Call him. See what he knows."

"Leo doesn't do phones. Says you never know who's listening." Marco pushed the cadaver back into the refrigerated drawer, where it would wait for Knight's final signature, and opened the door to the left, where yet another cadaver waited for him. "What do you think, Mr. Movie Star? Should we go out tonight?"

Isaiah Harrison lived at Sixth and Lombard, across the street from the Mother Bethel Church, a few blocks from Washington Square Park. Gilbert parked the car, and they climbed out.

"You know, I don't think I've ever been down here," Edie said. "My father always forbid us from crossing Broad Street when we were on our own."

Gilbert wasn't surprised; the neighborhood was historically Black, and the Shippens kept their daughters on a tight leash. "It's crowded down here," he said, pointing to the row of houses. "A lot of these houses have three, four families in them."

"That's horrible," Edie said. "Why isn't more housing being built? How can anyone live like that?"

"Those are questions for your father," Gilbert pointed out. "It's been like this for years, and it's only getting worse."

Much like Manayunk, this part of the city was working class, only its plight was made more difficult by the races of its occupants. While there was no official policy of segregation, as was in the case in more southern cities, Philadelphia's neighborhoods were divided on strict racial and ethnic lines. Gilbert had himself experienced this. His family had first lived in Pennsport when they arrived from Ireland, then moved to a white, Catholic, and Irish section of Manayunk by the time Gilbert was twelve. Gilbert's family had found a measure of stability when Mr. Lawless became a foreman at the yarn mill. They were able to purchase their snug home on Manor Street for a reasonable price. The city's African American population had boomed in recent years, but few white landowners wanted to rent their homes to the newcomers—or else they charged a premium for deplorable conditions.

Gilbert would never claim that growing up an immigrant—especially from Ireland, where his people were crushed beneath the boots of the British Empire—was easy. But it wasn't made harder by the color of his skin. Penelope, with her American accent and pale skin, could move into almost any neighborhood in the country without protest. Isaiah Harrison's children would be risking their lives to do the same.

"Here we are," Gilbert said, locating the address. He knocked on the door, and they waited.

After a moment, it creaked open. A woman with dark brown skin peered out, her eyes suspicious. "Can I help you?"

"We're looking for Dr. Harrison. I'm a colleague of his from the morgue," Gilbert said. "Is he at home?"

"I'll check." She shut the door firmly. A few minutes passed. When it opened again, Isaiah stood on the landing in his shirtsleeves.

"Gil? What are you doing here? And who's this?"

"Miss Edie Shippen, this is Dr. Harrison." Gilbert breezed through the introduction. "Isaiah, I know it's your day off. But we're hoping you can help us."

Edie pulled a flask from her bag, which held a sample of the liquor they'd found in Duncan's dressing room. Pyle would be furious if he knew that they'd removed evidence from the studio, but police had left the bottle undisturbed.

That meant either they'd ruled it out as the murder weapon, or they'd missed it entirely. Edie had wanted to take the entire thing, but Gilbert had insisted on a sample. A small enough amount to test, but not enough that anyone would notice. If the test came back clear, no one would ever have to know.

If it was poisoned . . .

Well. They'd cross that bridge if they came to it.

"We need to know if this contains enough cyanide to kill someone," Edie said.

Isaiah stared at them for a heartbeat, then sighed, shaking his head. "You don't do things by halves, do you, Miss Shippen?" He took the bottle and tucked it under his arm. "I'll run the tests *tomorrow*. When I'm at work. That fit with your schedule?"

"Thank you," Gilbert said, and he meant it. "We appreciate it."

◆ ──── ◆ ──── ◆

The next stop, of course, was to check in on his family. Lizzie had promised that everyone was safe at the Shippen's house on Rittenhouse Square. Gilbert couldn't quite believe it was real, even as Edie was perched on the sofa beside him, legs crossed primly at the ankle, staring adoringly up at Aoife Lawless.

"Thank you, again, Miss Shippen, for opening your home to us. We'll do our best to stay out of the way," Gilbert's mother said. "We won't take advantage."

"You're welcome to stay as long as you need," Edie insisted. "There's plenty of room."

Aoife Lawless gave a grateful smile. "Once the glass is fixed, we'll get the rest sorted. The police said it must have been thieves after money. Why they picked our house, I'll never know."

Gilbert and his father shared a look. He had an idea of who had broken into their house, and if he was right, it hadn't been for money. It was a warning from Tommy Fletcher.

"I'm just glad you weren't hurt," Edie said.

"That's what I said too. Things can be replaced, but people cannot." Aoife patted Edie's arm. "Anyway, it's not the first time we've had to put the house back together. You should have seen the mess these two caused as wee uns. Always scrapping and causing trouble."

Edie schooled her face into a look of surprise. "Lizzie, for sure. But not . . ."

"Bertie? Hell on wheels, that one," Aoife said. "Always causin' a ruckus with Finn and Tommy. If I had a nickel for every time the coppers brought 'im home . . ."

"Alright, Mam, that's enough," Gilbert broke in, his face flushing. "Miss Shippen doesn't want to hear about that."

"Oh, but I *do*," Edie said. She clasped her hands together beneath her chin and leaned close to his mother. "I want to know everything. How many times did the police bring him home?"

"Once," Gilbert said, and at the same time his mother said, "At least six."

Edie's entire face lit with delight. She turned on Gilbert, eyes twinkling. "Why, Dr. Lawless, you never told me about your brushes with the law."

"Tommy was the one always getting us into trouble," Gilbert said. "And anyway, I was never charged with anything. None of us were."

"That's because Bobby Flanagan kept his eye on you lads and brought you home before you could do anything too stupid," Aiofe said. "May the Lord rest his soul."

"Mr. Flanagan passed on?" Lizzie appeared in the doorway, notebook in hand. "Are you sure, Mam? I swear I heard him snoring during Mass just last weekend."

"Aye, last year. The drink finally caught up with him. You were hearing Mr. Boyle at Mass. That man can never make it to the second reading." Aiofe leaned forward and patted Edie's knee. "Now here I am, blathering away, Miss Shippen. I'm sure you have more questions for me."

"Many," Edie said.

"I actually need to speak with you," Lizzie said. "Sorry, Mam. Duty calls."

Edie winked at his mother and stood. "No rest for the wicked, I'm afraid. I'll have to hear what's left of the story later. Has Penelope seen the nursery yet? There's a dollhouse up there she might like to play with."

"I want to see!" Penelope looked up from where she was playing on the rug with her kitten and Aphrodite, who watched the feline creature with a mixture of fear and adoration.

"It's at the top of the stairs. Third door on the left," Edie said.

"Let's go, shall we?" Aoife stood, holding out her hand to her granddaughter. As soon as they were out of earshot, Edie turned to Gilbert. "I like her," she stage-whispered.

Gilbert pretended he didn't hear her.

The nursery was a large, airy room painted a pale green. Penelope beelined past the identical canopy beds, making her way to the dollhouse still set on a table in the center of the room—it was a scale model of the very house they were in, down to the wallpaper. A small doll family—a dark-haired woman, tuxedoed man, and two small, dark-haired girls—were arranged in various rooms. The woman sat at a piano in the parlor where they had all been gathered in real life just a few minutes before. The man stood in the library. One of the girls was in the bathtub on the third floor. The other was tucked into her bed in the green-walled nursery . . . complete with a miniature version of the dollhouse.

Penelope squealed with delight. She reached for the dolls, her little hands moving furniture and arranging things just so. Gilbert's heart swelled as he watched her, guilt and love warring in equal measure. Her mother had grown up in a house like this. Sarah had wanted for nothing, the same as Edie and Frances. He could imagine an almost identical dollhouse in the now-demolished townhouse a few blocks away.

If Sarah had lived, would they have eventually made amends with her parents? Would Penelope have had access to a life like this?

Gilbert would never know. He could never know. He was a fool for even thinking about it, thinking about her.

Aoife put her hand on her son's arm. "You're a good da, son."

"I want to give her a good life," he said. His voice was thick with emotion.

"It's all we ever want as parents," Aoife said. "It's why your da and I left home and brought you here. You and your sister—and Pen—are our greatest treasures."

Gilbert could only nod and watch Penelope play. She was his reason for everything—for getting up in the morning. For pushing himself physically and mentally in the boxing ring, for weaning himself from morphine, for agreeing to act in the damned film.

He'd give her the life she deserved.

Chapter 20

The Lawless family were grateful, if a touch perplexed, at Edie's insistence that they stay at her home for the time being. Edie's father accepted the news with surprising calm—and then suddenly announced he had plans to dine at his club that evening. The usually empty townhouse seemed full of life in a way it hadn't been since Edie was a child.

A smile broke across Gilbert's face as he leaned down to whisper something into his daughter's ear. The girl giggled, clapping her hands over her mouth, and Edie's own lips curled upward in response.

She loved seeing Gilbert with Penelope. Gilbert's entire demeanor changed when he was around his daughter, as the heavy weight usually settled over his brow lifted. He stood taller; his eyes shone brighter. Even the tremor in his hands seemed to lessen.

Edie drank her water slowly. There was a pressure building in her temples—a headache had been threatening all day. She leaned back in her chair and closed her eyes, the thoughts in her head a jumbled mess as the low hum of conversation faded into nothingness, drowned out by a high-pitched ringing.

She needed her tincture. She couldn't afford a spell now—she had too much to do. There was too much at stake.

"Excuse me," she said, and lurched from her seat. Gilbert jumped up and was beside her in an instant, his hands steady on her elbows.

"I'll see you upstairs." His voice brokered no argument, and Edie nodded. Gilbert's parents and Penny watched them with fascination.

"Be right back, mo leanbh," Gilbert told his daughter. "My friend Miss Shippen isn't feeling well, and I'm going to help her."

Penelope nodded, like she was used to her father leaping up and steering helpless women from the dining table. Perhaps she was—Edie hadn't the slightest clue what dinners were like in the Lawless household. Judging from this evening's supper, it was nothing like the silent, formal affairs she had endured as a girl. Edie's grandmother was of the strict opinion that children should be seen and not heard. She had the feeling that Penelope, as the only child in a household full of adults who doted on her, had never been introduced to the concept.

"Is it your head?" he asked, his warm breath against her ear.

Edie nodded, leaning on Gil's arm as they made their way upstairs. She didn't fuss as he guided her to the chaise beneath the window, kneeling on the floor at her feet. He unbuckled her shoes and slipped them off one at a time. His thumbs made firm circles on her ankle bones, his touch gentle. Intimate.

Edie closed her eyes, a little sigh slipping from her lips as his hands moved lower, massaging the arch of her feet.

"During the war," Gil said, his voice low, "I met a fellow from Hong Kong. A medic, who came from a long family of doctors, though he was the first to train in London. He said there were points in the body that, when the proper amount of pressure was applied, could relieve a variety of ailments—stress or chronic pain. Headaches."

His thumb worked into the ball of her foot. Edie let her head fall back, her eyes closed. A low moan escaped, and she sank against the back of the chaise. "I've tried a lot of things, Dr. Lawless," she said, "but never a foot rub."

"He was also of the opinion that needles applied in specific places could have a similar effect. Interesting fellow."

"Needles?" She shivered. "Do you think that could really help?"

"It may be worth a try," he said. "There's a practitioner in Chinatown who specializes in that sort of thing. I can introduce you." His hands worked their way up her calves to her knees. He looked up at her, a gentle smile on his face.

"Only if you take me out for chop suey afterward," Edie said.

"It's a date."

Edie gave a small sigh of relief. The pressure in her temples was still present, but the muscles at the back of her neck had relaxed enough to relieve some of the dull ache behind her eyes. Enough that she hoped she'd be able to take her tincture and be as right as rain in an hour or so. She opened her eyes and smiled at him.

Gilbert sat back on his heels and looked up at her. A flash of longing swept through his gaze, gone as quickly as it came on. He rubbed his hands on his thighs as he stood. "I should get back downstairs."

"Wait." The word slipped out before Edie could stop it. Gil froze, and Edie wondered if he was thinking about the last time they had been alone in a room like this, or about the way he'd pressed her against the car a few short hours ago.

Gilbert waited. "They're all downstairs," he said. But he came closer, and Edie's heart sped up as he leaned down, brushing his nose against hers.

"I don't care," she whispered. She captured his mouth with hers, winding her arms around his neck, tugging him down onto the chaise. He toppled over, a laugh huffing out between their lips. And then there was no laughing, or talking, only their two hearts beating as one.

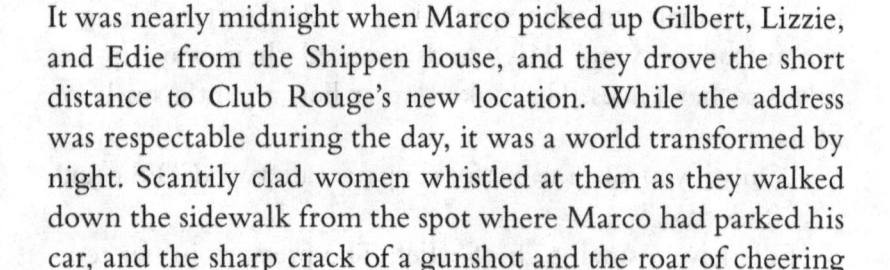

———◆◆◆———

It was nearly midnight when Marco picked up Gilbert, Lizzie, and Edie from the Shippen house, and they drove the short distance to Club Rouge's new location. While the address was respectable during the day, it was a world transformed by night. Scantily clad women whistled at them as they walked down the sidewalk from the spot where Marco had parked his car, and the sharp crack of a gunshot and the roar of cheering men erupted from a nearby building. Beside her, Lizzie let out a little scream, and Gilbert, on her other side, went still, his face shuttering.

"Shooting gallery," Marco explained quickly. "Nothing to worry about. Walk calmly, and don't make eye contact with anyone, Miss Shippen."

"I have been here before, you know," Edie said, stepping around a broken bottle on the sidewalk. "And anyway, why aren't you saying the same thing to Lizzie?"

"Because Leo's made it known that no one gets near Lizzie," Marco said. "And because Lizzie knows how to take care of herself."

"I'm perfectly capable of taking care of myself," Edie said. She dipped her hand into her purse and pulled out the snub-nosed pocket pistol she'd purchased over the summer, taking care to keep her finger clear of the trigger. "See?"

Marco burst out laughing, his arms going around his middle. Lizzie squeezed her eyes shut. And Gilbert, fast as a snake, reached out and clamped his hand around her wrist.

"Jesus, Mary, and all the saints," Gilbert growled. He stepped closer, his toes nearly brushing hers. "What is that?"

"It's a gun," Edie said. She tilted her head up, looking him in the eye. "Is your night vision going, Gil?"

"I can see it perfectly well," he said, exasperated. He looked down at her, his dark gaze serious. "What I don't understand is why you have one and why you're waving it around on the street."

"Oh, it's all on the up-and-up," Edie said. She gave him a prim smile as she pulled her arm free and tucked the gun back into her handbag. Then she reached forward and laced her fingers through his, giving his hand a reassuring squeeze. "Detective Pyle helped me pick it out while you were in the hospital, and he taught me how to use it. Turns out I'm a crack shot."

Marco let out a wheeze.

"You're a crack shot." Gilbert stared down at her as he repeated the words. He didn't pull his hand from hers, which Edie took to be a good sign. Maybe he wasn't actually mad about this.

"Detective Pyle was very impressed," Edie said. Then she turned her attention to Marco and added, "Should we go in?"

The interior of the club was packed full of revelers. Deep reds and rich golds swathed every surface. A long bar and a stage graced either end of the dance floor. The far side of the room held a row of secluded booths, draped behind deep red curtains, where patrons could meet in private. A narrow hall beside the last booth led backstage, where Leo kept his office and the performers had their dressing rooms. A few tables were scattered near the front of the room, and on the floor everyone was dancing.

"Don't drink a thing," Gilbert said quietly. "We don't know what liquor has been cut."

"Leo's at the bar." Lizzie was already heading toward her on-again, off-again beau. He resembled Marco—olive skin and dark hair—but where Marco tended toward a lanky etherealness, Leo was shorter and solid, in a well-tailored suit. He looked up as they approached.

"Lizzie, baby!" He stood, some of the hardness disappearing from his mouth. He plucked up Lizzie's hand and pressed a kiss to the back of it. Then he pulled her close, nuzzling his face into the crook of her neck as Lizzie giggled and wound her arms around him.

"Hi, Leo."

"All right, that's enough," Marco said. "We're in public, Leo."

Leo made a rude gesture behind Lizzie's back. Gilbert shifted from one foot to the other, pointedly looking anywhere but at his sister. Edie, who had borne witness to even more enthusiastic reunions between the pair, waved down the bartender.

"Hey, handsome," she purred when he approached. "How are you this evening?"

"Everything's jake, miss," the young man said, his accent light and from somewhere Edie couldn't quite place. He was good-looking, with sparkling brown eyes, light brown skin, and dark hair parted sharply down the middle. Edie hadn't seen him here before, which worked in her favor—he wouldn't know who she was. "What's your poison, beautiful?"

Edie's heart skipped, though not from the compliment. "Come on. I bet you say that to all the girls," she demurred.

He leaned close, his elbows resting on the bar top. "Only the pretty ones," he said, winking. "And I've yet to see anyone as pretty as you."

Edie let herself preen a bit and walked her fingers toward him. He watched her, something hungry and almost predatory in his dark eyes; it should thrill her, really. But instead, she glanced back over her shoulder, to where Gilbert moved between the tables, talking softly and collecting glasses. Gil turned his head, as if she'd called him, and frowned as he dumped the contents of the glass in hand to the floor, his gaze bouncing back and forth between her and the bartender.

Focus. Edie forced her attention back to the bartender. He waggled his eyebrows. Edie leaned closer, propping her own elbows up on the bar. "I have a proposition for you," she whispered. "Want to hear it?"

"I'm all ears, doll," he said. His breath was warm on her cheek, nearly close enough to kiss.

"I'll give you a hundred bucks if you don't serve anyone else tonight," she said.

"What?" The bartender narrowed his dark eyes at her. "Is this some sort of joke?"

"I'm serious. The easiest money you'll ever make. All you have to do is dry this joint up." She slipped the bill from her handbag and placed it on the bar between them. "Duck soup."

"Go climb up your thumb." He didn't move, though. A hundred dollars was more than he probably made over the course of a few nights, maybe even a week.

Edie shrugged. She put one finger on the bill and slid it back toward her. "All right."

"Wait." The bartender covered his hand with hers. "That's it? Just don't serve anyone? What's it to you?"

"What's it gonna be?" Edie raised her chin.

He took the money, and the vise around Edie's chest eased. One fewer drink poured tonight hopefully meant one fewer body in the morgue. A hundred bucks was nothing in comparison to a human life.

By the time she turned back around, Leo and Lizzie had disentangled themselves from each other, and Leo was looking at his youngest brother with a wrinkled brow.

"Cut?" Leo said. "What do you mean, *cut*? What are you implying, little brother?"

"I'm not implying anything, Leo," Marco said.

"You think I'm that stupid, to kill my own customers? Is that what you're saying to me right now?"

"Mr. Salvatore," Edie interjected. "Please. Perhaps we should speak in private?"

"Yeah. All right." He pointed his chin toward the corridor behind them. "My office."

Much like the office he kept in a converted warehouse downtown, where he organized illegal boxing matches, Leo's office at the club was the surprisingly snug office of a gentleman, not a thug. The furniture was heavy and Victorian, the desk almost identical to the one her father kept in his office at City Hall. A Tiffany lamp hung overhead, its red- and gold-hued glass throwing the room into warmth.

Leo shut the door behind them. He gestured toward the bar, the barest hint of a smile on his face. "I'd offer you a drink, but considering the circumstances . . ." He let the sentence linger. "Sit. Everyone."

They did, the four of them settling themselves on the sofa and armchairs. Leo leaned back against the bar. "So, if I am to understand this correctly," he said, holding his hand out in front of him, "there are at least four men dead after drinking in my club because someone cut my liquor with wood alcohol." He rubbed at his face, then looked straight at Gilbert. "If your boy Tommy is trying to get cute with me because he thinks I messed with his drivers, I swear, I will make his mother regret the day he was born. I will drench that hill of yours in so much blood, I will—"

"Hold it, hold it," Marco said quickly, cutting his brother off. Lizzie shifted closer to Edie, and Edie wondered, not for the first time, what Lizzie was doing with a man like Leo.

"I've known Tommy my whole life, Leo. He wouldn't do this. If the two of you had a deal, he'd honor it." Lizzie's voice was clear and calm. "There's got to be some sort of explanation. It's new, the two of you working together, isn't it?"

"Yeah." Some of the fire left Leo's gaze. "Yeah. We've got a whole operation. Tommy has the booze and the trucks and the muscle, and I've got contacts all up and down the East Coast. Tommy's a smart fella, but he's Irish. No offense," he said quickly. "It just means he's gotta work harder to get into places I've been in my whole life. I move his booze, and we both make money."

"Who made your latest delivery? Is there a record?" Gilbert looked at Leo, who was already moving behind his desk, pulling a ledger from the top drawer and flipping it open.

"September twenty-ninth." Leo ran his finger down the column. "Yeah. We got in four cases of whisky. The driver signed here—HB. What did you say that fella's name was?"

"Homer Byrne." Edie rubbed at her temples. "Why does it keep coming back to Homer Byrne? Mr. Salvatore, do you have any idea who would poison your liquor?"

"I do." The gangster was grim. It was then Edie noticed the dark circles under his eyes, the pinched line of his brow, the deep groove bracketing his mouth. He looked exhausted. "I don't have a name, not exactly. But I'd bet a cool grand that whoever offed your movie star is behind this too."

Marco frowned, his stance mirroring his brother's. "What does Duncan Carroll have to do with you, Leo?"

"I invested twenty grand in Norwood Studios just last month. Duncan Carroll came here himself to close the deal. I figured it was a good way to take some of my less . . . legal income and turn it legitimate. Now he's in the ground, the studio's on the verge of failing, and someone is targeting the club."

"No offense, Mr. Salvatore, but that's quite the conspiracy."

"It's no conspiracy, Miss Shippen." He rifled through his desk drawer and pulled out a slim manila envelope. He flipped it open and thrust the contents toward her. "See? Proof."

The envelope contained exactly one item: a single sheet of paper, and on it, written in careful black letters:
There is thy gold, worse poison to men's souls,
Doing more murder in this loathsome world
Than these poor compounds that thou mayst not sell.

Chapter 21

Someone had sent Leo Salvatore Shakespeare. Gilbert and the others crowded around the desk, looking down at the page. He hadn't taken the gangster for a thespian, but Leo read the verse aloud with the gravitas of a stage actor, then looked up at them, helplessness written across his face.

"It's meant for me," he said. "Romeo was an Italian. *I'm* Italian," he added, in case any of them had forgotten. "That arrived the day after Duncan died."

"The question is, are they blaming you for it, or taking credit?" Marco picked up the paper, reading it again. "'Doing more murder' seems pretty pointed."

"Did anyone beside Duncan know about your investment in the studio?" Gilbert asked. "Or your partnership with Tommy?" An alliance between the two gangs stood to shift the balance of power in the city's underworld. The other major players, like Max Hoff, would be high on the list of prime suspects.

What if Pyle had been coming at this from the wrong angle? What if the killer wasn't coming from inside the studio? Was Duncan Carroll's death simply the collateral damage caused by the opening salvos of a brewing gang war?

He looked over at his sister as fear stabbed beneath his skin like a thousand and one syrettes. If whoever was behind this was willing to kill a movie star Leo had met twice, in order to hurt him, it stood to reason that they wouldn't hesitate to hurt the woman Leo loved. Someone had broken into their house. He'd assumed it was Tommy, as a warning to hurry up the investigation, but what if it hadn't been?

Lizzie was in danger.

His entire family was in danger.

The edges of the room tinged black. His heartbeat slowed as his vision tunneled and the walls squeezed in. He pitched forward, his hands gripping the edge of the desk, bracing himself for the onslaught of memory, to be dragged from this reality into one warped with the phantoms of his past. His chest grew tight, and he couldn't hear, couldn't see, couldn't breathe. Couldn't even think. Only one thing looped through his brain, repeating like the figures on a zoetrope.

His family was in danger.

"Gil?" Lizzie was somehow between him and the desk, pressing her cool fingers to his chin. "Breathe. In and out. It's all right. You're here."

"He's shell-shocked?" Leo's voice came from somewhere far away, like he was speaking from another room. "Christ, Marco. Get me ice from the bar—quick."

Gilbert squeezed his eyes shut. This wasn't like his other episodes. There were no whistling bullets, no soul-shattering screams or bone-rattling explosions. He reached for his chest pocket, where his vials of morphine used to rest, but the pocket was empty. He had no relief, no treatment.

He couldn't breathe.

He couldn't breathe.

He clutched at his chest as he fell to his knees. His vision narrowed, and he thought, for one absolutely terrifying second, that his heart was giving out. Edie and Lizzie's worried faces hovered above him. And then Leo Salvatore was pressing a bag of ice to the back of Gilbert's neck. The sudden cold was shocking to his system, forcing him to gasp for air.

"Steady, man," Leo said. "Just breathe."

Somehow Gilbert did just as he was told. He took deep breaths, in and out, and gradually, the room came back into focus, his heart slowed, and his hand steadied. Lizzie led him to the sofa, where he sat, his elbows on his knees, cradling his head in his hands.

The mood of the room, already subdued, grew somber. "I'm sorry," Gilbert rasped suddenly. "I don't know what came over me."

"I thought you said they were getting better," Lizzie said quietly. Her voice sounded as if she was on the edge of tears, and when Gilbert raised his gaze to hers, his sister's face was flushed. Angry. "That's what you told Mam. That's what you told me."

"Liz."

"That's not better," she said. She stood, blinking rapidly. "I—I need a minute. Excuse me."

The door slammed behind her. The two Salvatore brothers exchanged glances, and Leo stood. "I'll talk to her," he said. Then to Gilbert he added, "It's not your fault."

Edie stood in front of him, her hands twisted in front of her and, etched across her face, a look of . . . sadness? Pity? "Gil," she said softly.

"I'll go get some coffee. Coffee?" Marco asked, and then left, not waiting for a reply. The door clicked shut, echoing through the office like a shot.

Gilbert ran his fingers through his hair. "Go," he said, his voice hoarse. "I know that's what you want to do."

"You aren't half as good at reading my mind as you think you are." Edie didn't budge. Instead, she came closer, kneeling before him. She put her hand on his arm. "Gil."

"You heard what Leo said. He wasn't wrong."

"I don't want to hear it from Leo or Marco or even Lizzie. I want to hear it from you," she said. "Whenever you're ready to share it."

"I'm a coward." He couldn't look at her when he said it. But he had to tell her; he owed it to her to tell her.

"You're not, Gil, you're—"

"I am." The words exploded from him, sharp and devastating. He had to tell her before he stopped himself again. "I tremble, and I see things that aren't there. And I can't stop seeing them. Because my body may have come back from the war, but my brain? It's still over there. Sometimes I think—sometimes I wish—that I had died over there."

"That's what happened this morning too," Edie said. "When I found you at the studio."

"Was that only today? Christ." He let out a little self-deprecating laugh. "Listen to me, Edie. I'm no good for you. I should have told you all this before. I'm sorry I didn't."

Edie didn't run screaming from the room. She didn't move her hand either—she just kept stroking his arm, the pressure gentle. Steady. "Lizzie said she thought you'd gotten better," she said. "She knew?"

Gilbert ducked his head. "Yeah. And it has. When I first came home, I could barely speak. I was in bed for months. It took morphine to make it bearable. A lot of morphine. I—I used it every day. For years."

Edie's gray eyes were soft. "And now? Do you need it now?"

He let out a huff. "No. Not since . . . not since the spring. I weaned off it. I've been boxing instead. I'm better, yeah. But I'm not fixed. That's what she doesn't understand." He had to make Edie understand this too. That he could push his body to exhaustion, he could numb his mind through drink or drug, and there would still be days when he would be right back in that muddy trench, fighting a war only he could see.

"Some days are harder than others," Edie said. "I understand that. Do you think less of me for my headaches?"

"No. Of course not."

"Do I not deserve love, or patience, on the days I can't get out of bed?" She stared at him then.

"You always deserve love," he said. "Edie—"

"And so do you." She stood then and gave him a sad smile. "I want to be with you, Gilbert. Whatever that looks like. Whenever you're ready."

He nodded. He stood too, his sweat-soaked shirt sticking to the skin of his back. He rubbed a hand across his face. He didn't know what to say to her, what to say to that. Thankfully, Edie's attention had been caught elsewhere. She leaned forward and picked up the note from Leo's desk.

"Gil, look at this." She handed it to him. "Look at the letters."

He stared down at the note. She was right: they'd seen that handwriting before. On the life insurance forms Harold Fox had filled out for Duncan Carroll.

A soft knock at the door announced Marco's presence. He had a mug of coffee in his hands, which he handed to Gilbert.

"All right?" Marco asked.

"Yeah." Or he would be, if they'd all leave well enough alone. They had more important things to do than to focus on him. He needed a good night's sleep and a round in the boxing ring.

But they had one more thing to clear up before any of that could happen.

"What do you know about something called la futura?" Edie asked, once Lizzie and Leo had returned to the office.

Leo's head whipped up. "What did you say?"

"La futura. What is it?"

A series of emotions flickered across Leo's face. Surprise, then confusion. Disbelief. "Why are you asking me about that? Who told you about that?"

Gilbert and Edie exchanged a glance. Leo's reaction mirrored Celeste's—both had recoiled, almost as if they were afraid of the term. "Celeste DuPont," Gilbert said. "She said you're the only one who knows who's behind it."

"No one was supposed to know," Leo said. His knee began bouncing, and he looked to Marco, his eyes serious. "You remember what it was like, don't you? When Pops was alive?"

Gilbert had never heard Marco speak of his father. He knew that Marco—and the rest of his brothers—loved their mother with an almost religious devotion. The woman, whom Gilbert had never met, was by turns saintly and terrifying.

"Yeah." Marco seemed to shrink in on himself, drawing his knees closer to him, hunching his shoulders. He looked at Gil and Lizzie. "Pops was a hard man. Life made him hard. And he took it out on us."

"And on Ma." Leo's knuckles were white on the edge of the sofa. "I could take whatever he wanted to give me. Whippings, beatings—whatever. But Ma didn't deserve that," he said, his voice hushed. "I would try to step in whenever I could—to take his attention away from her, and from them," he added, tilting his chin toward Marco. "He was just a kid. They were all just kids."

"You were just a kid too," Lizzie said softly.

Leo shrugged. "Anyway, one day, I got tired of it. One of the other boys on the block said there was a strega—a witch—who could help. Said she sold something called la futura. Some sort of spell that would change a person's future. So I went to her. She was an old lady—all stooped over, dressed in black. Her niece helped her to the front room. The niece was about my age and real cute.

"The strega made me tell her everything about Pops. And I did. And she and that girl looked at each other, and the witch nodded. The girl went to the back of the house and came back with a little jar of liquid. She said that the spell was inside. She said that there were two possible outcomes to la futura, and they depended on Pop's heart. If he had a pure heart under all that anger, he'd be fine. He'd stop drinking and his anger would vanish. But if his heart was black . . ."

"Leo." Marco's voice was sharp with disbelief. "You believed her?"

"I was a *kid*." Leo stood up. "There's this old lady, telling me there's a magic potion that could make our lives better, that could make Pops better? That would have him leave you and Ma and the others alone? I was going to try it." He paced the room, hands raking through his hair. "So I bought it. I slipped it into his soup that night, and boom. He dropped dead at the dinner table."

"Ma said he had a heart attack," Marco was on his feet, his voice rising to an anguished pitch. "It's why I went to medical school. I thought I could have saved him."

"Marco." Leo stepped forward, hand reaching, but Marco pushed his hand away and stormed from the room, slamming the door behind him. Leo watched him leave, his hand still outstretched.

Leo closed his fist, lowering his arm. He shook his head, as if clearing his thoughts, and turned back to the others.

"I dropped out of school and took over the butcher shop after that. And I tried to forget about it, because Ma was finally happy. And then I tried to forget about the whole damn thing. Anyway, one day, a few months ago, Celeste brings me a girl who needs help. More help than Celeste can give. I open the door—and it's the damned girl from the strega's house. All grown up and fresh out of the slammer."

"So what did you do?" Edie asked.

"She said I owed her a favor. So I set her up with a little house near South Street."

"Near Dante and Luigi's?" Gilbert asked. La futura's trail seemed to lead them in circles.

Leo's brow creased. "Yeah. How'd you know?"

Edie and Gilbert exchanged a glance. She took a breath, then explained, "A friend of Lily Byrne's gave me the address. I let her believe I was having problems with my love life, and she said that this woman could help. But when we got there, the house was abandoned. Some kids were there and told us to go to Madame Midnight if we were looking for the strega.

When we talked to Celeste, she sent us to you. Said you would know who she was."

Leo pursed his lips. He looked down at Lizzie, then back to Gilbert and Edie. Gil leaned forward. Leo had to tell them who the woman was.

"I promised her I'd never tell," Leo said. "You've got to understand. She . . . she's the real deal. She told me that if I told anyone, she'd put the evil eye on me."

"She's not a real witch," Lizzie said gently. "Things like that aren't real. She was trying to scare you."

"If it wasn't real, how come my dad died? I saw it work, Liz."

"I'd bet money it was cyanide or some other poison," Gilbert said. "It's too late to tell now, obviously, but it would fit the pattern. Lily Byrne went to this woman as well, for help with an angry husband: la futura. She gives it to him, and he drops dead. It wasn't magic, Leo. It was poison."

"I killed him." Leo looked down at his hands. Gilbert was sure he'd taken other lives without blinking an eye, but this death—his father's death—seemed to shake him. "She tricked me?"

"You saved your mam and your brothers, Leo," Lizzie said gently. "You didn't know."

"I should have." He looked up, then, right at Gilbert. "Her name is Lucia Olivetti."

Chapter 22

Finnegan Pyle sat behind his borrowed desk at Norwood Studios and frowned at Edie. "You think this woman—this Lucia Olivetti—has something to do with Byrne's death? I thought you said you were sure it was the wife."

"I think Lily gave Homer the poison, yes. But I think she purchased it from this woman."

"And what does that have to do with Burkhart's death? Or Duncan's, for that matter?"

"I'm not sure." Edie and Gil had been up until the early hours of the morning, trying to link it all together, but there were too many missing parts. "But look at this."

She pulled the folder from her purse and spread its contents out on the desk. "We learned last night that Leo Salvatore gave Duncan Carroll twenty thousand dollars to invest in this film. We also learned that someone here at the studio—presumably Harold—took out a life insurance policy on Duncan around the same time and cashed it out immediately on the day of his death. That same day, this arrived for Leo Salvatore." She presented the note.

Pyle took the note from her, his lips moving soundlessly while he read. "That's nonsense," he said.

"It's Shakespeare. More specifically, it's *Romeo and Juliet*. Leo seemed to think he'd received it because he was Italian"—Pyle let out a snort at that—"but I think it's more likely that he received it because someone wanted to blame him for Duncan's death. Look at the handwriting."

"It matches the note on the life insurance paperwork." Pyle leaned back. "So someone here at the studio sent that note? But who?"

"Who has access to the files in Fox's office? Start there."

Pyle nodded. "All right, Miss Shippen. Anything else?"

"Actually, yes." Edie filled him in on the conversation she'd had with her grandmother. "Duncan's common-law wife was sent to Sing Sing. Is there any way you can track down her name or see if she's still in prison?"

"Sure." Pyle gave a shrug. "But I keep these," he said, pointing down to the files. "Oh, and Miss Shippen? I'd tell your friend to get a lawyer. Things aren't looking too good for her."

Edie froze. "What do you mean?" she asked. "I just showed you that Harold took out an insurance policy on Duncan, and you're telling me that Ava is still your prime suspect?"

"Your friend stands to inherit upward of ten million dollars," Pyle said. He leaned forward, propping his elbows on the desk. "And I have evidence that the marriage was all a sham. I have a statement from Mr. Fox that says Ava has been—and I quote—'involved in a number of lesbian relationships that have endangered the reputation of this studio.' Seems he arranged the marriage to squash any rumors. Killing him would be a quick way to make it rich."

The floor felt like it had opened up beneath Edie's feet, and she was falling, tumbling into an endless abyss. How awful things would be for Ava if Pyle revealed this to the press. Her career would be over in an instant. "He told you that? Does Ava know?"

"Thanks for the tip," Pyle said. He stood, motioning for the door. "I'll see what we can find out about this ex-wife. And this Olivetti woman. Now run along, Miss Shippen, and let me get back to work."

Dismissed, Edie left, fuming. The nerve of that man! She'd thought that they'd achieved a positive working relationship—that he took her seriously. But just now, he'd treated her as little more than an annoyance.

Edie rubbed at her forehead, feeling so defeated. She still didn't know who'd killed Duncan. She couldn't figure out whether or not Lily Byrne had killed her husband, without finding this Olivetti woman. And she still wasn't sure if Frank Burkhart was an intended victim or if he just had the bad luck to get out of prison and end up in the wrong place at the wrong time.

Wait.

Frank Burkhart had been released from Sing Sing only a few months ago . . . the same as Duncan's ex-wife. Edie knew nothing about prisons, let alone maximum security prisons in New York. She had to assume that the men's and women's populations were kept separated. But could it be a coincidence?

Or could it be a connection?

Ava and Gil were reshooting a scene today. She made her way down to the studio where they were working, so deep in thought that she didn't see Della O'Malley until she'd nearly run the girl over. They collided hard. Edie reached out, steadying the girl, as the monkey on Della's shoulder screeched and climbed atop its mistress's head.

"Miss O'Malley! I'm so sorry. I had my head in the clouds."

"It's all right, Miss Shippen. I did as well." Della gave her a small smile as she stepped back, rubbing at her shoulder. She plucked the monkey off her head and cradled it in her arms like a baby. "We're all right, aren't we, Jade? And you, Miss Shippen? Were you thinking happy thoughts, I hope?"

"Not particularly, I'm afraid," Edie answered. The girl was wearing another red dress, long sleeved, with a skirt swinging around her knees. She wore a little brooch on the collar—a white enamel cat holding a red heart. "That is the most darling brooch I've ever seen," Edie said. "Where did you get it?"

"Oh!" Della looked down, her fair skin turning pink. "It was a gift from Duncan. My birthday was a few weeks ago, and he and Ava threw me a little party. I don't know where he got it, but I thought I'd wear it today. To remember him."

"That's sweet of you," Edie said. She reached out to touch the girl's arm. The monkey bared its teeth at her, and Edie retracted her hand. "How are you holding up?"

"I'm all right. I just wish . . . well. I heard you were some sort of detective," Della said, dropping her voice, a hint of shyness creeping in. A blush bloomed across her cheekbones. "Is that true? Are you trying to figure out who killed Duncan?"

"I am," Edie said carefully. "Mostly as a favor for Ms. Sylvester. She's very upset about the whole thing, as I'm sure you all are."

"It's been awful," Della admitted. "I've never met a lady detective before. Is it hard work?"

"Incredibly," Edie said. She was flattered by the girl's attention. "But there are so many times when the world won't believe a woman, simply because of the nature of her sex. I want to change that."

"I think that's swell, miss," Della said, almost breathless. "Please, let me know if there's anything I can help you with. I grew up here at the studio. I can answer any questions you might have."

Edie considered it. The girl was practically vibrating, so eager to help. Edie remembered what it felt like to be sixteen years old—not yet a woman, but no longer a child. She'd been desperate to be seen by the adults around her.

What would have happened if one of them had given her a chance? Would she have fallen so completely beneath Theo's spell? Or would she have chosen a different path earlier? Would she have been more like her cousin Rebecca—someone who was sure of herself and her place in the world?

"Actually, that would be very helpful, Della. Thank you."

"Oh, of course." Della looked at her expectantly. "What do you want to know?"

"Right now?" Edie looked both ways down the corridor; it was deserted. "Well, I'm wondering who is the person in charge of Mr. Fox's files? Surely, he has a secretary or an office assistant?"

"Oh! That's easy—my mother handles most of it. I help her sometimes when it gets busy. Why?"

"I'm simply curious," Edie said. "I was wondering who I should ask if I have a question about the cast."

"My mother, definitely," Della said. "She's been here since the beginning. Uncle Harry says he doesn't know what he'd do without her. The whole operation would fall apart."

"I see." Edie was struck by another realization. "Della, are your mother and Harold siblings?"

"Oh no. My father was Harry's stepbrother," Della said, "but they were raised as siblings. My father's father married Uncle Harry's mother when they were small children. They started the studio together. Mother was hired to be their secretary, and eventually she and Father fell in love and married. After he died, Harry insisted we come and live with him. We've been here two years now."

Mrs. O'Malley was a widow—that made sense. As did the fact that Della's father had been Harry's brother by marriage. It explained the total lack of family resemblance. "And the finances," Edie asked carefully. "Does Harold handle those himself?"

Della barked out a laugh. "Oh heavens, no," she said. "Uncle Harry doesn't have a head for numbers. He says they make him dizzy. Mother handles all of it, and he makes the movies."

Well *that* was an interesting piece of information. Mrs. O'Malley handled the business end of the studio, and Harold Fox concerned himself with the films. Had Mrs. O'Malley sent Duncan to ask Leo Salvatore for the money?

"Thank you, Della. This has been very helpful," Edie said. She smiled at the girl, who beamed in response. "I won't keep you any longer—it looks like you were on your way somewhere in a hurry."

"Anytime, Miss Shippen," Della answered. "Say goodbye to Miss Shippen, Jade," she told the monkey, raising its paw in a little wave.

Edie watched Della hurry off down the corridor, humming to herself as she went. The more information Edie gathered, the more confused she became. She headed to Ava's dressing room, let herself in, and pulled her notebook from her purse. She sat at Ava's dressing table, and wrote:

Mrs. O'Malley—manages money, files. Perhaps insurance? CHECK HANDWRITING.
Ava—rumors of lovers? Does Harold have proof?
Duncan—why Leo Salvatore? Did Harold know?
Della—clearly enamored with Duncan.
Harold—asked Daddy for a loan but was turned down. Arranged Ava's marriage to save the studio.

Beneath that, she wrote:
Frank Burkhart—check date of release from Sing Sing
Lucia Olivetti—connection to Duncan?
Dead men in cell—who poisoned Leo's liquor?

She tapped the end of her pen against her lips. None of it made sense. Every conversation revealed another suspect she hadn't considered. Perhaps Lizzie would be able to give some additional insight later this afternoon. She was going to take whatever information Leo had and try to track down Lucia Olivetti.

The door to the dressing room opened, and Ava stepped inside in full costume. Edie closed her notebook quickly and dropped it into her handbag at her feet. "You're done early," she said.

Ava smiled at her. She'd already scrubbed off the cake makeup she had to wear during filming, though she still wore the long wig that transformed her into Juliet. She looked younger, with the blond curls tumbling over her shoulders. Lighter. More like the Ava Edie had known in California and less like the serious, troubled creature that Ava had transformed to in the year since they'd last seen each other.

"Your doctor is a natural," Ava laughed. She slipped out of her shoes, unfastening her earrings as she crossed the floor. "Harold was happy after just two takes, if you can believe it. It's a shame he went into medicine instead of acting. Maybe this will change his mind."

"I doubt it," Edie said.

"Help me with these buttons?" Ava turned, gathering the hair from the nape of her neck. The dress she was wearing buttoned from her neck to below her waist. Edie stepped close, and made quick work of the task, her fingers brushing against the soft skin of Ava's back. Ava's breath caught, and Edie stilled.

"Ava," she said. She wasn't sure what she was going to say next—the name just slipped past her lips in a little sigh. Ava turned suddenly, her eyes dark. She slid her hands into Edie's black bob and kissed her.

Edie froze, her own hands on the gentle curve of Ava's waist. Ava made a little noise in the back of her throat and pushed closer until their bodies were pulled flush together, and she was so warm and soft, and how many times had Edie thought about this when they were back in California? Those nights she'd lain beside Ava, close but not quite touching, every inch of her skin electrified, wondering what would happen if she just moved her hand an inch, if she rolled over. If she'd find the other girl staring back, the same longing etched across her face. If it would be different kissing a girl than it had been kissing Theo. But she'd been so afraid—what if she'd misread Ava's looks? Her lingering touches? What if Ava didn't want Edie the way Edie had wanted her?

And now Ava was here, in her arms. Wanting her, her lips soft and warm.

And now it was Edie who hesitated.

She'd promised herself once that she'd never be anyone's second choice. That she wouldn't get caught up again in unrequited love. Ava was here, mouth pressed to Edie's, hands stroking gently up and down the length of Edie's spine, turning all Edie's nerves to mush, and yet all Edie could think about was Gilbert.

It wasn't fair to make Ava her second choice.

She stepped back suddenly, pulling away from Ava's kiss. The other woman looked up at her, blue eyes widened in surprise. "Is something wrong? I thought—"

Edie rushed to make it better. "I'm sorry, Ava. I can't. We can't."

"Did I misunderstand?" Color flooded Ava's cheeks. "I wanted to wait, to make sure that you were like me. I thought—I thought—"

"Wait." Edie reached out and threaded her fingers through Ava's. "You didn't think wrong. I . . . I used to want this. Dream about this. About you, back when I thought I'd be in California forever. But things have changed, Ava."

"You're worried someone will find out. But no one has to know," Ava said. "Harold knows about me. He . . . he'll protect us. We can be happy together. We can keep it a secret. Or we can run away and tell everyone here to kick rocks. We can go to Paris, like Gertrude Stein or Natalie Barney. Movies are made in France, too. We can be happy."

Edie's heart skipped in her chest. "No, Ava. It's not that. I'm not afraid of scandal." Edie knew what Ava was saying. She knew there were places—there were circles—where they could be together unbothered. Ava was right—they could go to Paris or New York and make new lives for themselves. Plenty of other women had done it, both at home and abroad. It wasn't unheard of, even if it was unorthodox. But that wasn't the issue. She brushed the other woman's hair back from her cheek. "I can't give you what you need, because I'm in love with someone else."

Love. She hadn't meant to say it. Hadn't even thought about associating the word with Gilbert, but the moment it left her mouth, she knew it was true. Her heart soared, thinking about him—about the way he looked at her like she was a puzzle he couldn't quite solve, the way his hand lingered on the small of her back. The way he'd looked at her when he thought he was dying, when she thought he was dying, his blood on her hands as she fought to save him.

"The doctor." Ava licked her lips and stepped back. She'd schooled her face into something cool and composed. Distant. "He told me there's nothing between the two of you."

They'd spoken about her. Edie didn't know why that knowledge stung so much. "He's right," Edie said. "There isn't. But I can't change how I feel about him."

"So you'd rather . . ." Ava's eyes filled with tears, and she shook her head, her voice trailing off. "No. Fine. Forget it. I'm such a fool. She told me I was a fool, and I should have listened to her. She's always right."

"Ava—"

"Get out." Ava flung her hand toward the door. "Just—just leave, Edie. I can't even look at you right now."

"Ava, please—"

"Go." Ava was near tears, and Edie couldn't stand to see her cry. She left, hurrying out of the room, wincing when the door to the dressing room slammed behind her, the sound reverberating through the corridor.

Damn it all.

Chapter 23

The day passed in a blur. Gilbert moved from scene to scene, changing from one costume to the next, reshooting frames that Harold had found some flaw with, or capturing entirely new footage. Some of it seemed laughable—Gilbert leaning against a pillar. Gilbert walking down a street. Gilbert staring up at Ava in Juliet's tower, arm raised, begging her to come down. By the time Harold called, *"Cut!"* for the last time, Gilbert was exhausted. He was thrilled when the makeup crew scrubbed his face clean of the heavy cream and powders they'd applied and reapplied throughout the day, and almost sighed with relief when he slipped back into his own street clothes in the privacy of his own dressing room.

"Good work today, son." Harold said, when Gilbert emerged. He was waiting across the hall, leaning against the wall. "A few more days of that, and you'll be done. I can't thank you enough."

"You're welcome," Gilbert said. He didn't know what else to say, and so he said nothing as Harold fell into step beside him.

They had almost reached the end of the corridor when Harold said, quite suddenly: "I feel as if I'm in desperate need of a good Kentucky bourbon, but my late father made me promise to never drink alone. Would you join me, Dr. Lawless?"

Gilbert paused. He wasn't much of a drinker—he'd had the same bottle of whiskey tucked into his dresser drawer for years—but he was still feeling off-kilter from the night before, and how Edie's face had looked when he finally told her the truth about his shell shock. She was right—he was being unfair. He was just as much to blame for what happened to Penelope as she was. He was Penelope's father, and he had been so focused on his sister that he had sent her and Edie straight into harm's way. He didn't know.

And neither did she.

He closed his eyes.

Christ almighty, he was a failure. Of a father, of a friend. Of a man.

He turned around.

"Yes," he said. "Yes, sir. I'd like that."

"Please. Sit." Harold led Gilbert into the office he kept in the studio building and motioned to the sofa. He pulled two crystal tumblers from a desk drawer and opened a nearly full bottle of bourbon. He poured two fingers in each cup, then swirled them as he walked over to Gilbert, and handed one over before settling in on the sofa beside Gil. He stretched one arm along the back of the sofa, close enough that his fingers could brush Gilbert's arm if Gil were to shift even an inch closer.

Gil moved back, closer to the arm of the sofa. He stared down at the sparkling brown liquid, swirling in the bottom of his glass. Did he trust Harold enough to drink? He thought he'd watched carefully as the older man poured, but what if he hadn't? What if he'd missed something?

Would he risk it?

Harold spoke first. "This damned movie might be the end of me," he said, his voice cutting through the silence. "I've wanted this for so long, but I'm starting to wonder if my sister was right. That maybe it's all more trouble than it's worth." He drained his glass and stood, then walked back to the desk and poured another, this one double the amount of the first.

"It can't be that bad," Gilbert tried to say, but Harold didn't hear him.

"He started on the stage in New York, you know," Harold said, instead. "His first role was Hamlet, if you can believe it. He made quite the splash and was set to play Romeo when he simply vanished. He was gone for almost a year, and none of his previous directors would touch him. He turned to film, and I took a chance on him. We made quite a few films, but his heart was on the stage. I think he thought that doing this—playing Shakespeare's greatest hero—would reopen some of the doors that he'd found slammed in his face.

"I thought having the two of them get married would help. The rumors about Ava and her . . . tastes. The whispers about Duncan's missing year. The way he was so damned unhappy. It could help his career, and then he could be happy. He could go back to the stage." He turned pleading eyes to Gilbert. "It isn't unheard of, an arrangement like theirs. It would have worked, as long as Ava kept things discreet. They didn't look at each other the way that you and Miss Shippen do, but they could do a convincing job at being in love."

Gilbert looked down at his glass. Love.

Did he love Edie? On paper, he knew what it looked like . . . She was impatient and impulsive and intriguing, and it would be irrational to love her. Irresponsible.

Incredible, a tiny voice inside him whispered.

Inevitable, a second voice said.

In denial, a third added.

Images flashed in rapid succession. Edie, tilting her chin up to his as they danced that night. Edie, eyes sparkling in the rain. Edie, her body warm and soft beneath him in her bedroom.

The way she'd looked at him when he told her the truth last night.

Love.

He took a drink.

"It is remarkable," Harold said suddenly. "The resemblance between the two of you, I mean." He took a long swallow from his glass. "He was like a son to me, you know. I never had children of my own—never had the time—but Duncan was everything I'd want a son to be. And seeing you here . . . It's almost like he's sitting here beside me again."

"I'm sorry," Gilbert said softly, "but I'm not him, Mr. Fox. And I never will be."

His own heart broke a little as the older man's face crumpled. He understood the pain in Harold's gaze. For years after Sarah's death, he'd have given anything to see her just one last time, to speak with her. He thought of Fatine, a pretty blond girl he'd met on R&R in France, who stood the same height as Sarah, had the same soft curve of her hip, the same bounce to her hair. How he'd wept in her arms, and she'd held him and stroked his hair until he fell asleep. How he'd woken alone and ashamed and missing Sarah more in that moment than he had since the day they'd buried her.

Grief, after all, was the price of love.

Was he willing to pay it a second time?

Gilbert stood. He took the glass from Harold's hand and placed it with his own on the desk. The other man hung his head, and Gilbert paused, hand on the door. "I'm sorry," he said, again. And left.

Mrs. O'Malley was leaving her own office, locking the door with a key from a large metal ring. She saw Gilbert emerge and stopped short.

"Dr. Lawless," she said. "You startled me. I didn't see you there."

"Don't mind me, Mrs. O'Malley. I'm just leaving." He ducked his head and tried to hurry past, but she reached out, stopping him with a hand to his arm.

"You were in Harold's office, I take it?" she asked. She looked up at him, her dark eyes shrewd. "Is he at it again?"

"Pardon?" Gilbert, his mind still reeling over thoughts of Edie. "I'm not sure what you're referring to."

"Sure you aren't." She pressed a hand to her forehead as if she were thinking. "I'll take care of it, Dr. Lawless. Like always. Lord knows what he'd do if I wasn't around to clean up his messes."

She hurried off, muttering under her breath.

"Clean up his messes."

It was an innocent comment. The type of thing people said all the time.

Nevertheless, Gilbert couldn't help but wonder, as she disappeared down the hallway, how far exactly Mrs. O'Malley would go to clean up Harold Fox's messes.

◆━━━━━━━◆◆◆━━━━━━━◆

"Dr. Lawless, you have a call," Martinez announced when he arrived back at the big house. "Dr. Harrison, from the City Morgue, has requested that you call him back at once."

Harrison. He'd almost forgotten about the bottle they'd found in Duncan's dressing room. He thanked the butler and hurried into Harold's office. It was hard to believe that it had only been a day since he and Edie had sat here, learning about the break-in at the house in Manayunk. He'd felt as if he'd aged a year in that time.

"City Morgue, how may I direct your call?" Cecelia's voice was light over the phone.

"Hi, Cecelia, it's Gil," he said. "Harrison called. Can you put me through to the lab?"

"One moment." Any trace of warmth in her voice had vanished. The line clicked over, and he waited.

And waited.

"How may I connect your call?" The operator's voice came back on the line; Cecelia must have disconnected the call. The door to the big house slammed shut, and other voices followed—Mrs. O'Malley's, raised in anger, and Harold's pleading. Martinez, placating.

The voices moved down the corridor.

"City Morgue, please," Gilbert ground out. He understood Cecelia was angry; hell, he was angry with himself. He'd never been the type of man to lead a woman on. In fact, he could count the number of women he'd ever been out with on one hand. Sarah, of course. Fatine, in France. And Edie.

But he needed the information Harrison had. He'd grovel if that's what it took.

"Cecelia," he said, as soon as the line clicked over, "I know I hurt you, and I'm sorry. I'm sorry. But please, please— put me through to Dr. Harrison. Please."

There was a beat of silence on the other end. And then a voice that was decidedly *not* Cecelia's asked, "Dr. Lawless? Is that you?"

"Bette?" Mortification flooded Gilbert. "I'm sorry, I—"

"Save the apologies for Cecelia," Bette said. "She deserved better."

"I know." He squinted up at the ceiling. "Please put me through to Dr. Harrison, Bette. It's important."

"Hang on." The line clicked over, and for a moment, Gilbert was worried that she had also disconnected the call. But then Harrison's warm voice said, "Laboratory, Dr. Harrison speaking."

"Isaiah. It's Gil."

"Mr. Movie Star." Gilbert could almost hear the smile on Isaiah's face—and he was going to murder Marco for bestowing that nickname on him. "I was hoping you'd call back. I had a chance to run that sample you brought me."

"And?"

"No dice. It's just your run-of-the-mill bathtub gin," Harrison said. "No traces of cyanide. I even ran tests for arsenic and a few other substances, just in case—all clear. That bottle of liquor didn't kill him."

Damn. Gilbert thanked him and hung up. So the bottle was a dead end after all. Just like everything else.

He found Edie waiting for him at the car. She looked as discouraged as he felt. She climbed to her feet as he approached, brushing the dirt from her maroon skirt with a glove dyed the exact same shade.

"Hello," he said. He leaned in, brushing a quick kiss across her cheek. "Harrison called." He filled her in as he opened the car door, hating the way her face fell. She recounted her conversation with Pyle, one that had proven equally frustrating. But when she mentioned what she'd discussed with Della, Gilbert straightened. He told Edie what Mrs. O'Malley had said to him—that she was always the one cleaning up his messes.

"I hope Lizzie had better luck today than we did," Edie said. She went to climb in the car, then stopped short.

"You all right?" he asked. "Is it your head?"

"I'm fine," Edie said automatically. "It's just . . . my bag. I forgot it."

"Where?"

"Ava's dressing room," Edie said. "I left in a hurry. We had a bit of a row."

"You had a row?" Gilbert looked over at Edie. "Over what? I thought you were close." Harold's words echoed through his head: *"Ask Miss Shippen."*

"Over you, actually," Edie said, though she didn't look at him.

"Me?" His heart kicked up in his chest. "Why in the world would you have a row over me?"

"Don't be dense," she told him, like he should know exactly what she meant.

"They didn't look at each other the way you and Miss Shippen do . . ."

He'd seen the way Ava had watched Edie. The way that Edie had flushed in the other woman's presence when they'd first arrived at the party. There was a history there that Gilbert wasn't privy to, and he certainly wasn't going to ask. Whatever had happened between Edie and Ava didn't change the way Gilbert thought of Edie, and he knew that Edie's business was her own. She was a grown woman, capable of making her own choices.

"I'll walk with you," he offered. When they reached Ava's dressing room, Edie knocked on the door. It swung open soundlessly, the interior of the room dark. Gilbert found the chain for the overhead light and tugged.

Edie's bag was on the floor beside the dressing table. She bent to pick it up, then stood, furrowing her brow.

"What's wrong?"

"My notebook's not here." She rifled through the bag. "That's odd." She turned back to the vanity table, frowning at the mess scattered across it. Papers and makeup and jewelry . . . but no notebook, at least not one that Gilbert could see.

"Do you think Ava took it?" Gilbert asked.

"Why would she take it?" Edie replied. "No, it has to be here somewhere." She ducked her head beneath the table. "Aha. Here it is, and . . . oh. Ow!" Edie stood so fast she knocked her head on the edge of the table. She wobbled slightly.

"Are you all right?" Gilbert asked, reaching out to steady her.

"No," Edie said. She held up her hand between them, a small bottle pinched between her index finger and thumb. It was a little larger than her gloved hand, with a bulbous bottom filled with a swirling liquid. A green glass vial etched with a skull and crossbones, just like the prop that Duncan had used during his last scene.

A vial no one had been able to find.

"No," Edie said again. "I'm really not all right at all."

Chapter 24

Edie knew they should do three things: one, alert Pyle that they'd located the vial; two, find Ava and ask what she was doing with the vial; and three, take the vial to Dr. Harrison so he could see if it contained the cyanide that killed Duncan Carroll.

She knew that she should do these things and yet she couldn't quite find a way to make her legs move. She stood, frozen, holding the vial up to the light.

Gilbert moved first. He wrapped his big hand around hers, gently prying the glass from her hands. "We need to take this to Pyle."

"It's not hers," Edie said. She knew that Ava was many things—wild, impulsive, reckless. Ambitious. But she wasn't a killer. Edie was sure of it.

Gil's dark brown eyes were full of pity. "Edie," he said, his voice soft. "Why would she have this?"

"It's not hers," Edie said again. She refused to believe it. She pushed past him. "Let's go ask her. She'll tell us."

"*Harrison* will be able to tell us if it's poison," Gilbert pointed out. "If it's not, there's no reason to alarm anyone. But if it is . . ."

"Someone is trying to frame her," Edie insisted. "Someone has been trying this entire time, because . . . because . . ."

"Because she's a homosexual?"

Edie stared at him. "How did you . . . ?"

"Harold alluded to it earlier. He said he'd arranged the marriage between Ava and Duncan to stave off any whiff of scandal."

"Which is exactly why Ava would have no reason to kill Duncan. He was protecting her." Edie needed Gilbert to understand. "Don't you see? Whoever did this is trying to hurt her too."

"All the more reason to tell Pyle it's here," Gilbert said. "He can take it in as evidence, and have it tested to see if it contains poison. He can dust for fingerprints. If someone other than Ava left that there, he can prove it."

He was right. Edie hated to admit it, because she couldn't help but wonder what she would do if it turned out that she was wrong about Ava all along.

She exhaled. She had to trust Gilbert. Trust Ava.

"Fine. I'll go find Pyle. Stay here in case Ava comes back. Keep an eye on this," she said, giving the vial between them a little wiggle. She set it down on the vanity, above the spot on the floor where she'd found it, and hurried out before Gilbert could insist on going instead.

She found the detective quickly enough. He was in his office on the other side of the studio, with the lights turned off, scowling, as the film reel of Duncan's death flickered over the blank wall opposite from where he sat. Edie couldn't take her eyes off Duncan's form as he strode across the set, his face a mask of agony as he came across the still form of Ava's Juliet. Edie could almost hear the way his footsteps echoed, and the horrified pitch of his voice as he called out his lines, despite the fact the only sound in the room was the constant clicking of the film as it ran through the projector beside him.

"Can I help you, Miss Shippen?" Pyle asked. He had his feet propped up on the desk and his arms crossed over his chest. He kept his eyes on the screen.

"We found the vial," Edie said. Her pulse thundered in her ears. On the screen, Duncan held the bottle high.

Pyle sat straight up at this. "What? Where?"

"Ava's dressing room." She couldn't stop watching the scene in front of her, even though it was seared in her memory. Duncan raised the bottle to his lips and drank.

Pyle switched off the film projector. It whirred to a stop, the silence in the room disorienting, and the image of Duncan on the wall vanished into darkness.

"You coming with me or not?" Pyle huffed from the doorway.

"Right. Sorry." Edie gave her head a little shake and followed him back to the dressing room, where Gilbert was waiting.

"Do I even want to know what the two of you were up to in here?" Pyle asked. "Where is Miss Sylvester, anyway?"

"I left my purse here earlier, and I came to retrieve it. As for Ava? I haven't a clue. The room was empty when we knocked." Edie had no intention of telling Pyle about what had occurred prior to her forgetting the bag. Not about the kiss and not about the way Ava's face had crumpled when Edie rejected her.

"And it was just—what? Sitting out here on the table?" Pyle seemed incredulous.

"It was on the floor beneath the vanity," Edie said. "My bag must have tipped over, and my notebook fell out. I bent down to look for it, and the vial was there."

"And you moved it." Pyle's face flushed, a deep red spreading up his jaw in splotches. "Did you stop to think about fingerprints? Or any other evidence you could be disturbing?"

"I was wearing my gloves," Edie offered.

"Miss Shippen—" Pyle whirled on her but never got the chance to say whatever it was he meant to. Gilbert inserted himself in between Edie and the detective in a flash.

"Fin," he said, his voice dangerously low, "that's enough."

Pyle stared at Gilbert for a heartbeat. "It's gonna be like that, Bertie?"

"We came to get you right away. If you have a problem with anyone, it should be with the officers who searched this room. How long has that bottle been wedged behind the dresser?"

"How do I know your girl didn't drop it there herself?"

"Why would I do that?" Edie'd had enough of the masculine posturing. She didn't need Gilbert to protect her, as much as she enjoyed it. She shouldered her way in between them, hands on her hips. "If anything, this is evidence against Ava."

And it was. Damning evidence, if it contained poison. Edie's pulse quickened. Had she been wrong about Ava this entire time? Had she hidden the bottle . . . or had it been planted by the true killer?

Pyle seemed to be considering the same question. "All right," he said. "Here's what's going to happen. The two of you are going to take that down to the lab. I'm going to telephone the district attorney."

"The district attorney?" Edie's own voice sounded far away over the blood rushing in her ears. "Why are you calling the district attorney?"

Pyle gave her a pitying look. Gilbert slipped a steadying hand around Edie's waist. Neither of them had to say it.

If the bottle contained poison, Pyle would arrest Ava. She would be charged with murder.

Harrison was still in the lab when Edie and Gilbert arrived. He took one look at the vial and raised an eyebrow.

"Let me guess. You want me to test this?"

"Please," Gilbert said.

"You know, I do have actual, honest-to-goodness work I could be doing right now," he said. He crossed the room to a metal cabinet and pulled a set of beakers from one of the glass shelves inside. "Actual work, paid for by the city of Philadelphia. And yet."

"It's official this time," Edie said. "Pyle sent us."

Harrison let out a snort. "That's a first. Hold this." He handed one of the beakers to Edie and turned to another cabinet. He stacked a set of glass jars on the table, each with carefully labeled contents. "Thank you." He took the beaker back and set it over a small burner. He put on a pair of thick rubber gloves, then precisely measured out the contents of the jars, dropping them into the beaker one at a time. He adjusted the heat and turned to Gilbert.

"I'll take that now." He took the vial and uncorked it.

"Do you smell that?" Edie asked. "It smells like . . ." An almondy scent filled the room, reminding Edie of marzipan and Christmas cookies. Or the cherries on top of a sundae.

"Cherries," Gilbert and Harrison spoke the word at the same time, then gave each other a knowing look.

"Technically, it smells of bitter almonds. The cherries on a sundae are flavored with almond essence," Gilbert explained. "Not everyone can smell that, but it points to cyanide."

"There's one way to find out for sure," Harrison said. He picked up a small glass tube with a rubber balloon on one end and inserted it into the bottle. "Watch."

A single drop of liquid hung suspended from the edge of the tube. Edie waited, barely breathing, as the drop fell. It hit the surface, painting the solution inside with streaks of bright, brilliant blue. Another drop fell, adding more blue to the beaker.

"Cyanide," Gilbert said.

"Cyanide," Harrison agreed. He replaced the cork on the bottle, set it on the table, and carefully removed his gloves.

Edie stared down at the green glass vial. Poison. Ava would be charged with murder, and she, Edie, would... what? Watch her friend suffer through a trial? Be strapped into an electric chair? Ava had her secrets, yes. But did that make her a killer?

No. Ava hadn't killed Duncan. And now more than ever, Edie had to find a way to prove it. Her mind whirled, and she barely heard what Gilbert and Harrison were speaking to each other, their voices fading into noise.

So much rested on this vial and the poison it contained. Duncan had barely taken a sip from it, but that had been enough to kill him. But who had put out the vial for the scene? Had it been Harold? Edie thought back to that day on set—Harold had called, *"Cut,"* and she'd gone to the restroom. She remembered speaking with Della. Ava had spoken with Frances and Lizzie. Edie couldn't remember where Mrs. O'Malley had been during the break. Perhaps she had used the opportunity to slip the poisoned vial onto the set, instead of the ones they'd been filming with?

How far would Mrs. O'Malley go to protect Harold Fox?

"Where would the killer have gotten this poison?" Edie asked suddenly. "You can't just walk into a shop and buy something like this, can you?"

"You'd be surprised," Harrison said. "It's used as a pesticide, mostly. Kills bugs, rats. You can buy it at the hardware store."

"Frank Burkhart's parents own a hardware store," Gilbert said slowly. "And he was in Sing Sing. Same as Lucia Olivetti."

"What if Frank wasn't killed by accident? What if Lucia killed him, trying to cover her tracks? If he gave her the cyanide to begin with . . ."

"That's all well and good," Harrison said, "but neither of you Sherlocks have explained how there's any connection between this Lucia Olivetti woman and that film studio. You're pinning a lot of assumptions on a woman who may as well be a ghost."

"It all comes back to Leo Salvatore," Edie said. "He's the one who set Lucia up when she got out of prison. Byrne and Burkhart delivered liquor to Leo's club . . . liquor that was tampered with and cut with wood alcohol. Duncan Carroll also went to Leo to secure funding for Harold's film. And then . . ."

Edie stopped, her voice trailing off. She was missing something. She knew it. "Gilbert, do we know how Mrs. O'Malley's husband died?"

"Harold's original partner? No." Gilbert paused, thinking. "But if it happened here in Philadelphia, there will be a record of it upstairs."

The records room at the City Morgue took up the entire top floor. Gilbert greeted the archivist, a brown-haired, middle-aged woman with a pretty smile and a thick pair of spectacles, and explained their request.

"Do you have a date?" The woman asked.

"Probably 1919," Edie said. "But we don't know the exact date."

She showed them to the appropriate filing cabinet. "Things are organized by month and then alphabetically by the decedent's last name."

They found the file quickly enough: "O'Malley, Gregory." Gilbert pulled the file free, flipping the folder open. Two metal bands at the top secured the report to the folder. The front page was a copy of the death certificate. "Gregory O'Malley, age forty-seven. Place of birth: Scranton, Pennsylvania. Place of death: Roxborough, Philadelphia, Pennsylvania. Cause of death . . ." He looked up at Edie. "Suicide. The code here is 165—that's suicide by poison."

Edie leaned close. "Does it say which poison?"

"We did an autopsy," Gilbert said. He flipped through the pages, frowning. "It's thorough. The autopsy noted high oxygenation of the blood and a cherry-red appearance of the skin. It looks like Knight presided, with Dr. Vincent assisting. He's retired now," Gilbert added, as an aside. "It says symptoms are concurrent with cyanide poisoning. But I can't find any evidence of testing."

Cyanide. The same as Duncan Carroll.

Gilbert flipped back to the first page, to the death certificate. "Gregory O'Malley," he read again. "Age, forty-seven. Birthdate: November 12, 1872. Marital status: Married. Name of spouse . . ." He paled, and looked up at Edie.

"What is it?"

"Name of spouse," he said, voice shaking. "Helena O'Malley, née Olivetti."

Olivetti.

They had to call Pyle and get back to the studio at once.

If Mrs. O'Malley was the killer, anyone at the studio could be in danger.

◆―――――◆―――――◆

Pyle met them in Harold Fox's driveway. The big house was silent. Every light was off, and no one, not even Martinez, answered when they knocked on the door.

"Hello?" Edie called. "Mr. Fox? Mrs. O'Malley?"

There was no answer.

"Should we split up? Check the rest of the house?" Edie asked. "You two can each take an upstairs wing, and I'll look down here?"

Gilbert shook his head. His fingers squeezed hers, warm and reassuring. "We'll stay together," he said. "Maybe they all went out."

"Even Martinez?" Edie asked.

"Maybe it's his night off," Gilbert said, even though he sounded like he didn't really believe it.

"Bertie's right," Pyle said. "We stay together."

There was no sign of anyone on the entire first floor. Harold's office was pristine, with not a pencil out of place. The dining table was set for five, though the ice had already melted in the water glasses, the condensation leaving growing rings on the white tablecloth. The parlor, too, was empty, as was the library.

The east wing of the house, where the cast quartered, was equally abandoned. Edie hesitated in the door of Ava's room. Something about it felt . . . odd. Edie had spent hours in Ava's room in California. The other woman made Marco look natty in comparison. She was always tossing her things here and there, kicking her shoes off as soon as she crossed through the door and dropping her handbag on the nearest surface. But the room was a disaster, even beyond Ava's usual mess. Clothes were everywhere, and the bed was unmade, the linens piled on the floor.

"Someone was looking for something," Pyle said. "And they were in a hurry."

"What do you think they were looking for?" Gilbert asked.

"The vial?" Edie couldn't puzzle it out. If Ava was the killer, she wouldn't ransack her own room. No—this suggested that the real culprit found the vial missing and panicked.

Panicking people made mistakes.

"We need to search Mrs. O'Malley's rooms," Edie said.

They crossed the landing to the other side of the second floor, where Harold, Mrs. O'Malley, and Della resided. Their rooms were part of the original farmhouse and felt older. The wood-paneled walls were darkened with age, and the electric lighting gave way to gas lamps on the walls.

Della's room was first. It was small, about half the size of Ava's. A cage for the monkey sat on the dresser, the door opened. Her narrow bed was neatly made, the covers pulled tight. Undisturbed. Photos clipped from magazines covered the wall above her bed—a pinned constellation of movie stars and jazz singers. Duncan appeared several times—in press photos from his films and in lifestyle spreads. Even his headshot was pinned up there, directly above her bed. Other movie stars were featured as well, though nowhere near as prominently—Edie noticed a photo each of Buster Keaton and Rudolph Valentino. A handful of Clara Bow and Alla Nazimova. A handwritten note was pinned among the clippings. Edie leaned forward.

Della, Happy Birthday! Can't imagine life here without you. Love, D.

Harold's room was much the same. The windows were open, and the curtains swayed in the breeze, filling the room with an autumnal chill. But in sharp contrast to the rooms in the other wings, his looked pristine.

The last room belonged to Mrs. O'Malley. It was almost identical to her daughter's, down to the narrow bed pushed against the wall she shared with Della. The top of her dresser was neatly organized—a few tubes of lipstick and a compact of pressed powder beside a bottle of perfume on a silver tray; a hairbrush and mirror; and a small collection of framed photos. The first was Della in what looked like a professional headshot. The second was a family photo—Mr. and Mrs. O'Malley, with their arms around a grinning, gangly Della. The third was a wedding photo. Mrs. O'Malley smiled at the camera, her arm around her groom. A younger man, clearly Harold, stood beside him, smiling, and beside Mrs. O'Malley was a blond girl of about sixteen or seventeen, in a large hat, holding a bouquet of flowers.

Edie recognized her instantly. She'd seen her just a few days prior, weeping at her husband's funeral.

Lily Byrne.

With trembling fingers, Edie turned the frame over. She slid off the back, carefully removing the photograph from the glass. On the back, in a thick, bold hand, was written:

Wedding Day, June 1903. Harold Fox, Gregory O'Malley, Helena O'Malley, Lucia Olivetti. St. Joesph's Church, Phila.

Lucia Olivetti was Lily Byrne.

Lucia Olivetti was Mrs. O'Malley's sister. Mrs. O'Malley, whose handwriting matched the note sent to Leo Salvatore, and the life insurance policy on Duncan.

Lucia Olivetti, who peddled poisonous potions to rid unhappy wives of their husbands.

Edie looked up at Gilbert. "I know who can help us find Lucia Olivetti," she said. "But you aren't going to like it."

Chapter 25

Gilbert kept white knuckles on the steering wheel as he parked the car on Cresson Street, a few blocks up from the shoe shop turned speakeasy where Tommy spent most of his time. He had no idea how Tommy would react to the news that Lily Byrne wasn't who she said she was.

Unless he already knew.

Unless he thought it was a way to spook Leo Salvatore so badly, the deal fell apart.

But no. That didn't make sense. Tommy was a lot of things—a criminal. A killer. But he never went back on his word.

Unless.

Gilbert's parents had assumed the break-in at the house was random. Tommy himself had apparently assured them of that. He'd promised to use his men to get things back to rights. But what if he'd lied? What if he had been behind it? What if it had been a warning for Gilbert? He had assumed that Tommy had wanted him to help Lizzie and Edie investigate the Byrne murder, but what if it was the opposite?

What if Tommy was trying to tell him to stay out of it?

"Tell me you have your gun," Gilbert said suddenly.

"I have my gun," Edie said. "Why do you want to know if I have my gun?"

"In case I have to shoot Tommy Fletcher," he answered. His voice came out more calmly than he would have thought. Edie, however, looked alarmed at this.

"If anyone's shooting my gun, it will be *me*," Edie said. "You didn't even want me to have it in the first place. You said—and I quote: 'Edie, that's the worst idea I've ever heard.' And now you want to borrow it? Tough luck, Doc."

"Edie."

"I'm a crack shot, remember?" She grinned at him, though her smile didn't quite reach her eyes. "Let's go."

The late afternoon sun painted her in burnished golds as she climbed out of the car, adjusting her hat and gloves, her handbag snug on her wrist. For a moment, all he could do was look at her, his breath caught in his chest. Edie looked like they were about to waltz onto the pages of a fashion magazine, not into a dusty shoe shop operated as cover for an underground speakeasy, a pistol in her handbag. She beckoned him, impatient, and he hurried out after her. Gilbert took her hand, and they strode into the shop. The bell overhead jingled, but this time, Gilbert didn't bother waiting for anyone to come fetch him. He had business with Tommy. And he was going to settle it.

The heavy steel door at the bottom of the stairs was shut tight. Gilbert raised his fist and pounded on the metal, the booms echoing through his bones.

Edie leaned close, her warmth grounding him to the present. Her fingers tightened around his, steadying him. She whispered, "Should I take the gun out now?"

"Not yet," he replied.

After what felt like a geologic age, the peephole at the top of the door slid open.

"Doc? Is that you?" Jack McConnell's blue eyes peered out from the other side of the door. He yelled back over his shoulder, "Tommy, it's Doc!"

There was a pause on the other side of the door. And then Tommy's voice: "Let him in."

The door creaked open. Jack stepped back to allow them to pass, a wide smile on his face. Tommy stood in the middle of the floor. A bar stretched along the back wall. There wasn't much else in the room—a stack of crates containing bottles, most empty. A billiards table. It was a far cry from the splendor of Club Rouge. This was a neighborhood establishment, a place for hardworking husbands and fathers to gather after a long shift in the mills.

"Afternoon, Doc. And . . . Mrs. Doc?" Jack was staring at Edie with naked fascination, his gaze sweeping from the top of her head to the tips of her toes.

"Keep it in your pants, McConnell. She's a lady. Miss Shippen, this miscreant here is Whistlin' Jack McConnell."

Edie held out her hand. "Pleasure to meet you, Mr. McConnell. You're a boxer, aren't you?"

He took her hand and bent to press a kiss to the back of it, like she was a medieval lady. When he looked up, a ruddy flush had spread across his cheeks. "Yes, ma'am. You've heard of me?"

Her eyes flashed to Gilbert. "I have. And I'd love to tell you all about it, but we're actually here in a bit of a hurry."

"What's going on, Bertie?" Tommy asked. "You figure out who killed my boys?"

"She did," Gilbert said, pointing to Edie. "And I'm not sure you're going to like it."

Tommy and Jack turned their attention to Edie. She'd settled herself on one of the bar stools, legs crossed at the knee. "It all started in the year 1919," Edie said, a little dramatically. "Well, actually, I guess if you're going to get technical about it, it started even before then. What year did Leo take over his father's gang?"

"Oh-nine, I think," Tommy said. "Maybe a little earlier."

"All right." Edie cleared her throat and tossed her head, pushing her dark waves back from her face. Gilbert could only stand and watch her.

"It was the year 1909," she began again. "Leo Salvatore was tired of watching his father cruelly abuse his mother and younger brothers. Barely more than a child himself, he heard rumors of a woman in the neighborhood who could help. A witch—or a strega—as he called her. She promised him a potion that would either stop his anger or kill him. I think we all can guess what happened there.

"Let's skip ahead to the summer of 1919. Red summer. The war was over. Unrest gripped the country, drawn along racial and political lines. In New York City, a young actor had fallen in love with a woman of Italian heritage. They fell into a group of Bolsheviks, wanting to change the world by any means necessary. They planned to do this by trying to loosen organized crime's grip on the working man. Unfortunately for the actor and the woman, they were arrested in the Palmer Raids, and sent to Sing Sing. The actor came from a powerful family, so he was released unscathed, but she was left to rot."

"Is there a point to this, Miss Shippen?" Tommy asked.

"Shush." Edie gave him a look she must have copied from a governess at some point, as chilling as any Sister Thomas Aquinas had delivered while Gil and Tommy had been in school. "I'm getting there. Don't be rude. Now. Where was I?" She paused, tapping at her lip. "Oh. Yes. Sing Sing. I think we know someone else who spent some time there, don't we?"

"Burkhart!" Jack nearly shouted from beside Gilbert. Edie beamed at the boxer.

"Burkhart. According to my assistant's research, Frank Burkhart was also arrested during the Palmer Raids. He knew this woman before prison, and it was just his luck that they were released at the same time. They both came home, to Philadelphia. Frank came to you, Tommy, and the woman went to someone else. She'd heard of a mystic woman here who was able to help women in need: Celeste DuPont. Celeste, sensing this woman needed more help than she could provide, sent her to Leo Salvatore. He recognized her at once—she'd been the niece of the strega who had given him the potion that killed his father. He set her up with a nice little house in South Philly, and for a few months she did all right. She set herself up as a witch and sold potions from her living room. Then one day, she disappears completely. Vanishes.

"Except she doesn't. Not really. She's gotten married, you see? Takes a job at Wanamaker's. And somehow, the people who need her find her. Her neighbors report she's got a stream of visitors in and out of her house at all hours. But her marriage isn't all it's cracked up to be. Especially when she sees the true love of her life—the young actor who was arrested with her—is starring in a movie filming right here in the city! And he's changed his name and seems to have forgotten all about her, but she's never stopped plotting revenge on the man who walked free while she was in prison. He's moved on with his life—he's a star! He's eloped with his gorgeous castmate! She gets angrier and angrier—how dare he? He betrayed her. So she sets a plan into motion, made easier because her sister practically runs the film studio. She poisons her husband. Frank, of course, knew too much, so she had to kill him too. And then she makes her way to the film set, where her relative works, and kills Duncan Carroll as well. The end."

That wasn't quite the ending Gilbert had been expecting. He blinked. He had followed Edie's thinking for most of it, but there were some places where her ideas seemed . . . thin.

Tommy, too, seemed confused. "So Lily Byrne is actually some communist witch? That's what you're telling me?"

"That's my theory," Edie said. She crossed her arms. "I had to extrapolate, of course—but if you tell us where Lily is, then we can see how correct I am."

Tommy rubbed a hand over his face. "Fine. I'll take you there myself."

Tommy explained that after the funeral, Lily hadn't been able to afford rent payments on the house she'd lived in with Homer. He'd helped her by setting her up in a boarding house near Main Street, a short walk to the train station and near the church where Gilbert's family attended weekly Mass.

An elderly woman answered. "Mr. Fletcher," she said. "I didn't expect to see you back so soon. Is there a problem?"

"No, ma'am. I'm here to check on Mrs. Byrne. I bought some friends."

The woman's face pulled down into a frown. "More people to see Mrs. Byrne, hmm? All day long, this doorbell rings, asking to see that woman. Pfft! I had to tell her that I'm her landlady, not her secretary."

"She's had visitors today?" Tommy asked.

"Yeah. One right after the other. Someone might still be up there—I went to the market and just got back. I'm not in charge of her social calendar," she added as she stepped aside to let them in. "You remember which room is hers?"

Tommy remembered. He led them to a room on the third floor, near the front of the house, with windows overlooking the street. Gilbert frowned; if Mrs. Byrne had been looking out of the window, she would have seen them coming. She could be long gone by now.

Hello?" Edie called as she stepped through the door, then stopped short. Gilbert nearly stepped on her, catching himself on the frame in the nick of time, and saw what had stilled her.

Mrs. Byrne's room was actually a set of rooms—a larger sitting area, and a smaller alcove through a doorway with a beaded curtain. There, on the floor, was the prone form of a blond woman, face down, a pool of blood spreading beneath her. Edie let out a strangled little noise and turned, hiding her face in Gilbert's shoulder. His arm came around her, and he held her for a moment, mentally cataloging the scene. There were two teacups on the table, both empty. A heavy candlestick was on the floor beside her, the bottom edge stained with dark brown blood.

A small sound, too weak to be a moan, came from the woman, and that spurred Gilbert into action. She was alive, which meant she could be saved.

Gilbert let go of Edie and dropped to the floor beside the wounded woman. "She's alive," he barked out. "Help me. I need something to staunch the bleeding, and a pillow to put beneath her to elevate her head and shoulders. Quickly!"

Edie grabbed a pillow from the settee and knelt beside Gilbert too, not caring about the blood on the floor or how expensive her skirt was. Together with Tommy and Edie, Gilbert was able to reposition the woman to her back, taking care to stabilize her neck. Once she was in position, her eyes rolled, and her pulse fluttered beneath Gilbert's fingertips. She'd clearly been hit over the head with the candlestick hard enough to knock her senseless and split open her scalp. But the blow hadn't been hard enough to kill her.

"Here," Edie said softly, handing him a tea towel.

Gilbert pressed the towel to the wound on Lily's head. Her eyes fluttered, and she let out another whimper; she was barely holding on to consciousness. "We need to call an ambulance."

Tommy stood. He stared down at the woman. His dark gaze was flinty, his mouth a hard line. He eased his gun from the holster beneath his jacket and pointed the black muzzle at her.

Gilbert's heart stopped. Beside him, Edie froze too. "Tommy," Gilbert said, his voice soft. Gentle. He inched his hand out, trying to angle his body between Edie and Tommy. Between Edie and the gun. "What are you doing?"

"You're saying she's the one who killed my guys?"

"I believe she did, but I think the bigger question now is who did this to her?" Edie's voice was steady. She asked the question like a schoolteacher—like she knew Tommy already knew the answer.

Tommy let out a short, barking laugh. "Someone who needs me to finish the job."

"Don't you want to know why?" Edie continued. "She's clearly made someone very angry. Was she merely a disgruntled wife, or was she working for someone else?"

Gilbert saw where Edie was going with this. He needed to help her. Tommy was a violent man, but he was also shrewdly rational. He hadn't risen to power in Philadelphia's crime world by virtue of his kindness and compassion. "She's right, Tommy. It can't be a coincidence that she and Burkhart both came from New York. That liquor he and Byrne delivered was tampered with. Someone wants your deal with the Salvatores to fall apart. They want Leo to think you sold him bad booze."

Tommy's hand wavered. "It was her," he said. "That's why she killed Byrne and Burkhart."

"But who gave her the orders? Look at her, Tommy." Gilbert motioned his hand over her still form. "She's going to see justice for what she did to your men. But she needs medical attention. And if she dies—or if you kill her—you'll never know who tried to sabotage your deal. She knows something, man. And we can only find out what that is if you let us call an ambulance, and she goes into police custody. Understand?"

Tommy stared at Gilbert. As boys, Gilbert had always been the one person who was able to talk any sort of sense into Tommy. He hoped that he still held a shred of that trust. Time slowed, the seconds stretching into forever, as Gilbert held Tommy's gaze, silently pleading with his childhood friend to change his mind.

Finally, Tommy lowered his gun. "Damn you, Bertie," he said. "You'd better be right. But we aren't calling an ambulance. I'm not letting her out of my sight until I deliver her straight to Pyle. Can she be moved?"

Gilbert wasn't going to press his luck—or Lily's. "I think most of the bleeding has stopped. Her airway seems clear. I'd rather her get to a hospital, but she seems stable enough for now."

"I'll call him." Tommy held out the gun, butt first, to Gilbert. "If anyone who isn't me comes through this door, shoot them."

Gilbert stayed still. "You know I won't be doing that."

"Worth a try." Tommy holstered the gun. His footsteps thundered down the stairwell as he headed to the telephone, and the taut string holding Gilbert upright snapped. He turned to Edie, who was already moving toward him. They crashed together, wordless.

"Are you all right?" he asked.

"Am I all right? Are you?" Edie asked, breathless. She pressed a kiss to his cheek. "That was some quick thinking. I only hope he isn't too mad when he figures out who really hit her."

"What do you mean?" Gilbert asked.

Edie held out her hand.

There, against the soft skin of her palm, a small brooch glittered.

He picked it up. It was a small brooch, maybe the size of a quarter. A small white enameled cat, holding a red heart.

"We need to find Della," she said.

Chapter 26

When Edie was sixteen years old, she had believed herself to be madly in love with Theo Pepper, the boy next door. He was two years older, and dashingly handsome, with soft blond hair and a quick smile. He was an artist; he spent long, lazy summer afternoons painting Edie in the slanted light. He'd made her promises too—promises that had her giving away parts of herself she'd never get back.

She knew what it was like to be young and impulsive. She knew what it was like to be swept up in love. Because she suddenly understood why Della had been weeping that day in the bathroom. She understood why Della covered her walls with photos of Duncan, the handsome older man who had shown her kindness. Why she'd pinned the note he'd written her above her bed, where she could see it every night.

Can't imagine life without you. Love, D.

She gripped the brooch in her hand as they drove back to the studio. They'd left Lily Byrne with Tommy. He hadn't been able to reach Pyle, and Edie could only hope that the gangster wouldn't kill the woman as soon as she and Gilbert left his sight. But they couldn't be in two places at once, and

Edie had slipped the brooch in her handbag before Tommy had come up the stairs.

They had to find Della.

Edie couldn't believe she hadn't connected the dots earlier. The girl was clearly in love with Duncan. Edie had assumed the tears in the bathroom were over her uncle's displeasure, but now . . .

Had Della known she was poisoning Duncan? Had it been intentional?

They passed through the studio gates. Another car was just ahead of them, Harold's roadster, with Martinez behind the wheel. They followed it up to the big house, where they parked practically on its bumper.

"I say, what's going on?" Harold asked, once he climbed out of the car. He held out his hand and helped Mrs. O'Malley exit. "Is everything all right?"

"Where have you been?" Edie asked, ignoring his question.

"We had a meeting with the insurance company in Center City," Harold said. "There was some sort of mix-up about Duncan's policy. Everything is sorted now."

"We need to know where Della is," Gilbert said. "It's important."

"Della's at home," Mrs. O'Malley insisted. "She wasn't feeling well."

"No, she's not." Edie handed the woman her daughter's brooch. "She went to go see your sister, I'm afraid. We found this."

"Lucia?" Mrs. O'Malley's face paled. She took the brooch with a shaking hand. "That's impossible. Della doesn't know my sister. I haven't spoken to her in years. Not since she went to prison. I—I wouldn't even know where to find her. Della knows nothing about her."

"That's not true," Harold said. He slipped his arm around his sister-in-law. "I should have told you. I didn't even think anything of it, really."

"Harry?"

"She came to see me a few months ago. It was right when she arrived in the city. I didn't know how to help her—I certainly couldn't have her hanging around the studio!—so I put her in contact with a friend of mine."

"Celeste Dupont," Edie said.

"Exactly right," Harold said. "Della and Duncan popped into my office when Lucia was on her way out. They both seemed to take an interest in each other."

"Did Lucia and Duncan speak to each other?"

"I can't remember. I—"

"Is Della all right?" Mrs. O'Malley interrupted her brother-in-law. She stepped forward, grabbing onto the lapels of Gilbert's jacket. "My sister is dangerous. You have to get Della away from her."

Gilbert put his hands over Mrs. O'Malley's, gently. "We just came from your sister's apartment. Della wasn't there."

"Your sister is hurt," Edie said. "Someone hit her over the head. We found this on the floor beside her."

Edie held out the brooch.

Mrs. O'Malley swooned. She let out a low moan and went limp, slumping forward against Gilbert. He staggered backward under her weight as Harry rushed to help.

"Come on now, old girl, we'll find her," Harry said. He tucked his sister-in-law beneath his arm, holding her upright.

"We'll fetch Detective Pyle, and he'll call for backup. We'll have the entire police department looking for her, if I have my way."

"The detective and Ava were having a meeting down at the studio." Martinez checked his watch. "They still might be there."

They raced down to the studio building. It was deserted, as it was just past five o'clock. All of the crew had gone home to their families, along with the assistants and the hundred other people who usually kept the building abuzz. They checked the office Pyle was using first—it was empty. As was Ava's dressing room.

A sick, worried feeling spread through Edie's middle with every empty room they encountered. Della could be halfway to New York or Pittsburgh by now. She'd had hours to vanish. A million scenarios ran through Edie's mind—Lily Byrne's landlady had mentioned multiple visitors. What if Della had happened upon her aunt with someone else? What if Gilbert's theorizing to Tommy had a kernel of truth—what if Lily Byrne had been working for someone else who wanted to keep her quiet, and Della had stumbled into the wrong place at the wrong time?

"This place is too big," Mrs. O'Malley said. "They could be anywhere."

"Let's split up," Edie said. "You two take the west side of the building, and we'll take the east side. We'll work faster that way."

Gilbert slipped his hand into Edie's, the weight of his palm warm and reassuring. They searched quickly, opening doors and closets filled with props and costumes that took ghoulish shape in the half-light.

Finally, they came to Studio A. Duncan had died there, and it had been roped off by police tape for the last week. Edie's pulse quickened. *Of course.* How had she not thought of this earlier? Where else would a heartbroken, helplessly romantic girl go?

They slipped beneath the police tape and into the cavernous space. It was dark save for a single spotlight over the sound stage. Della waited for them there, sitting cross-legged on the stone table where Duncan had breathed his last. Juliet's dagger sat in her lap, and her monkey, Jade, was perched on her shoulder.

"Let me talk to her," Edie whispered to Gilbert. "Stay here."

"Be careful," he said. She gave his fingers a squeeze.

"Della?" Edie's heels clicked across the studio floor. "Are you all right?"

Della looked up. Her eyes were red and swollen from crying. Edie almost would have felt bad for her if the girl hadn't killed one person and tried to kill another. "How did you know I'd be here?"

"It was an accident, wasn't it?" Edie sat down slowly, keeping a careful distance between herself and the dagger. Even blunt-tipped as the prop was sure to be, it could cause damage if Della wished it to.

"Of course it was." Della's monkey snuggled closer to its mistress, and Della absently patted it. "I wouldn't—I would never—" Della erupted in a whole new round of sobbing, drowning out whatever she was going to say.

"What did you think would happen?" Edie asked gently. "Did you want to make him ill? Did you give him too much?"

"Of course not! It was supposed to make him love *me*, not her! And she was making Duncan miserable. They fought constantly. He didn't deserve that. I never would have fought with him. I would have made him so happy! But that woman . . . she tricked me. She told me it was a love potion, but it *killed* him."

Edie had her suspicions about that. Lucia Olivetti, or Lily Byrne, or whatever she called herself, knew more about Duncan's character than anyone else. She had used her niece to get revenge on the man who had cast her aside back in New York, and she didn't care what damage murder would do to a young girl's psyche.

She didn't care that if found out, Della would be the one to pay the price.

"You switched out the vial during the break," Edie said.

Della hiccupped. "Yeah. Mother saw me and gave me a talking to about leaving the props alone. She had no idea what I was doing. No one did. And then, once he died . . ." Della wailed again.

"You made some bad choices," Edie said, keeping her voice calm. "But it's not over yet. You can still make the right choice."

Della looked up at her, eyes big. "All right," she said finally. "But I won't show you. I'll only show Dr. Lawless. He's been kind to me. And he's so handsome, isn't he?"

"He is." Edie had to suppress a smile. The girl was confessing to attempted murder, and still concerned with Gilbert's looks. She looked to the darkness near the door, where she knew he was waiting. "Gil?" she called. "Can you come here?"

Gilbert crouched down beside Della and listened intently to the girl as she repeated her story, his frown deepening as she spoke. He threw one last, alarmed look at Edie as Della declared again that she thought she'd purchased a love potion from her aunt.

"Did that make you angry?" he asked. He kept his voice gentle, his body loose.

Della seemed to think about this. "I didn't mean to hurt anyone," she said again. "Even today, when I went to see Aunt Lucia, I just wanted her to tell me the truth. Instead, she laughed at me. She called me stupid." She picked up her head and stared at Edie. "I'm not stupid. She lied to me. I got so angry. She was really the one who killed him—it was her fault! I picked up the candlestick and I . . . I just saw red. And she fell, and she made such an awful sound, and I just . . . I killed her, didn't I?"

"No." Gilbert's voice was firm. "You knocked her senseless, but she's alive. And we'll make sure she'll pay for what she did. I won't sugarcoat things, lass. You're going to have consequences as well. Even though it was an accident."

"I know." Della's lip trembled. "You should probably take me to the detective now."

Della wept as Pyle directed her into the back of the police car. Mrs. O'Malley and Harold hovered. "Don't worry, dear girl," Harold called. "My attorney will meet us downtown. You'll be all right."

"What a waste," Gilbert said, coming up beside Edie, once the cars had departed. "All of that talent, all that potential. Wasted. Over what?"

"She said it was an accident," Edie said.

"You believe her?" Gil looked down, surprised.

"I think I do," Edie said. "She was young and jealous and irrational. She bought a love potion the same way thousands of other little lovesick girls did. She didn't know that Lily Byrne was peddling poisons. She didn't mean to kill him. Her aunt, of course, is a different story."

Ava stood on the steps of the studio. She looked tragically glamourous, with her blond hair beneath an inky turban, and swathed in an embroidered cocoon coat. "Miss Shippen, lady detective," she called out. "You pulled it off, after all. Even after . . ."

"I told you I'd prove you were innocent," Edie said. "I keep my word, Ava."

Ava's eyes glittered with unshed tears. She reached out and hooked her pinky through Edie's, giving a quick squeeze. Edie squeezed back. She hoped this meant that, even after all this, they'd be able to remain friends.

"Thank you," Ava said, voice soft. "I don't know how I'll ever repay you."

Edie grinned at her friend. The smallest sprout of an idea was rooting in Edie's heart. "Oh, don't worry," she told Ava. "I have an idea."

Lily Byrne looked older beneath the harsh lights of the police station. *Lucia Olivetti,* Edie corrected herself. Tommy Fletcher had kept his word and handed her over to Pyle at the first possible moment.

It was hard to reconcile that the woman sitting in irons at the table on the opposite side of the window was the same beautiful widow who had been weeping at her husband's funeral. A dark bruise stretched down the side of her cheek, from where Della had struck her the day before, and her eyes were ringed in dark circles. She had a petulant pinch to her mouth, and her blond hair hung in limp strands around her face.

"She can't see us?" Edie asked. The room they were in was dark, illuminated only through the window that faced into the interrogation room. Edie had heard of one-way mirrors; they were the stuff of dime-novel detective stories, but she'd never seen one in person.

"No, but I'm sure she knows we're here," Pyle said. "This isn't her first trip around the block."

But it was Edie's. The unspoken weight of Pyle's words settled on her shoulders. She'd never even stepped foot into Central Police Station before that morning. She'd never sat face-to-face with a criminal—let alone a murderess—and tried to coax a confession out of them. Which, if she was being honest with herself, was exactly the reason why Lucia Olivetti was refusing to speak with anyone but *that snooping dame*.

"I'll be right here in case anything goes sideways," Pyle was saying. "But don't worry too much, Miss Shippen. She's in bracelets, and poisoners don't tend to be the type who get their hands dirty."

As if to illustrate his point, Lucia rested her forearms on the table in front of her. A chain secured her to the floor, long enough to allow her to shift positions, but too short to allow her to stand.

"This is a terrible idea," said the man on the other side of Pyle. He hadn't bothered to introduce himself. Pyle had introduced him only as being from the DA's office. "Detective Pyle, I really do think you should be leading this interrogation, not this... this..." His voice sputtered into nothingness as he waved a hand in Edie's direction. "I mean, look at her."

Edie looked down at herself. She thought she'd dressed rather smartly for the occasion, in an inky-blue suit that swirled around her calves and a long jacket over a white silk blouse. Her hat was even demure—a blue wool cloche, nary a feather in sight. She looked over at the man and gave him her biggest smile. "I don't believe we've been introduced. I'm Miss Edie Shippen, lady detective."

"You know her father," Pyle supplied helpfully. "Ned Shippen?"

"Councilman Shippen." The man paled. He adjusted his tie and shook Edie's hand. "Of course. I'm Dexter McGill, assistant district attorney."

"Excellent. May I?" Edie's pulse was thundering, but she couldn't let these men see even an ounce of weakness. The fact that she was here...

Well. She'd have to prove she could handle it.

Pyle opened the door to the interrogation room. Lily Byrne shifted in her seat, chains clinking against the metal table.

Edie settled herself on the chair, the cold metal seeping through the wool of her skirt. The room was freezing. She wasn't sure how Lily, in her thin, city-issued dress, wasn't shivering down to her bones.

"Mrs. Byrne." Edie inclined her head as if she were meeting the woman for tea at the Crystal Room, not in a police interrogation. "I hope you're feeling better."

Lily let out a snort. "Skip the niceties, Miss Shippen. We both know why you're here."

"You asked to speak with me." Edie held the other woman's gaze. "I'm curious about what you have to say."

"Mr. Fletcher told me about you. He said you're some sort of detective. That you want to help women who can't help themselves."

"I am." Edie leaned forward. "But you seemed perfectly capable of helping yourself, Mrs. Byrne. You've left quite the trail of bodies behind you."

Lily Byrne, to her credit, didn't look ashamed of herself. She crossed her arms over her chest. "Most of them deserved it," she said. She glanced over to the mirror on the wall, where Pyle and McGill were waiting behind the one-way glass.

"Like Duncan?" Edie needed her to say it.

"*Especially* Duncan. I gave him my youth. Years of my life. And he walked away, free as a bird. I spent three years in the slammer for his ideas," she said, her voice dripping with rage. "Three years in Sing Sing. When that brat of my sister's came to me? It was too good to be true."

"She said she asked you for a love potion. Did she know there was a risk of killing him?"

Lily snorted. "Idiot girl. I told her it would make him fall in love with her. If she thought it would hurt him, she'd never have swapped out the vials."

Edie's heart lifted. This, hopefully, would be enough to spare Della the worst possible outcome. It established her as a patsy to her aunt's crimes, not a cold-blooded murderess. Especially after the girl had confessed earlier in the day to sending the threatening note to Leo Salvatore. She'd learned of Leo's deal with Duncan and thought the gangster had killed him in revenge.

Thinking of Leo reminded Edie that there was still one loose end, however. Something Edie had to know.

"On the twenty-ninth of September, your husband and Frank Burkhart made a delivery of gin to Club Rouge. It was denatured with wood alcohol. Why?"

Lily's eyes flashed. "Go on, Miss Shippen."

"It seems an odd thing. Especially with them both dying a few hours later."

"I was sorry about that," Lily said. "Well, not about Homer. He was a brute. But Frank? He was a good man. We came out of Sing Sing at the same time, you know. I didn't want to kill him. But I didn't really have a choice."

"Why not?"

"It was me or him. I had my orders. We both did: we were to find a way to sabotage the deal between the Salvatore Brothers and the Cresson Street Crew. Poor Frank never stood a chance."

Now they were getting somewhere. Edie leaned forward. "Who gave the orders?"

"Oh no. That's all for today," Lily said. She stood up, as far as her chains would let her, and gave a wave to the mirror. "I do hope you'll come see me again, Miss Shippen. Us clever girls should stick together. Just know one thing: he's only just getting started."

Edie stayed in the interrogation room long after Detective Pyle led Lily Byrne back to her cell. The cold had seeped into her bones, into her soul. She shouldn't care what happened to Tommy Fletcher or Leo Salvatore. They were criminals with blood-soaked hands. They lived in a world that was kill or be killed.

But she thought of Lizzie and the way she smiled when Leo held her hand.

She thought of the Lawless family and a tiny kitten in a little girl's arms.

Whoever had threatened Leo and Tommy wouldn't hesitate to hurt the people Edie loved. And she couldn't let that happen.

Chapter 27

October 25, 1921
Mount Airy, Philadelphia

Gilbert closed his fingers over the key in his palm. It was small and brass, and the tag attached had the address of his new house. He could still scarcely believe it. It hadn't seemed real when the check had arrived from Norwood Studios a week prior. He'd stared at the envelope for an entire hour before being brave enough to open it, and then, when he saw the amount, followed by Harold's swirling signature, he had to put it back down and take a short walk around the block. His hands shook when he took it to the bank to deposit, and again when he signed away most of it as a down payment on his new house a few days later.

The house itself felt like a marvel—a stone-fronted twin in the leafy Mount Airy neighborhood across the Wissahickon from Manayunk, within walking distance to the train station. It was three floors, with a basement, and a garage out back for the car. The paint was peeling, and the floors were dusty—it had been vacant for some time—but Lizzie would have her own room, and so would Penelope. Room for his parents, even, if they ever decided to leave Manor Street. It wasn't perfect.

But it was his.

He fit the key in the lock and turned. The door swung open, and his footsteps echoed through the empty rooms. His empty rooms. All his.

He couldn't wait to bring Penny here. She was in school until three—he'd pick her up, take her for a water ice, and let her roller-skate through the first floor. His chest swelled with warmth and pride and most of all . . . hope.

He couldn't remember the last time he'd felt hope.

Upstairs, a door creaked. Gilbert froze, a spike of fear cooling the warmth in his veins. No one should be in the house. He'd only gotten the key himself less than an hour before.

Maybe it was the neighbor on the other side of the wall. That's what he told himself as he started up the stairs, turning at the landing and coming up to the second floor—all matter of noises could carry through the walls, and some people were louder than others. All of the doors were closed. The front room, which would be Lizzie's, was washed in sunlight; the fully plumbed bathroom, complete with shower, beside it. His own door, straight back, was shut tight.

But Penelope's, the last door on the left, was open. Dappled sunlight spilled onto the hall floor. Soft humming, high and feminine, came from within, and the hair on the back of Gil's neck prickled.

Someone was here.

"Hello?" he called out.

The humming stopped. "Oh!" Edie's voice came from the room. She appeared herself a moment later, wearing a dark orange knit dress and a matching hat. "You're here! I was supposed to be gone by now. This was supposed to be a surprise."

He pressed a hand to his chest, where his heart was threating to beat out of his chest. "Jesus, Edie. What are you doing here? How'd you even get in here?"

"I picked the lock," she said. She was pouting, her hands on her hips. Her lips were dark again, a perfect cupid's bow. "You ruined my surprise, Gil."

"What surprise?" He stepped closer. She was maddening, really. Absolutely maddening. He wasn't even going to acknowledge her comment about picking the locks.

"Well, you're here now." Edie held out her hand. He took it, and he let her tug him into Penelope's room. The last time he'd been in here, it had been empty save for dust bunnies and peeling wallpaper. But now . . .

Gil's hand tightened around Edie's, and his heart swelled in his chest, threatening to explode. The room was a little girl's dream—the wallpaper had been torn down and replaced. Gone was the sad, peeling green, and in its place were purple and blue birds and flowers on a field of cream. There was furniture too—a white framed bed with a blue canopy, a low dresser with a mirror, and a small bookshelf, stocked with children's books. A wicker pram, with a doll, waited in the corner, and beneath the window was a dollhouse version of their stone twin, with a little red-haired girl, a red-haired woman, and a dark-haired man.

Penelope. Lizzie.

Him.

"Edie." He didn't have words. He turned and found her standing in the door, hands twisting.

"It's too much, isn't it?" she said. "I wanted it to be perfect for her. I wanted her to—"

He didn't think twice. He crossed the room in two steps and took her face between his hands. He kissed her without thinking, acting purely on instinct as his entire body vibrated with joy, with wonder.

With love.

Edie kissed him back, pushing her hands into his hair, and he pulled her close.

It was time for a new beginning.

Acknowledgments

Sophomore books are notoriously difficult creatures, and mine proved no exception, compounded by the back-to-back losses of my grandfather and great-grandmother while writing and revising this book. But—we did it! It's real!

My endless gratitude to my editor, Melissa Rechter, for her patience and enthusiasm for this book and her belief that I would get it done (even when I wasn't so sure myself). Thank you, again, to the rest of the team at Crooked Lane for their hard work: Rebecca Nelson, Thaisheemarie Fantauzzi Pérez, Cassidy Graham, Dulce Botello, Stephanie Manova, and Matt Martz; and a special thanks to cover artist, Jessica Khoury, for knocking it out of the park once again.

I wouldn't be doing this without my agent, Amy Giuffrida. Thank you for answering every question with grace and reassuring me it was absolutely okay to ask for deadline extensions when I needed them.

A million thanks to the members of my writing village: my Hopefully Writing crew, my fellow 2024 Debuts, and A-Team agent siblings. Kimberly G. Giarratano, Katie Tietjen, Nekesa Afia, and Stephen Spotswood, thank you for welcoming me into the mystery community. Maria Turead, Sarah T.

Dubb, and Kyrie McCauley, thank you for reminding me that first drafts are allowed to be a hot mess. Teagan Olivia King, thank you for always being quick to reassure me that I can, in fact, write a novel.

Speaking of writing novels—it's a hard enough job on its own, let alone writing and revising a book to publication in less than nine months while balancing a full-time day job and motherhood. Thank you to my friends, neighbors, and colleagues for asking me about the book, showing up at events, hosting playdates, and cutting me slack. I appreciate you all.

I can't imagine doing this without the support of my family. My parents, siblings, aunts, uncles, cousins, grandparents, and in-laws: thank you, thank you, thank you for showing up at (almost) every signing and event to heckle me and buy books. I'm exactly who I am because of each and every one of you (and maybe we should stop and think a little bit about why it is I grew up to write murder mysteries).

And last but not least: Eric, I couldn't have survived the last year without you. Thank you for holding us together through the sad tears and the happy ones. For cooking me dinner and reading whatever I sent you and reluctantly humoring some of my ideas (like adopting Mister and moving into the house next door), and vetoing others (like throwing my laptop into the sea and giving up on this whole writing thing entirely). I love you.